Sue Minix is a member of Sisters in Crime, and when she isn't writing or working, you can find her reading, watching old movies, or hiking the New Mexico desert with her furry best friend.

The Murderous Type

SUE MINIX

avon.

Published by AVON
A division of HarperCollins*Publishers*
1 London Bridge Street
London SE1 9GF

www.harpercollins.co.uk

HarperCollins*Publishers*
Macken House
39/40 Mayor Street Upper
Dublin 1
D01 C9W8
Ireland

A Paperback Original 2023
3
First published in Great Britain by HarperCollins*Publishers* 2023

A catalogue copy of this book is available from the British Library.

ISBN: 978-0-00-858465-8

Typeset in Sabon Lt Std by Palimpsest Book Production Limited,
Falkirk, Stirlingshire

Printed and Bound in the UK using 100% Renewable Electricity at
CPI Group (UK) Ltd

To Cara Chimirri for her dedication, patience, and undying enthusiasm.

CHAPTER ONE

By the last Saturday in June, outdoor activities in Riddleton, South Carolina, were like a bad marriage. You could survive more or less unscathed if you got out early enough. Wait too long, though, and it turned to hell in a hurry. With that in mind, today's Riddleton 10k began at six in the morning. Two cups of coffee short of complete brain function, my caffeine-deprived body was camped out on the sidewalk in front of the town hall, at the finish line.

Throngs gathered along the race route to cheer on the runners, and my ears vibrated with the echoes of a hundred conversations, which played snare drum in my head. Mostly arguments about who would win the competition. Although, a young couple behind me argued over whether to spend money they didn't have on a new fifty-inch flat-screen on clearance at Walmart. No surprise, he was the yes, she the no.

Once a stagecoach rest stop halfway between Blackburn and Sutton, Riddleton had grown when engineers built the dam to create Lake Dester. It remained a small town, though, rife with the typical small-town mentality. Everyone knew everything about everyone else, and help during troubled times was never more than an arm's length away. It suffocated me as a kid growing up here, and I couldn't wait to escape to college in Blackburn. When I moved back to town last year, however, I learned how reassuring having people around who cared about me could be.

However, surrounded by densely packed humanity, I shifted my feet and struggled with what to do with my hands. No room in the pockets of my getting-tighter-everyday jeans, so I lowered them to my sides. Unfortunately, my puppy Savannah's leash occupied one of them.

"Ouch!" A tiny drop of blood welled on my index finger. I stuck the offended digit in my mouth and glanced down. My German shepherd puppy fixed her warm brown eyes on me, ears back, tail wagging. I squatted to her level. "Now see here, Savannah, just because you own a maw full of razor blades doesn't mean you're allowed to slice me to ribbons every time you want a little attention."

She licked my cheek, her silver muzzle prickly against my skin. So much for scolding.

Brittany Dunlop, her flyaway blond hair taking off in the breeze, squeezed in beside us. "A kiss counts as an apology, wouldn't you say, Jen?"

Brittany had adopted me in kindergarten, and we'd remained best friends ever since. Although she topped the tape measure at a whopping five foot two, she was a formidable presence in my life, and I don't know how I would've survived my childhood without her. The voice of sanity whispering in my ear when my stepfather Gary was having one of his out-of-control days, and home became crazy town.

Savannah leaped towards her in greeting, and her tongue flared like a lizard snapping breakfast off a branch. Brittany yanked her hands out of the danger zone and clasped them behind her back, having already experienced her share of rapier-like love nips.

"Close to one as I'm going to get, I'm sure." I told the pup to sit, then pushed gently on her hindquarters until she complied and leaned on my leg, tongue dripping saliva on my brand-new Nike cross-trainer. The exercise was a trial for us both, given the distraction of the masses around us. "She needs to potty, but escaping the crowd will be an adventure."

"Want me to run interference for you? I'm a librarian, remember? People have to listen to me, or I'll shush them." Brittany knelt to scratch Savannah's chest, an offer of some much-needed attention to the self-proclaimed neglected puppy.

"No, you hold our place. I want to see Eric win." Eric O'Malley—the tall, lanky, red-headed leader of the Riddleton Runners, a group I'd reluctantly joined last year—also represented the police department as a patrol officer. No question about which role meant more to him today, though. He chased the finish line like it was an armed robbery suspect trying to get away.

Brittany pursed her thin lips and inched her oversized, tiger-striped glasses back up to the bridge of her nose. "You think he's fast enough?"

"Hard to say, but a win would mean a lot to him. Besides, I've learned to appreciate his friendship, so I should root for him, don't you think?"

She raised her so-pale-they-could-barely-be-seen-in-the-sunlight eyebrows. "Yeah, like that's the only reason."

I sent her an eye roll. "Please! I'm well aware of what you're thinking. He's my running buddy, and a win would make him happy, which is my only interest."

"If you say so." Brittany crossed her arms. "Wanna put your money where your mouth is? I say the chief's a shoo-in again."

My mind generated a picture of the graying fifty-something who carried his thirty-plus years on the force, the last ten spent behind a desk, like ankle weights. In comparison, Eric was a gazelle being chased by a lion through the Serengeti. A gangly, red-headed gazelle in baggy green shorts and a red tank top. "That old man? No way. I'll risk five bucks."

"Throw in lunch, and you've got a deal."

"Done." I allowed Savannah to maneuver us through the multitude, and smiles flashed from friends and strangers alike. Nothing like puppies and babies to grab attention. Most people were suckers for the young and the helpless. Like *The Young and the Restless*, only cuter.

A youthful—compared to my ancient twenty-nine, that is—woman in a Sutton High School Track T-shirt peeked around the muscular biceps of the middle-aged man who stood in front of her. She squealed at a pitch an octave above my comfort zone. "Hey, aren't you Jennifer Dawson?"

Here we go. I resisted the urge to cover my ears as I suspected Savannah wished she could. "Yes."

She powered the rest of the way through and almost trampled the bounding puppy since Biceps Man's leg blocked her escape route.

Muscles flexed under his tight, black Gold's Gym T-shirt, he exposed what he clearly believed to be an irresistible smile.

Nice try, fella, but I don't think so.

"I'm so excited to meet you," the young woman said. "Catching that killer by yourself was amazing. You're a real hero."

Vacant eyes stared up at me from the first floor of the Cunningham house. When Aletha—bookstore owner, muse, and friend—was murdered last year, I became embroiled in the investigation because evidence pointing to me was found at the crime scene. I shook away the memory. At least the woman didn't have a question about my stalled second novel. "Thank you, but I got lucky. Had lots of help, too."

"Well, I think you're terrific. Also, I loved your book, by the way. When's the next one due out?"

My faux smile made its first appearance of the day. "Soon." Otherwise known as never, at my current rate of progress.

Savannah stretched to the end of her leash, giving me the perfect excuse to make an exit. If only she could write the novel for me, the question would never arise again. Did they make laptops with German-shepherd-sized keys?

American flags wilted on the lampposts lining Main Street under a sunny, eighty-five-degree sky at seven in the morning. The humidity-thickened air left me with the sensation of trying to breathe underwater. A skill I'd never mastered, even when someone tried to drown me last year. Fortunately, I'd mastered the skill of holding my breath instead.

Savannah towed me past Bob's Bakery to the grassy strip in front of the post office, across from the library. Actually, it was more like a post closet, the parking lot being twice the size of the structure itself. The architect must've suffered from a bad case of wishful thinking.

At the moment, the post office was the only structure in town besides my bookstore devoid of decorations. I had no idea when the tradition began, but all the local shop owners decorated their windows for every major holiday. The town council even hosted a contest for some holidays, which sometimes included a prize for the best display. The Independence Day reward was the opportunity to be the grand marshal of the parade. When I inherited the bookstore from Aletha, that responsibility became mine. Unfortunately, I had the artistic ability of a blender.

Riddleton mayor, Teresa Benedict, came out of the building—short, brown hair as spiky as her disposition pinned by the phone headset she spoke into. She flapped a fistful of town correspondence from her mailbox—probably destined for the suitcase she called a purse—at me and lifted her chin away from the microphone. "You ever gonna finish that book, Jen?"

I stifled a groan and gave her a thumbs-up in place of the finger I wanted to use while Savannah searched for the perfect spot to do her thing. Her requirements remained a mystery to me, but after four or five false alarms and a peanut snatched out of the dirt, she made her selection.

As I bent to retrieve the results with a plastic bag, the mayor strode past us toward a black, late-model Ford Expedition. A cloud of lavender wafted over me. She might want to cut back before a swarm of bees investigated the all-you-can-eat buffet.

With murky brown eyes flashing, Teresa said into her headset, "Well, he won't be chief of police much longer if he doesn't change his mind. It'll be the last decision he ever makes." She tucked into the driver's seat and shut the door behind her.

I shook my head at the mayor's hyperbole. The more contentious, the better she liked it. I ran a hand down my puppy's spine and scratched her favorite spot at the base of her tail. "Uh-oh, Savannah, sounds like the chief did a boo-boo."

She thrust her rear up against my fingertips and snuffled my other hand, floppy ears perked, tongue hanging out the side of her mouth.

Goofball.

Would her ears ever stand up? When she ran, she resembled a baby bird that fell out of its nest, flapping useless wings all the way down.

"You're right, little girl. He must've pooped on the rug."

We meandered back toward the town hall and edged our way into the horde near the bakery, directly across the street from the town hall. Bob had sketched his obligatory window display but hadn't painted it yet. This year's offering? In his trademark tri-corner hat, George Washington crossed the Delaware with a mug of coffee in one hand, a donut in the other, and a big smile on his face. An interesting twist on the old adage, "An army travels on its stomach."

Electricity crackled as wannabe critics argued the merits and demerits of Bob's work. To me, the scene was entertaining. To them? The wedge on which the whole world teetered. Good thing I wasn't one of the judges. I might not live long enough to complete my book.

On our way back to the finish line, Savannah scarfed the remains of two hot dogs and an apple turnover off the ground. Poor baby never ate. Two gargantuan bowls of puppy chow and a gazillion treats a day notwithstanding, of course.

I rested my arm on Brittany's shoulder while the pup flopped down on my feet and sniffed the sidewalk for more nibbles. "Any sign of the runners?"

"Not yet, although I've heard a commotion from up near the park. How was your walk?"

"Eventful." I held up the bag, then chucked it into a nearby trash can, decorated with posted remains from our last election. Perfect place for it. "The mayor is mad at Chief Vick. I overheard her on the phone just now, and he did something to stir up her venom."

A snigger escaped Brittany. "Might be anything. I think we've all been infuriated with Tobias Vick at one time or another. It seems he goes out of his way to irritate people."

"Ain't that the truth. Like the day he sent Eric to give me a ticket because my muffler sounded like a cement mixer. He only gave me a warning, though, and even helped me fix it the next day. Of course, I shouldn't complain. That's how we became friends. Still, I've seen people with car parts falling off, and the chief never bothered them."

"No kidding. I guess it depends on his frame of mind each day."

Since my return to town a year and a half ago, the only moods he'd exhibited were foul, fouler, and foulest.

Brittany continued, "He's been a huge supporter of the library, so I can't complain too much." Hands stuffed in her shorts pockets, she turned to me. "Speaking of which, are you game to help me set up for the fundraiser?"

As the town librarian, Brittany was responsible for raising money to cover shortfalls in the budget. The annual fundraiser auction provided much of the necessary funds. "Absolutely! Antonio's has the food covered, right? I love that restaurant."

"Yup, and a bottle of wine for the auction. All we need to do is prep the dining room."

"Generous."

"Definitely. You know, I think it's the expensive one the chief likes so much."

"Guess we'd better make sure he has the highest bid to stay on his good side. I might have muffler trouble again." I scratched Savannah behind her ears. "I wouldn't want to be within a hundred miles of him if he loses. Doubt anyone else'll try for it, though. Everyone knows how much he wants it."

"After what he did to me the other night, I'm bidding on it."

We turned to find rookie RPD Officer Leonard Partridge behind us, his navy-blue uniform crisp, creases perfectly centered down his legs. His cousin Greg stood beside him, munching on a hot dog slathered with mustard, some of which had escaped to worm its way down his scruffy chin.

A hot dog at seven in the morning? My belly flipped. "What'd he do?" I asked.

Leonard ran fingers over his chestnut mustache. "I had a date at Antonio's. The chief staggered by our table, knocked a whole glass of wine in my lap, then kept going. No apology. Nothing. And, I couldn't say anything because he's my boss."

Brittany touched his arm. "Perhaps he didn't realize what happened."

He tipped his chin and thrust out his chest, the protective vest straining the buttons on his shirt. "He knew, all right. Did it on purpose 'cause his son likes the girl I was with. It worked, too. She's ghosted me ever since. Third time he's embarrassed me like that."

I suspected the girl's reaction had little to do with Chief Vick's son. Or the spilled wine. Leonard seemed okay, and Eric hadn't mentioned any problems with him as a patrol partner. However, he did once say the man complained a lot. Still, Leonard made the hair on the back of my neck dance a jig every time I encountered him. Like a goose walked over my grave, as my grandmother used to say. No idea why.

In the distance, a roar went up from the spectators along the race route, which built in intensity as it traveled toward the finish line. The runners were almost home. Who would be first? On my tiptoes, I peered past the flat-screen couple, who'd managed to creep up to the street. Eric and Chief Vick, reminiscent of the Scarecrow and the Cowardly Lion, galloped side by side around the corner of Pine and Main, a hundred feet away.

A few yards behind, a short, squat man I didn't recognize fought to shorten the gap. At the same time, Lacey Stanley—the manager of my bookstore, Ravenous Readers—closed in on him with long, elegant strides. A former Olympic hopeful with dreams derailed by a torn ACL in college, Lacey was now a married mother of two who threw herself into the bookstore with the same gusto she once used to train for gold.

We ran together every Saturday morning, yet I'd never realized how speedy she was. She must've saved all her energy for race day. Or, more likely, she didn't want me to get discouraged about being the tortoise to her hare. Especially since, in real life, the hare never stopped to take a nap.

Eric sprinted ahead at the straightaway, stick-figure arms pumping like coupling rods on a locomotive. He increased his lead to a full stride. The chief labored to catch up, face fire-engine red, chest heaving. No surprise since Eric told me last week the old man unbuttoned his pants to sit down when he thought nobody was looking. The separation diminished an inch at a time. From the look of it, the guy would either win or die trying.

Ten feet from the finish line, they bumped shoulders again. Chief Vick clipped his front calf with his back foot and collided with Eric, who stumbled and hit the ground two feet short of the tape spanning Main Street. His arms and legs jumbled together like pickup sticks, blood oozing from a gash in his right knee.

The crowd gasped.

The chief of police lunged through the two-inch-wide plastic ribbon with his hands high above his head.

CHAPTER TWO

I arrived at Antonio's Ristorante, my usual five minutes late. Tony Scavuto—khaki cargo shorts and a paint-splattered lime-green T-shirt with a two-inch hole in the middle covering his solid frame—daubed gray, swirled clouds across the top of his window, humming "C'è La Luna" under his breath. Below the brewing storm, he'd created a revolutionary battle scene including a rotund British soldier with a Dick Dastardly handlebar mustache firing meatballs out of a cannon at a group of blue-and-white-clad American soldiers with napkins tucked into their shirt collars, brandishing knives and forks.

Inside, the rattle of pots and pans fought for my attention, along with the smell of roasted beef. A red and white Riddleton Library Fundraiser banner was strung across the back of the room. The Tiffany lamps suspended overhead reminded me of the last time I'd been here. A disastrous dinner date during which I'd had way too much wine and made a fool of myself.

Brittany breezed by with an armful of pristine, snow-white tablecloths, a towel tucked into the back of her shorts like a mud flap for her butt. I followed her to a row of empty wooden tables. "Sorry, I'm late. Savannah dillydallied on her walk. I'm amazed at how many fascinating trees and mailbox posts Riddleton has, but I don't understand why she needs to stop and sniff every one of them. I can't imagine what she smells."

Brittany deposited her load on the sideboard. "Believe me, Jen, you don't want to be able to smell everything she can."

"True. A permanent head cold sounds more appealing."

She clutched a tablecloth at one end and handed the other side to me. A flick of our wrists floated it into place like a parachute wafting back to earth. One down, thirty-nine to go. Plus, place settings, glasses, and silverware. This afternoon might last three weeks.

The library needed the money, though. The town didn't collect enough revenue to support it without help. If our library closed, Brittany would lose her job and move in with me. A Hindenburg-level disaster. We'd considered sharing an apartment once, for a minute, but realized that decision might lead to the end of our lifelong friendship. Opposites attract, but only in small doses.

We'd better hurry up and finish our work since the fundraiser had to be successful for that reason if nothing else. Besides, Brittany might have enough left to buy a copy of my book for the shelves. Then more people could ask about the second one.

Yippee.

We moved on to table number two, and I grabbed my end. "Tony worked hard on his decorations this year, didn't he? I love the Dastardly Redcoat. Kinda reminds me of Angus."

Her guffaw drowned out the kitchen clatter. "Don't let *him* hear you say that."

13

"Okay, he can be Muttley. The good guy."

"I don't know. I think he'll ban us from his restaurant, and you'll starve to death."

My running partner—short, stout Angus Halliburton—owned the Dandy Diner, where I ate most of my meals. "Not necessarily. Plenty of puppy food in my house."

"I think it's safe to assume the diner's cuisine tastes better. Besides, I doubt your dog would share. Or that there'd be enough for both of you."

With a new cloth in hand, I headed for the next table. "No kidding. That hound eats more in a day than I do in a week. Why couldn't the lady in Savannah breed Chihuahuas instead?"

Brittany wagged her finger at me. "Jennifer Marie Dawson! That woman gave you a thousand-dollar dog because she felt sorry for you. Really! I wonder about you sometimes."

And Savannah's mother saved me when I was stranded after the almost-drowning episode. My own fault, though. I should've stayed out of the investigation. Olinski tried to tell me, but I didn't listen as usual. Of course, I didn't listen to him the whole time we were dating in high school, either. Why should things be any different now that he's a police detective?

I stuck out my lower lip. "You're right. Consider me chastised."

She suppressed a smile. "I'm a little surprised Tony bothered with another elaborate holiday display after the chief nosed him out last time. He insists the contest is rigged because the Vicks always win."

"Silly man. Anne-Marie Vick shoots the works on their house for every holiday. Flags, bunting, lights, you name it. That's why they always exhibit the best

14

display. I wouldn't be surprised if they hosted a Revolutionary War re-enactment on their front lawn this year. Or a North Pole-style snowball fight next Christmas." I hadn't spent much time with Anne-Marie since my return to town, but I recognized a workhorse when I saw one.

I straightened the corner of the tablecloth into an equilateral triangle. "Too bad donating an expensive bottle of wine for the auction won't improve Tony's chances to be the grand marshal. The chief isn't one of the judges."

"Worse than that, Angus told me Tony messed up the chief's order the other night, and Vick gave him a negative review on Yelp."

"Petty, but typical. I guess the chief just can't help himself."

Tables clothed, I wandered over to check out the auction items while Brittany collected the place settings Tony had loaded on a cart for us. Almost every business in town had made a donation. The two gas stations each offered a year's worth of free drinks. The Riddleton Bank donated a complete financial checkup. I provided a hundred-dollar gift certificate from Ravenous Readers, and the Piggly Wiggly tendered the same amount in groceries.

Brittany returned with a double-decker trolley loaded with plates, glasses, and silverware. My life for the next two hours. All for a good cause, though. Tony—close-cropped black hair plastered to his olive skin by sweat—followed on her heels with the bottle of wine that would highlight the auction. I held out my hand, and he passed the prize to me. I examined the label. What made this particular vintage so unusual? I shot

15

him a curious glance and set it on the table with the other contributions.

He ran a hand over his hair and gestured toward the donations. "A 2018 Bibi Graetz Testamatta Toscana. Excellent wine, rich and full-bodied." He kissed his bunched fingertips. "*Perfetto*. If the rest of my wine-lover customers join in, it should bring in a ton for the library."

"Thanks, Tony." Brittany squeezed his arm. "Quite generous of you."

"My pleasure." Red-faced, almost-black eyes glistening, he pulled back his broad shoulders, kissed Brittany's hand, and returned to the kitchen.

I folded my arms over my chest. "What's that all about?"

She blushed and tucked a strand of blond hair behind her ear. "Nothing. He was being gallant."

"You sure? That's not what your face says."

She grasped a handful of plates and centered one on each side of the table. "Don't be silly. Nothing is going on between Tony and me."

"Well, you better not let your pal Detective Olinski see that kind of nothing going on. He's got a green streak a mile long. I should know. He drove me crazy with it in high school."

"Oh, please! We've been on a couple of dates, neither of which included our wedding. Besides, people change."

"Are you kidding? To Stan Olinski, your second date *was* the wedding. He brought you a dozen roses *and* chocolates. Ghirardelli, no less. You're lucky I didn't break into your apartment and steal them after you went out." I laid silverware beside the dishes. Fork on the left, knife—blade toward the plate—and spoon on the right. My mother would be proud. "Remember how

16

he reacted when I went away to college? He stayed angry for ten years."

"I don't see the comparison. You two dated all the way through school. Everyone expected you to marry." Her lips twitched. "I think you're jealous."

"Ridiculous. If Olinski cared about me as much as he cared about that blue uniform he wanted so much, he'd have understood being a writer was my dream. Something I'd never accomplish if I became Mrs. Stanley Olinski at eighteen. I needed to experience more of the world outside this little Podunk town." To be honest, though, Brittany and Olinski had much better-matched personalities than he and I ever did.

She studied me. "I understand, but what about now? Why won't you let anyone in?"

"Come on, Britt. All my relationships end in disaster. Olinski hated me when I left for college, Scott abandoned me for a job in Paris, and you know about the last one. Face it. I have lousy instincts when it comes to men. And that obviously hasn't improved with age." My hand shook a bit as I laid down a fork. "I want to concentrate on my work. This second book is what I need to put my life back on track."

Brittany hefted another handful of plates. "Your experiences are discouraging, but don't give up. What about Eric? He's a good guy."

We made it to the last table. Finally. "Eric O'Malley is a friend."

"Uh-huh. Keep telling yourself that. You know he wants more."

True, but the thought of another relationship right now had me headed for the hills like a bandit who'd just robbed the Wells Fargo stagecoach. I placed the final wineglass and stepped back to admire our work. Not bad. Almost professional. "I know, but friends are more important at this point in my life. It's been less than a year since my last fiasco. I'm not ready to think about anything else yet."

"Well, you need to. You spend too much time alone."

I tapped her with my elbow. "That's what I have you for."

With only an hour left to turn our pumpkins into coaches and don our glass slippers, Brittany and I scurried home to our apartments across the hall from each other. Savannah greeted me with her usual fervor, and I scrambled to protect my arms and legs from her enthusiasm.

At fifty-seven pounds and growing, her behavior had evolved from koala to velociraptor on steroids. The next time I took her in for shots, I'd ask the vet about a trainer. Never having owned a dog before, I needed help before I ended up with an eighty-pound, four-legged whirling dervish.

We played tug of war with her leash until I feinted her out of the way, clipped it to her collar, then navigated the steps down to the street. Savannah mercifully skipped a few of her prime stops, and we returned home in a jiffy. I shoveled another load of food into her dish to fill her back up again. While she gobbled it down, I hopped in the shower to sluice away the day's dust and grime.

I could've sworn my meager wardrobe giggled at me as I decided what to wear. Fortunately, the casual dress code for the fundraiser made khakis and a red cotton blouse an acceptable choice. The time required to relocate the clothes from the hangers to my ever-broadening physique and plaster down my recalcitrant short, black hair left me five minutes to return to the restaurant. I met my blue eyes in the mirror and thumbed my thin nose at myself, then remembered I had to go. The only way I'd even be close to on time would be to drive.

I tossed Savannah a rawhide chew stick, which looked and tasted nothing like a shoe, in the hope she'd someday learn the difference. In the parking lot, I jumped into my new, old car—a silver 2015 Dodge Dart—and traveled the three blocks to Antonio's. I missed my Sentra, but the damage done when my vehicle was searched by the bad guy during the Cunningham investigation cost more to repair than the Nissan's value. The one time I'd ever regretted passing on the comprehensive insurance option.

Parked cars lined Main Street for blocks, and I had to circle twice to squeeze between a light-brown pickup truck and a red Honda on Pine Street in front of the post office. After a short stroll past the bakery and the drugstore, I got another look at the Dastardly Redcoat. I smiled and shook my head as I opened the door. Tony really should win this time, but he probably wouldn't. Chief Vick would be sitting on the back of Riddleton High School Principal Alan Goldfarb's candy-apple-red 1965 Mustang convertible, as always.

The crowded restaurant buzzed like an overhead power line. The competition had begun before the auction even started, with people arguing over who wanted what more. Except for the wine, the items available for bids possessed little monetary value, but the social status achieved by the highest bidder would turn some egoist into this year's whale in a puddle.

The race was also high on the topics-of-conversation list. Apparently, Brittany and I weren't the only ones to place bets on the outcome. Leonard's cousin, Greg, argued with his friend, who refused to pay off his wager while Leonard looked on.

"Not my fault your guy fell on his keister," Greg said.

"Fell, hell! The chief pushed him."

"He did not. It was an accident. Chief Vick won fair and square."

At the back of the room, Tony stretched his stocky five-foot-plus frame to the library banner, which tilted down on one side. Adjacent to the lectern, more patrons clamored for service at the bar than the fire department would appreciate, given current capacity limits. I caught Brittany's eye and smiled. A well-lubricated crowd meant a more successful auction.

I sank into the vacant seat next to Angus, designated by my name card. He'd gone all out and donned a blue suit and green tie. Spiffy, although he tugged on the collar of his white oxford shirt at every opportunity to make room for his double chin. At least I'd spend the time with my favorite diner owner and friend. "Did I miss anything?"

"Nope. Brittany hasn't opened the festivities yet." With hands clasped over his ample midsection, Angus set his sights on the table near the podium, occupied by the mayor, the chief of police, and their respective spouses. "I'm amazed they can all sit together. They have more nerve than I do, that's for sure."

"What's wrong with them sitting together?"

Angus leaned closer. "I probably shouldn't tell you this, but our mayor and the police chief were a hot item until he dumped her last week."

A long sip of Moscato fueled my response. "You ought to lay off the rumors, Angus. I was nearly arrested for murder because of gossip." The fact I inherited the bookstore didn't help much either. "People can be hurt."

He studied his fingernails. "You're right, but this isn't hearsay. I saw them together in the diner several times. Sometimes talking business, like the time he asked her how she managed to accumulate so much money in her campaign fund when the donations didn't match up. But I also overheard some utterly unbusinesslike conversations."

I poked him in the arm. "Quite accidentally, I'm sure."

A crooked grin supplemented his sidelong glance. "Of course. What else?"

Brittany approached the podium and tapped the microphone. She killed the buzz and gained our undivided attention. "I want to welcome everyone to the seventeenth annual Riddleton Library Fundraiser." She waited for the applause to stop. "Thank you all for coming. Anyone can tell you I'm a reader, not a speaker, so let's move straight to the auction, shall we?" Another ovation mixed with cheers.

"Our first item up for bids today is Bob's Bakery's donut-a-day for a year." She pointed to a bearded man at a table near the door. "John, you've been enjoying Bob's donuts for the past year. Care to start us off?"

The bids continued at a furious pace until they peaked at three hundred dollars. Bob's donuts were the Mount Everest of pastries. Soft, moist, and over-filled every time. Worth every penny. The gas station drinks went for fifty dollars each, and town hall clerk, auburn-haired Veronica Winslow, invested two hundred dollars in a hundred dollars' worth of books

21

from my bookstore. A proud moment for me. Giving something back for a change.

Veronica paid regular visits to the bookstore, and her twins had come to love our daily Story Time. While I'd hoped our gift certificate would gain us a new customer, I was happy it had gone to someone who truly appreciated the value of a good book.

On the way back to her table, Veronica stopped at mine. "Hi, Jen. I can't wait to cash in your gift certificate. Will I be able to use this to buy your new novel anytime soon?"

I swallowed the panic wedged in my throat and painted a grin over the scowl determined to appear on my face. "I hope so. I'm hard at work on it."

She brandished her prize. "Well, hurry up! I can't wait."

The aromas of Tony's culinary efforts wafted from the kitchen, which rocketed the rest of the process along posthaste. In the past, they'd served the food right away and then held the auction. However, three years ago, only five people stuck around after dinner, so they reversed the order of events.

The decision resulted in livelier competition and more money for the library. Of course, an extra hour for people to drink alcohol on empty stomachs might've helped. The fundraiser had raked in five thousand dollars, give or take, so far tonight. I'd have to remove my shoes for a more accurate count.

Tony's wine came up last. Leonard kept his word and drove the price up to almost a thousand dollars before he dropped out. I was surprised he allowed it to progress that far. A thousand dollars is a lot of money on a patrolman's salary. What would he have done if the chief quit first?

Chief Vick waved his prize overhead. Typical. "To victory! Two in one day. Can't beat it with a tree trunk."

His wife, Anne-Marie, pasted a weary smile onto the thick layer of makeup covering her burgeoning wrinkles. Years of apologies for her boorish husband had clearly drained her. Perhaps a win in the decoration competition would generate some enthusiasm in her. Tony appeared at the chief's side with a corkscrew and whispered something in his ear.

"Heck yeah," the chief said loud enough to draw all eyes to him. He handed over the wine bottle. Probably not a great idea since he already had an array of empty glasses a collector would be proud of on the table in front of him.

Tony inserted the corkscrew and turned until the wings were ready for takeoff. A push and a pull resulted in a pop, and the room erupted in cheers. He poured a half-glass for each of the table's occupants, but the chief drank down his glass and gestured for more.

After everyone had claimed their prizes, Tony and his staff served the cuisine that had tantalized us all afternoon. Gravy-smothered roast beef or broiled chicken for the main course, baked potatoes, and asparagus on the side. Antonio's hadn't let us down.

With his refilled glass in hand, Chief Vick rose to his feet. A few taps with his knife garnered everyone's attention. "Hey, folks, I know you're all ready to dive in, but I wanted to thank each and every one of you for making this fundraiser such a rousing success. Now, as Tony would say, *mangia*!" He drained his glass again before anyone else even had a sip.

Brittany joined us, and I dug my crumpled five-dollar bill out of my pocket and handed it over. Nobody would ever accuse me of weaseling out on a bet. Even if the chief did cheat.

Angus tucked his napkin into his shirt collar and ensured proper coverage.

A smirk played around my lips, and I fought to contain it.

"What? It's a brand-new shirt!" He sliced off a hunk of dripping roast beef and moaned appreciation as he chewed.

Sure enough, in the middle of the bib, he'd left behind two splashes of brown gravy. Score one for self-awareness.

As I stabbed my first asparagus spear, a scream split the air. Anne-Marie Vick stood with her hands fastened to her ears. My chair flipped as I jumped up. Chief Vick twitched and jerked on the floor. Saliva foamed out of his mouth, and blood and vomit pooled beside his head.

CHAPTER THREE

By the time the paramedics loaded Chief Vick on the gurney, his breaths had ceased, and his heart rate and blood pressure neared the bottom of the scale, according to the paramedic who measured it. His pasty skin projected a reddish tinge, and his arms and legs clenched every so often as if prepared for battle. They transported him to the ambulance, a stretcher wheel crying out for a splash of WD-40. One paramedic pushed while the other forced air into the chief's lungs with an Ambu bag fed by a portable oxygen tank.

Anne-Marie followed behind, and mascara-laden tears fashioned a black river down her cheeks. Her highlighted brown hair stuck out on the sides where she'd seized it with her hands, and her amber irises drowned in a sea of red. They'd been married for decades. A tumultuous marriage, perhaps, but still a long time to devote to one person who was suddenly unable to breathe for himself.

Try as I might, I couldn't keep my inner mystery writer at bay. Were Anne-Marie's tears a demonstration of genuine grief or the product of a crocodile? She was a real estate agent with excellent enough performance skills to convince prospective buyers a condemned dump was a fixer-upper. Still, as the spouse, she would be the first person the detectives would question if this turned out to be more than a simple medical condition. What would they find? What clandestine secrets lay deftly shrouded in the Vicks' bedroom closet?

The instant the ambulance doors closed, whispers flew like hummingbirds with too many feeders to choose from, rumor and innuendo making up the nectar.

"I overheard his wife telling someone the other day he and his whiskey enjoyed a closer relationship than the two of them did. Maybe it finally did him in."

"Nancy over at the Snip & Clip said the same thing! Poor Anne-Marie. His roving eye put her through so much. She never knows what he's doing or with who!"

"Are you kidding? He's been involved with the mayor for over a year now. That's why he won't investigate her campaign fund."

The men expressed some thoughts on the subject, too. "The dude had it coming, man. Looks like karma to me. What goes around comes around."

"At least he ain't hassling me for a change."

Tuning out the birds' chatter, Brittany and I clustered at our table with Angus, who had nothing to say for once. His silence disquieted me. Most times, I found his constant prattle reassuring. A reminder that no matter what happened, the world continued to turn. Not this time.

Brittany picked her napkin off the floor and folded the cotton fabric into a perfect square while Angus tugged at his collar. I collapsed into my chair and shoved my plate away to clear space for my elbows. And give my fluttering stomach time to settle. The asparagus spear, still attached to the end of my fork, sparred with the roast beef that once enticed me. My belly heaved, which forced acid up into my throat. This might be my last appearance at the Riddleton Library Fundraiser. Perhaps the restaurant, too. I couldn't imagine ever enjoying a meal here again.

Eric responded to the 911 call from the police department. His shirt, sized to cover the protective vest he wore underneath, included short sleeves hanging over his elbows, and his spindly legs wallowed in his uniform pants. He was thirty-one. Way past time for Opie Taylor to grow into his clothes.

Leonard, tidy in his blue sport coat and gray slacks, had managed the scene while awaiting backup. Meanwhile, Eric spoke with Mayor Benedict and her husband, Xavier. My effort to catch Eric's eye produced no results. He displayed his blank, professional expression, but I suspected his emotions roiled inside. The tension dwelled in his rigid limbs and fidgety fingers. He'd worked with the chief for five years and lost a race to him under problematic circumstances only a few hours ago. A race he'd trained for daily, for months. A race he'd intended to win. The conflict wouldn't keep him from doing his job, though.

In my head, Tobias Vick continued to writhe on the floor. The image of arms and legs jerking while foam poured out of his mouth and drained down his jaw would be superglued to my brain for the foreseeable future. Another project for my shrink, Dr. Margolis. As if I didn't have enough problems to entertain him with already.

I rested my hand on Angus's shoulder. "You ever run across anything about Chief Vick having a seizure disorder?"

Angus edged his tie down an inch and unbuttoned his collar, red-faced with a coat of sweat across his forehead. He blotted it with his napkin. "No, never. Nothing wrong with him, as far as I could tell. He always claimed he was healthy as a horse. Certainly ate like one. Bolted his lunch in my place every day. Sometimes breakfast and dinner, too. Although, someone told me his uncle suffered from epilepsy. Perhaps he inherited the condition."

Why did the chief eat so many of his meals at the diner? The grapevine asserted Anne-Marie possessed the culinary talent to write her own cookbook. No idea about the veracity of the story. She'd never invited me over for a meal. "Might've been a well-kept secret. I doubt the department would want anyone aware one of its officers might fall out any minute. Not suitable for their image."

Brittany pushed her asparagus into a circle around her white stoneware plate. "Actually, Jen, I don't think he could've joined the force if he had difficulties with seizures. Not even now, with all the drugs available. He's been around almost thirty years. No way would the police have hired him back in the Dark Ages. The state wouldn't have given him a driver's license."

"In that case, what happened to him? Why was he thrashing around in a puddle of his own puke?" My stomach threatened to add my dinner to the mess on the floor, and my foot kicked the table leg. "The vomit was bloody."

She shrugged. "Maybe he was poisoned? It's the only thing I can think of that might explain the symptoms. Unless he had an allergic reaction. I've never heard of one like that, though."

"Cyanide," Tony said as he came out from behind the podium.

I turned around. What was he doing back there? "What?"

He wrapped his arms around his chest and lowered his voice to a whisper. "It has to be cyanide."

Perspiration dotted Angus's face again. "What makes you think so?"

Tony's almost-black eyes flashed. "Classic symptoms." He turned on his heel, strode to the kitchen, and disappeared through the double-swinging doors.

Angus and Brittany gawked at me, mouths agape.

I elevated my hands, palms up. "Don't ask me. I have no idea."

Brittany fiddled with her fork. "How does he know what the symptoms of cyanide poisoning are? Guess I need to do a little research on Tony."

"If they ever let us out of here." Angus pinched his lips. "I wonder what they're waiting for."

The door opened, and Detectives Olinski and Havermayer marched in.

With a nod toward the front of the restaurant, I said, "Them."

It was the first time I'd seen either of the detectives since that night at the Cunningham house last year. Other than the peek I had the night Olinski had brought the flowers and candy to Brittany. My heart ricocheted off my breastbone as the memories rushed back. Vacant eyes. Smoke. Fire. Terror.

Deep breath in, slow breath out.

Olinski was his usual frumpy self as if he'd crawled out of a college student's laundry bag. He had a hound dog aspect to him, one in desperate need of a home.

29

In reality, however, his analytical mind could slice through granite. A walking, talking Ginsu knife.

His antonym, Francine—although I'd never heard anyone call her that—Havermayer starched her clothes into place, no matter the circumstances. She could dig ditches and walk away without a speck of dust on her. Me? I got dirty stepping out of the shower.

The detectives took control of the scene and directed the patrol officers to collect contact information from everyone present. Eric approached our group while Leonard started on the other side of the room. Olinski and Havermayer took over the conversation with Teresa and Xavier Benedict.

Would the mayor tell the truth about her relationship with the chief? Did the mayor actually *have* a relationship with the chief other than as his boss? Either way, I doubted she'd discuss it in front of her spouse. What I wouldn't give to be a piece of gum stuck under the tabletop for that little chat.

Armed with his notebook and pen, Eric asked us basic questions about what had happened before the incident. Our answers were unanimous: nothing unusual. He took our information, but I stopped him before he proceeded to the next group. "Are you guys going to treat this like a crime scene?"

One eyebrow went up. "Why would we? The chief had a seizure. Upsetting, but not illegal. We're questioning everybody. That should be enough for now."

I pointed to the detectives. "If you're so convinced there's no reason to be concerned, why are they here?"

His green eyes fired lasers. "Because the chief's one of our own. We're all hands on deck for something

30

like this." He took a deep breath. "Why are you trying to make more of this than it is?"

My dander rose to the occasion. "What if the chief didn't have a seizure? Shouldn't you collect the evidence to be safe?"

Eric tucked his thumbs into the top of his Sam Browne belt. Opie Taylor playing gunslinger. "What are you thinking?"

"He can't be epileptic, or he wouldn't be on the police force, right?"

"I'm no doctor, but I'm sure there are other reasons someone might have a seizure. We need to wait for more information."

"What if someone poisoned him?" I clenched my fists at my sides. "Evidence may be lost. The dishes and glasses will be washed as soon as you clear the scene."

"That's a gigantic assumption, don't you think?" He ran a hand through his almost orange hair. "The detectives are the best at their jobs. They'll consider everything. Right now, we have no reason to believe this is anything other than what it appears to be. A medical emergency." He gazed into my eyes, leaned in, and whispered, "I care about you, so please don't go running off half-cocked like you did last time. Nothing to worry about, until there is. When that comes about, we'll handle it. I don't want anything to happen to you."

When? Not if? So much for the medical emergency theory. "I think you know more than you're willing to admit."

His step back created space between us. In more ways than one. "No, I don't, and if I did, I couldn't tell you. Do me a favor, and forget about this, okay?"

Not really, but I had little choice in the matter. The alternative would turn the entire Riddleton police force against me. I had enough trouble keeping friends already.

Eric retreated, and the detectives filled the vacuum. We answered all the questions again. Havermayer squinted at me, lips pressed flat as if she had no problem suspecting me of murder. Again. No evidence to back up the insinuation this time, though. No motive, either. Chief Vick and I hadn't spoken five words to each other in the year and a half since I landed back in town. Not even during Aletha's homicide investigation. He'd left all the baseless accusations to Olinski and Havermayer.

Olinski rubbed the back of his neck and adjusted his dark-rimmed glasses. "Now, Jen, we gonna have any problems with you, or will you keep your nose to yourself, and let us do our jobs this time?"

"I don't recall giving you any trouble the last time. In fact, my memory is convinced I solved your case for you."

His nostrils flared. "Not quite what I remember. Regardless, no case to solve at the moment, so don't you go creating one. The chief had a seizure. I'm sure he'll be fine in a few days, and that'll be the end of it."

The paramedic who forced oxygen into him on the way out the door would probably disagree. "I hope you're right, but don't you think you should collect the evidence just in case? Why are you here, if not to investigate?"

"There you go again. There isn't anything to collect because, as far as we can tell, no crime has occurred. Why don't you go home and finish your book? I'm tired of hearing people talk about it."

So much for working out our differences on the ride home from Savannah when he dragged me back for questioning about Aletha's murder. No hope of our ever being friends. What did Brittany see in him? If he'd changed at all since high school, it was for the worse. "Fine. I'll go home and work on my novel if you'll at least consider the possibility there might be more here than a medical condition. You always accuse me of making assumptions. What do you think you're doing now? Tony thinks it's cyanide poisoning."

"He would."

"What does that mean?"

"Forget it." Olinski inhaled a deep breath and expelled the air a little at a time. "I still think you're overreacting, but I'll keep an open mind." After one more glare from Havermayer, the detectives headed for the next table.

Brittany turned to me. "Maybe he's right. We could be jumping to conclusions."

Wow. I never expected a statement like that from my best friend. She'd always covered my back, even when I was wrong. Too much time spent with Olinski? "You're on his side because you're dating him."

Her jaw fell. "I can't believe you said that." She put her hands on my upper arms. "All I'm saying is, I can't think of any reason someone would seriously hurt or try to kill Chief Vick."

I had no answer. He was an irritating, irascible man, but if that was a motive for murder, few men over fifty would still be alive. "Still, I'd expect you to back me up. I'm your best friend. He's some guy you've been on two dates with."

Brittany's face turned red, and her voice went up an octave. "I'm always on your side, but sometimes you're wrong. And I've known Olinski as long as you have.

He isn't some guy I just met in a bar. I'm sorry if you have a problem with our relationship, but I'm not going to stop seeing him just because you don't like it."

I bit back the nasty reply surging toward my lips. No sense in provoking a cornered animal. She'd cool off a lot faster if I let her be. The mayor and her husband drifted away from their table, and I wandered in that direction. All the plates remained where the occupants had abandoned them in the ruckus. However, the glasses, and the wine bottle, had disappeared.

CHAPTER FOUR

Sunday morning dawned hot and humid. Clouds wrapped the sky in a lackluster gray blanket, leaving the streets of Riddleton desolate and depressing. A perfect backdrop for my current mood. I drenched my T-shirt with sweat while Savannah completed her rounds. Sniff scratch squat, sniff scratch squat, all the way around the block, one tree, mailbox post, and fire hydrant at a time.

"Come on, kid, let's go. I'm ready for a shower."

She turned her head toward me, pulled her ears back, and waved her bushy tail back and forth through the dense, pre-storm air. Not much of a breeze, but my German shepherd loved me. That would have to be enough.

My ill humor, however, was unrelated to the weather or the dog, more like a night filled with scenes of Chief Vick writhing on the floor along with last September's fiery collapse of the Cunningham house combined in a horrific freak show. I awoke drenched with sweat, heart pounding. A peaceful snooze used to be one of my preferred ways to spend my free time. Not anymore.

Dr. Margolis suspected PTSS after the events last year. He offered to prescribe an antidepressant and something to help me rest, but the last thing I needed was some drug to cloud my already challenged creativity.

If I'd managed to survive a childhood with my irrational mother and psychologically abusive stepfather, I could pull through this. I *would* pull through this. The mantra the doctor taught me worked well enough when my emotions threatened to bury me under a pile of rubble.

Deep breath in, slow breath out.

The exercise calmed my racing heart but provided little help for the turmoil in my head. Did Chief Vick experience a sudden onset seizure disorder, as the police wanted to believe? Or was he poisoned, as Brittany and Tony had suggested?

And what happened to the glasses and the wine bottle? If someone took them because they contained evidence, the culprit stayed in the room with us all evening. Somebody hung around and answered questions as if they had nothing to do with the situation. As if they hadn't tried to murder our chief of police. The concept propelled my heart back into the Kentucky Derby.

Teresa and Xavier Benedict sat at the same table as the chief. Was she involved somehow? Revenge for the chief ending their alleged affair? A bit extreme, even for a woman scorned. A little vinegar in his precious vino, perhaps, but a toxic substance? Hard to say what she might've been thinking, though. The mayor would be considered above suspicion and would've had no trouble stashing the evidence in the duffel bag she called a purse.

What about her husband? Did he find out about the affair and decide to end the relationship himself? Could be, but how did he abscond with the glasses and bottle?

Unless he and Teresa were in on it together. *Nah.* More likely, someone started to clean up, and one of the detectives told them to stop. The cops would've retrieved the evidence or at least noticed it missing, right? I should ask Eric about that.

No, I refused to make their problem mine. Lesson learned about interference in police business. Despite the fact Olinski and Eric didn't believe it. Investigations were too time-consuming, too dangerous, and I had too much to lose. Like my freedom or my life.

Finally finished checking her pee-mail, Savannah dragged me to the steps of my apartment building, only one thing on her mind: breakfast. An enormous bowl of kibble and a couple of good-girl treats waited for her at the top. Coffee waited for me. The magic elixir, which stimulated my creativity, enabled my fingers to fly across the keyboard and, most importantly, kept my eyelids open.

The steps disappeared under our feet two at a time, both of us eager for our respective rewards. We'd established our morning routine by the time the pup had lived with me for two weeks. We walked, she ate and I sipped, then I showered while she napped away her Mount Whitney-sized belly on the bathroom rug. A workable situation, as long as I kept the water behind the shower curtain. An accidental splash sent her running from the acid rain. Couldn't wait to administer her first bath. I'd have to drape the walls and floor in plastic like a serial killer.

I threw on shorts and a Pat Benatar T-shirt and stared at my cell phone beside the coffeemaker. Should I call Eric and ask what they'd found so far? No, I needed to stay out of it.

But he was my friend, and I should check on him. He had a shock last night.

I picked up the phone and laid it back down. Was that actually why I wanted to contact him? Probably not. How about if I didn't mention the investigation? Then I could do my friendly duty without interfering, right?

I snatched the cell and thumbed the button before changing my mind again.

His groggy voice answered on the third ring. "Hello?"

I forgot he worked overnight. *Some friend.* "Hey, Eric. I'm sorry I woke you."

"No problem, I'm always awake for you. What's up?"

Always awake? For me? Brittany was right. Not making that mistake again, though. "Nothing. I just thought I should check on you. I suspect you were more upset last night than you let on."

He chuckled. "I'm okay, but that's not why you called."

Did everyone know me better than I knew myself? "Not true. Am I really such an awful person you'd assume I have an ulterior motive?"

"No, of course not. I understand you. The chief's illness is a mystery, and you can't help yourself. So, what do you want to know?"

I sipped my coffee. His assumption was correct, but I refused to make it any more obvious. "I do care if you're all right. Seeing Chief Vick like that had to be hard on you. You've been friends for a long time."

"I'd hardly call us friends. He's my boss. I'm not sure he even likes me."

That's new. "Why do you say that?"

"Just a sense. He barely listens when I talk to him, and when I asked for a new partner, he refused without explanation."

"What's wrong with Leonard?"

He sighed. "Nothing. I was only supposed to be his training officer, never his permanent partner. Time for him to move on."

Strange. Eric liked everyone. Why not Leonard? "Perhaps the chief has plans he isn't ready to tell you about. A restructuring or something."

"Maybe. Listen, Jen, I need to get some sleep. I'm back on shift this afternoon."

"Sure. I'm sorry. Just one more thing. Last night the wineglasses and the bottle disappeared from the chief's table. Did you guys collect them for evidence?"

"No, I don't think so. Someone from the restaurant staff must've picked them up."

The staff or the perpetrator? Either way, the cops blew it. Good thing I wasn't the "I told you so" type. "Thanks, Eric. I'll talk to you later. Sleep tight."

Savannah stretched down the length of the couch. Mount Whitney rose and fell with regularity, and her paws twitched. Mind whirling, I settled in front of my laptop. When my word processing program booted up, the cursor at the Chapter Fifteen decorating the other-wise blank page taunted me.

Write something, write something, write some-thing . . .

The midpoint. The twins, Dana and Daniel Davenport were hot on the trail of their father's best friend, Peter Robinson, convinced he'd killed their father, Victor. Of course, he had nothing to do with it, but all the circumstantial evidence pointed to him. Red herring was my favorite dish. I took a deep, cleansing breath, and my fingertips hovered, ready to pounce at the slightest reason.

Dana handed Daniel the slip of paper found in her father's sock drawer. "What do you make of this?"

Victor,
Meet me at your house at 2:30. It's important.
Pete

He shrugged. "So what? They met here a lot."
"I put away Dad's laundry the morning he died. The note wasn't in there."
"So, Dad stashed it sometime later."
Dana crossed her arms, meeting her brother's gaze. "Exactly. But Peter said he didn't see Dad that day."

Okay, now what? Dana will want to confront Peter. Daniel will insist they show the paper to Detective Abernathy. I needed them to challenge their father's friend into doing something stupid. Although, what that might be, I had no idea. Yet. Time for another sibling squabble. My favorite part to write. I guess because I never had siblings to squabble with.

Before I finished my third sentence, my phone rang. I wanted to ignore the thing, but Sunday meant the call could be from my mother. We'd developed a routine since she took care of me after my fiery night in September. We called each other on alternate Sundays. Our relationship was still adversarial at times, but at least she gave up the harassment about finding a "real job" and a husband. And she still pouted about not having grandchildren, apparently my sole reason for existence.

Inheriting the bookstore alleviated the pressure on the employment part. Though the store generated no

40

profits, she considered it a respectable occupation. In return for her rational behavior, I always answered her calls and remained civil for as long as she allowed. A win for both of us.

I picked it up on the third ring, disregarding Savannah's glare at the disturbance. "Hi, Mom. How are you?"

"How do you think I am?"

Uh-oh. "What's wrong?"

"You were supposed to call me this morning."

Switching hands, I tapped my fingers on the desk. "I called you last Sunday. Your turn this week."

"Oh, no. Your turn and clearly you didn't want to talk to me."

What's going on? She'd not had a day like this in a long time. "Not true. I'm sorry if I forgot I was supposed to call you today." Sometimes I was the only grown-up in our relationship. Scary concept. "Chief Vick had a seizure at the fundraiser last night, and my mind won't think about anything else."

No response. She sniffled in the distance, then huffed into the microphone.

I pulled my cell away from my ear. "Mom, are you all right?"

"What? I'm fine."

I rubbed the back of my neck to push the tension into my shoulders, then twisted my head in a circle, eliciting several satisfying cracks. "You're not fine. You're crying."

"Who says I'm crying? You're crazy! I'm hanging up now. Call me when you're ready to be reasonable."

Savannah lifted her head again, eyes focused on the dead phone. "I think something's wrong with Grandma."

41

She thumped her tail, raising puffs of dust. The cleaning fairy must've taken the day off again. "No, that's not a happy thing." She turned over on her back for a belly rub. I obliged. "Guess I'll give her time to cool off and call her back. I'm worried about her." Thump, thump, thump.

Two more sentences graced the screen before a knock on the door triggered an explosion of rumbling woofs. Olinski and Havermayer stood on the other side of the peephole.

What's with these two and Sunday mornings?

They showed up on a Sunday to tell me about Aletha, too. Perhaps they wouldn't ruin my day this time. But why else would they be here?

"Morning, detectives. To what do I owe the pleasure?" Their blank expressions proved the sarcasm in my tone had flown over them like a jet with a tailwind.

Olinski strode through the doorway. "We need to ask you some questions, Jen."

Havermayer followed him into the living room, glanced at the couch, and elected to remain standing. Savannah took advantage of the detective's indecision, jumping back into her favored nap spot. The fastidious woman pinched her lips and turned away.

I suppressed a smirk. *Who's a good dog?* "What's up? Is the chief okay?"

Olinski maneuvered his glasses back to the bridge of his nose. "Chief Vick succumbed to his illness early this morning."

Well, crap. First time in my life, I wanted to be wrong. "I'm sorry to hear that. Any idea of the cause yet?"

"We suspect cyanide poisoning, but we won't have confirmation until the medical examiner finishes her assessment. Which leads me to my first question: what made you so sure he didn't have a seizure?"

Since when did he pay attention to anything I said? "The chief had a violent reaction within minutes of drinking the wine that didn't look like anything medical I've ever heard about. When Tony mentioned cyanide, it made sense."

Havermayer folded her arms across her chest. "You were the last one with the bottle before the auction. Perhaps, you're the one who added the poison."

Here we go again. Didn't she have anything better to do than invent silly stories about me? Sounded like her wine came from sour grapes. "With Brittany and Tony cheering me on? Maybe the vineyard put something in before they shipped it. Makes about as much sense. Why would I want to murder Chief Vick?"

Her green eyes snapped. "You tell me. If you have a motive, we'll find out. Might as well tell us now."

I turned to Olinski. "Is she for real?"

He rattled the keys in his overcoat pocket, and a hint of a smile played around the corners of his mouth. "Detective Havermayer is exploring all possibilities."

My eyebrows lunged toward my nose. "Well, she's foraging in the wrong forest this time. I knew almost nothing about the man. All I did was put the bottle Tony gave me on the table with the rest of the donations. I had no opportunity to tamper with anything before the auction. Brittany can vouch for me."

"All right. Tell me how Tony came to mention the cyanide."

"Brittany, Angus, and I were discussing the possibility it might not be a medical issue because it didn't seem logical a cop would have a seizure disorder. Britt said

43

she would do some research, and Tony told her he recognized the symptoms of cyanide poisoning. When we asked him why he thought so, he walked away without a word. Ask *him* how he drew that conclusion."

"I would, if I could find him. Any idea where he is?"

A headache ballooned above my eyes. I massaged my temples. "No, I haven't spoken to him since last night."

Olinski stepped toward the door, Havermayer in tow. "If he contacts you, call us."

"You really think he could've had something to do with the chief's death?"

He shrugged. "We're not ruling anyone out at this point."

I closed the door behind them and rested my head against the cool, painted wood. No way I would be able to focus on my work anymore while Olinski's and my mother's words danced together in my head. A tango in which the roses were all thorns.

CHAPTER FIVE

Determined to salvage something of the day, I rescued Savannah's leash from the doorknob. "Come on, kid, let's go for a walk."

She slid off the couch, yawned, and stretched her way to the door.

"Try to contain your enthusiasm."

We skipped down the steps into the summer gloom. In the distance, storm clouds gathered. Nothing like a morning thunderstorm to brighten the day.

We drifted down Main Street past the Goodwill, where Sunday discounts had attracted their regular crowd of thrifty shoppers. The town hall and the police department seemed quiet as we headed toward the bookstore to check on Lacey and barista-in-chief, as he liked to call himself, Charlie Nichols.

Charlie was a thirty-five-year-old computer geek who could easily pass for a teenager camped out at the nerd table in the high school library. His parents finally pried him out of their basement last summer, and he'd moved into the apartment below mine.

When Aletha left me the business, I had no idea what to do with it. I was an English major in college with no relevant experience. The one thing I did know was she had a vision and tasked me with bringing it to fruition. And bring it to fruition, I would, for her sake if nothing else. With Lacey and Charlie's help, of course.

The bells over the door jingled as we entered, but the place appeared empty. Lacey had to be around here somewhere, though. She'd never leave the store unsecured. Although a town with a population of ten thousand or so and a crime rate near zero—if you didn't count last year's murders, which were completely unexpected—Riddleton did, however, have a miscreant or two. Usually a bored teenager after Mommy and Daddy's attention.

Savannah turned her tail into a propeller and cruised full steam ahead to the front counter, where Lacey kept the coveted bacon snacks. Unfortunately, no delicacies manifested out of the sea, and the pup voiced her dissatisfaction with a muted yip.

"All right, little girl, I'm coming. Hold your horses." Lacey removed the apron she wore over her uniform— khaki slacks and red Ravenous Readers polo shirt—when at work in the stockroom. She fumbled under the cash register for the treat bag.

Savannah spun in a circle, then trembled on her haunches in a struggle to maintain contact with the floor. Lacey tossed a meaty lifeline to the half-starved dog, turned on the lights, and flipped the sign in the window, which declared us open for business.

Ten o'clock already. Where had the morning gone? I removed a cup from the stack and filled it with fresh-brewed coffee. "Where's Charlie?"

"He ran over to Bob's to pick up the goodies."

My stomach grumbled at the mention of donuts, muffins, and croissants. My favorite kinds of empty calories. Hanging around here without parental supervision had already thickened my waistline by half an inch. Too much more and I'd need new jeans. Nope, not in the budget.

I roamed the store to ensure the tables were clean and the chairs straight. No need, though. Charlie just snapped his fingers like Mary Poppins, and the place cleaned and organized itself. Given our interactions when he first moved into the apartment below mine, I hadn't expected much when I hired him. He'd always seemed outrageous and irresponsible. But Charlie volunteered to work for what I could pay. As it happened, he would've been a bargain at twice the price.

Lacey was a lucky find, as well. The mid-thirties soccer mom type had helped out at the bookstore since its inception, and Aletha had taught her everything she knew about retail management, making Lacey the perfect person to step into the manager role. From a financial perspective, I should've run the business myself, but that wouldn't leave me enough time to write. Also, like Charlie, Lacey agreed to do the job for almost nothing until we turned a profit or I finished my book, whichever came first. I still didn't completely understand why, but I probably wouldn't have survived this long without her.

She picked up a feather duster and started on the cherry bookcases along the walls. "Difficult news about Chief Vick, huh?"

"No kidding. What an awful thing. I can't get the scene out of my mind."

"I'm glad I didn't see what happened. I'd be crawling into my kids' beds after bad dreams instead of the other way around. Anne-Marie must be devastated."

47

Lacey had a boy and a girl, six and eight, respectively, both prone to nightmares. She often found herself trying to sleep in a crowded bed.

"Yeah, I hope the cops won't harass her too much. I remember what they did to Tim Cunningham when they thought he was guilty."

She shifted from Art to Biography. "Why would they? Didn't the chief have a seizure?"

I seared my tongue on the not-quite-cool-enough-to-drink-yet coffee. "Olinski and Havermayer came to my apartment. They think he had a seizure as a result of cyanide in his system. He passed away this morning."

The duster hit the floor as Lacey smothered her mouth with her hands. "Oh! I had no idea he didn't make it. I must call Anne-Marie." She knelt and retrieved the fallen feathers. "Could it have been an accident? I mean, who'd want to kill him?"

Anyone who's ever met him? I leaned against the coffee bar and braved another sip. "Beats me, but the spouse is almost always the first person they consider." Although, Havermayer seemed happy to move me to the top of the list just 'cause. "You know her better than I do. Does she have any reason to want him dead?"

"Other than his personality?"

"Ha ha. If that was her motive, she'd have killed him years ago. It needs to be something recent that made her snap."

"Nothing I can think of. But who knows what goes on in someone else's marriage."

"True. Does she have anyone to help her sort everything out?"

"I suppose Teresa will. They've been friends for years." My voice dropped. "Oh."

"What's wrong?"

I filled her in on what Angus said about the mayor and the chief. "But you know him. The whole thing is probably a figment of his imagination."

"It's pretty crappy if true. Teresa having an affair with the husband of her close friend? That's low even for a politician. Besides, Teresa came in here the other day and said Vick planned to run against her in November. He had his faults, but I can't believe he'd do that to someone he cared about. Unless, of course, Angus was right, and it was one heck of a bad breakup."

"Could be, but would that be enough of a reason for her to murder him?"

Lacey shrugged. "Stranger things have happened. If she could do that to her friend, she could probably do just about anything."

"Maybe, but if they were in a relationship, and Anne-Marie found out about it, that might've been the trigger for her to kill him."

"Even if he ended it?"

"Could be."

"I just thought of something." Lacey tapped the duster against her hand. "When I was in the diner for lunch Friday, Anne-Marie was eating with a younger woman who was obviously pregnant. I couldn't hear what they were saying, but Anne-Marie was very angry."

"So?"

"So, what if the chief was the father? What if that's why he ended it with Teresa? But he refused to leave his wife, and the woman decided to take matters into her own hands."

I shook my head. "What if you've been spending too much time with Angus?"

Color rose into her cheeks. "You're right. It is a bit far-fetched. I got carried away."

"No problem. All we have is speculation at this point. Your theory is as good as anyone else's. However, Olinski also told me Tony is missing. They can't find him anywhere. Weird after he brought up poison as a possibility last night."

"Tony? What would he know about the subject?"

"I'm not sure. He made an odd comment about the chief being poisoned. An unusual thing for him to pull out of thin air. Olinski asked me about what he said, but I couldn't say what he referred to."

"What if he didn't pull it out of thin air? What if he's seen this before?"

Hmmm. "I never considered that. Might be worth some investigation."

Lacey smirked. "By anyone other than you, right?"

I did my Groucho Marx imitation—waggling eyebrows and imaginary cigar. "Of course. What else?"

I left Savannah, our official mascot, in the care of Aunt Lacey and Uncle Charlie to allow them to spoil her with treats and allow me to feign ignorance. Not to mention procure a healthier meal for me without a health department complaint against Angus for a dog in the restaurant. Nobody local would turn us in, but no way to predict who might pass through on a Sunday morning.

Activity at the police station had picked up some during my visit with Lacey; however, the town hall on the corner remained quiet. Angus had managed to get some work done on his windows yesterday. His sketch was complete, and all that remained was for him to color inside the lines.

The left window portrayed George Washington flipping burgers on a grill while American soldiers sat on the ground, muskets leaning against the trees, chowing down. The door showed a Minuteman carrying a loaded tray to the other side, where a British soldier on the right window waited to receive them. The remaining Redcoats sat on the ground, muskets leaning against the trees, waiting for their lunch.

Well done, Angus.

Once inside, I perched on a counter stool, and Angus directed his orchestra of cooks, busboys, and servers. His black combover flopped whenever he gesticulated a direction, but the white apron around his generous core still lacked its typical colorful ornamentation. By the end of the day, his protective cloth would resemble a Sarah Spitler abstract painting. He should sell the thing on eBay.

The restaurant contained a near-capacity crowd, which would evolve into standing room only when the churches let out. Down-home food, speedy service, and reasonable prices made the Dandy Diner perfect for me. My culinary skills would make a competitive eater retire.

A break in the action provided Angus the opportunity to come over. "Morning, Jen. The usual, or do you have a sense of adventure today? I can whip up some French toast for you. Eggs only, no milk. What do you think?"

The backflips my belly responded with indicated a solid nay vote. "The usual will do. Not feeling adventurous after last night."

"I understand. Coming right up. With coffee, of course." He flashed uniform, white teeth and patted my cold hand with one of his warm, moist ones. "A fresh pot is almost done."

The man always knew what I needed. Angus relayed my order to the tall guy at the far end of the grill, then returned with my java. Steam circulated the distinctive aroma, and I inhaled deeply, relaxing into it.

The man who cracked my eggs seemed familiar somehow, but he faced away from me. I pointed him out. "New cook?"

"Yes. He moved to town last week. In fact, he's a friend of yours. Marcus Jones?"

Aletha's ex-boyfriend. I never dreamed I'd run into him again. I took a large swallow of coffee. "He lives in Blackburn. How'd he end up here?"

Angus wiped the Formica beside me. "I'm not sure why he relocated, but he's in the diner because he needed a job, and I needed an experienced cook."

"Interesting." Did Marcus inform Angus about his past? Should I tell him? I caught my lower lip between my teeth.

"He told me he's on probation, if you're worried. He also told me you saved his life. All the résumé I required."

My shoulders relaxed. "Thank you. I appreciate you giving him a shot."

He winked at me. "Well, as they say, any friend of my favorite author . . ."

"Lucky for you my list of friends is quite short. Otherwise, your payroll would take a whole week to process."

Angus collected my breakfast and whispered something to Marcus, who accompanied him back. When he approached me, his chestnut-brown face split into a contagious grin. "Surprised?"

I shared his smile along with the memories of how

we'd rescued his kids when they were kidnapped. "I am. How are you and the girls?"

A cloud descended. "We're okay, considering. Mama died last month."

"I'm so sorry, Marcus. What happened?"

"A bad stroke. They couldn't save her."

Was Vangie's empty stare when we last met a precursor? "How are Larissa and Latoya dealing with it?"

"They're all right. Don't understand too much. One of the reasons we moved. Toya kept asking when Grandmama was coming home."

My heart expanded in my chest. Too difficult to explain death to a five-year-old. "Poor baby. Where are you staying?"

"With an old friend of my mama. Mary Washington. Her husband died around the same time. She lets us stay with her, and I help with the bills, so everything worked out fine. She also minds the girls when I'm here."

The cancer finally beat Harry Washington. That explained why I hadn't seen old Mrs. W. at the bus stop in a while. No need to visit him in the nursing home anymore. "I'm happy things fell into place for you. You and the kids deserve a fresh start."

Marcus pressed his lips into a line. "Well, I better go back to work before I'm unemployed again." He turned away, then back. "I never thanked you for saving us. When I think about what might've happened to my babies . . ."

"Sure you did. At the hospital, remember? Besides, you would've helped me too, I'm sure."

He tilted his head and frowned. "You're right, I would. Now, you better eat your food before icicles grow on it."

I concentrated on my plate full of eggs over medium, bacon, grits, and toast, but my appetite failed me. Strange because I hadn't eaten since lunch yesterday. The closest I'd come was the asparagus spear, probably still stuck to the end of my fork. I forced down a few bites to avoid hurting Angus's feelings and shoved the dish away. Coffee appeared to be the only thing my stomach would tolerate.

Chief Vick's death had no more to do with me than any other citizen of Riddleton, but I couldn't pry it out of my mind. Was it the challenge of a mystery? Idle curiosity? Neither one was a good enough reason to risk the wrath of Olinski again. Handcuffs made a lousy fashion accessory.

Anyway, where would I start? Anne-Marie Vick was the obvious choice, but I didn't have enough information about her to envision a motive. Unless she'd finally had enough of his womanizing. What if he really did father that woman's child, as Lacey suggested? That would set off even the most understanding of wives.

Would Anne-Marie risk going to prison for killing her husband? Silly when divorce was so much simpler. Easier to get away with, too. Did she have a financial incentive of some sort? Police work, while rewarding and necessary, didn't pay very well. I couldn't imagine the Vicks had a considerable investment portfolio Anne-Marie wanted all to herself.

A pregnant girlfriend would set off Teresa Benedict, too. Especially if the chief ended their relationship because of it. The mayor had a re-election campaign to worry about, though. The very suspicion of involvement in a murder would damage her chances. Plus, the word on the street—in other words, Angus—was Teresa had set her sights on higher office. Which one, I had no idea. Either way, her name couldn't come up in the investigation. Even if cleared, her political career would be in jeopardy. She'd be crazy to take the chance.

But what about her husband, Xavier? Did he find out about the affair and decide to end it himself, unaware the chief already had? He wouldn't care about his wife's re-election prospects if he was blinded by jealousy, and it wouldn't be the first time a man ever murdered his spouse's lover. Jealousy was one of the top three motives for homicide.

That left Tony. What did I know about him? Not much. His move here from Chicago came after a nasty divorce. Which could've been a handy excuse, though. I needed to look into the possibility he had experience with death from cyanide poisoning. Sounded like a job for Brittany. Assuming she wasn't too busy with Olinski, of course.

Why was I worried about this stuff, anyway? Not my problem. I had a mystery of my own to deal with, and it was sitting on my desk right now, waiting for me. I blew a hard breath out through pursed lips and sipped my coffee.

Angus took a break from his concerto. "Are you okay?"

I ran a hand through my hair and smoothed the tufts back down. "I'm fine. My brain won't let go of the chief's death. Like I'm an addict, or something. I can't interfere, though."

"Absolutely not. Olinski would eat you for breakfast."

"No kidding. By the way, have you seen Tony Scavuto today?"

"No, why?"

"Olinski and Havermayer are looking for him."

"Did they try his cabin? He has one up on the lake somewhere."

Someplace on the forty-one-mile-long, fourteen-mile-wide lake. Glad I wasn't the one who had to find him. "I didn't know that."

"He bought it last summer. Said it would be a great place to hide."

"Apparently, he was right. I'll have to tell the detectives."

He took my plate, scraped the remains of my food into a container, and handed it to me. A mid-morning snack for Savannah. "Too bad Eric didn't receive the promotion he wanted. He'd let you help."

"Promotion?"

"Yeah, when Larry Smith retired, a spot for a new detective opened up. The kid thought he had a real chance."

Disappointment for him welled in my chest. I took a swallow of my cold coffee. "What happened?"

"The chief shut him down. Told him, 'Over my dead body.' He didn't tell you?"

"No," I replied, irritation clenching my jaw. "He never said a word."

CHAPTER SIX

I exited from the artificial atmosphere of the restaurant into the blustery winds of a looming summer storm. The black sky headed our way. There was no rain here yet, but the squall would be a ripper when it arrived. Of course, I had no idea where my umbrella might be or if I even had one. Time to collect Savannah and proceed home.

When I crossed Pine Street, the town hall appeared desolate, almost abandoned. Next door, however, the Riddleton Police Department bustled. Uniformed officers entered and exited in groups, civilians one or two at a time. Amazing what a murder could do to kick people into motion. Especially with the chief of police as the victim.

Anne-Marie Vick and her son stood on the steps by the American flag wreath on the door. She brushed her highlighted brown hair off her cheek with an impeccably manicured hand. Her face had aged overnight, and dark glasses guarded her eyes.

Twenty-one-year-old Zach shoved his hands into the pockets of his jeans and shifted his weight from one Reebok to the other. His gaze darted as if tracking a bee he feared might sting him. However, it never landed on his mother. Not likely she'd be able to count on him for emotional support.

I started up the stairs toward them, carefully avoiding the red, white, and blue garland wrapped around the handrail. "Anne-Marie, Zach, I'm so sorry for your loss."

She lifted her glasses and dabbed at a tear with a crumpled tissue. "Thank you. It's a terrible shock."

Zach brushed his black hair—long on the top with buzzed sides—off his forehead and nodded. He laser-focused his gray eyes on me. "I *will* find out who did this."

The sensation of uneasy fingers tripped down my spine. Did he think I had something to do with it? Another visit from my old pal paranoia. "I suggest you be careful, Zach. In my experience, the detectives don't like when regular people interfere in their investigations."

His eyes flashed. "I'm not a regular person. I start at the police academy next month, and Dad told me a spot on the force would open up by the time I graduate. I'm practically a cop."

Anne-Marie jerked her head in his direction but said nothing.

Someone leaving RPD? Something else Eric never mentioned. "I'm sure your father taught you a lot about police work over the years, but I suggest letting the professionals handle it."

Zach folded his arms across his chest and glared at me. His lips twitched.

My stomach did a somersault. Trouble would be headed his way if he didn't give up the idea of finding the killer. I turned to Anne-Marie. "How are you?"

A flurry of sadness, fear, and anxiety zipped across

her face. "It hasn't sunk in yet." She removed her glasses and fixed her amber eyes on mine. Puffy dark circles documented a sleepless night. "I'm aware of what people say about him. He has . . . had . . . his problems, but he always put his family first."

Did she genuinely believe that, or was she protecting herself? The former meant she was unaware of his alleged affair with the mayor. But if it was the latter, then she assumed I was the oblivious one. It wasn't my place to inform her whichever way. I wanted to ask about her pregnant lunch date on Friday but didn't dare do that, either. "I understand. Our interactions with him were snippets out of time. You knew the man inside the chief of police."

Her lips creased into a sad smile. "I did."

"If you need anything, please tell me. I want to help if I can."

She stared down at her hands. "Thank you. I will."

I nodded to Zach, who picked at his thumbnail, seemingly oblivious to the world around him.

It had started to sprinkle, so I ducked next door into Ravenous Readers. No decorations yet. Lacey must still be working on her design for the contest. Something elaborate, I imagined, since she refused to allow me a glimpse of it.

I slithered into a seat at my favorite table by the window where I once spent so much time writing. Or trying to, anyway. But the space had lost the magic. Maybe it'd never been the space at all. Maybe I missed Aletha's warmth and support, my chest now filled with the responsibility of her legacy. I hadn't made much progress with the bookstore yet, but I hadn't burned down the place, either. A minor victory.

Charlie—in jeans, cowboy boots, western shirt, and cream-colored, ten-gallon hat—had returned from Bob's. I approached the pastry display case and peeked around, looking for his horse Trigger. No sign of him. Must be out back, grazing.

Savannah caught my scent and came charging. I braced for impact and addressed Charlie while she jumped against my hands in a desperate attempt to wash my face with her tongue. "Got a hoedown after work?"

He flashed his perfect teeth. "Nope, only feeling fearless today. Thought I should dress the part." He hitched up his britches. "At least I left the six-shooters home, right?"

I shook my head and scratched the somewhat calmer puppy behind her ears. There was no point in expecting him to wear his uniform. It wasn't in his nature, and I knew that when I hired him. "Don't gravitate from fearless to reckless, all right?"

"You bet, Boss." He handed me a cup of coffee—cream and two sugars, just the way I liked it.

I blew the steam away and took a small sip. "Where's Lacey?"

He moseyed toward me with thumbs hooked in his belt loops. "She's in the back, taking inventory. Want me to fetch her for you?"

"Nah. Tell her I'm going home if she needs anything. Thanks."

He offered me a lid for my cup, then tipped his hat. "My pleasure, ma'am."

I smiled and shook my head. When they made him, they broke the mold. Unfortunately, he was still in it at the time.

When Savannah and I scurried into the street, the temperature had fallen, the darkened clouds now accompanied by the wind in a Halloween-style duet. I ducked my head and jammed my hands into my pockets, Savannah's leash looped around my wrist. "C'mon, little girl, let's go."

She trotted beside me until we arrived at her favorite oak tree in front of the police department steps. She followed her nose around the trunk, inch by inch, and ignored all attempts to move her toward home.

"Looks like you're here for the duration."

I glanced back toward the familiar voice.

Eric stood with one foot on the bottom step, a clean uniform slung over his shoulder. His red hair was a burst of color framed by the gray sky.

"Indeed. Unless you have a bomb on you. That might budge her an inch or two."

He grinned and turned to my puppy. "Savannah!"

She spun around, flattened her ears, and charged him, her leap an inch shy of his face. He put out his free hand in defense. "Whoa! Easy girl." The pup calmed, and he scratched under her chin.

Savannah craned her neck to give him better access. I'd be jealous if I weren't so irritated with Eric. "Tell me about the promotion you tried for. The one the chief wouldn't give you."

His brows approached his hairline. "How'd you learn about that?"

"Guess."

He centered his green eyes on mine and gave me a half-smile. "Angus. But how did he find out?"

"How does he find out anything? He just does. Anyway, what happened?"

61

"Not much to tell. Larry Smith retired, and I put in for his spot. The chief turned me down."

"Did he say why?"

"A strange thing. When I asked, he became angry and said he had someone else in mind for the job but wouldn't say who."

Odd. Eric was the best officer in the department. He deserved to be a detective. I paused to allow my anger to pass, then said, "Who's more qualified than you?"

"Nobody I can think of. I'm the senior patrol officer. Unless he planned to bring someone in from outside the department."

"Rather unfair to not give you a chance."

He held his uniform in front of his chest. "I guess it doesn't matter now."

"No, probably not." Maybe whoever the new chief turned out to be would give him a fair chance. "It sounds to me like the chief upset a lot of people in the department. Maybe instead of only looking at towns-people you should consider looking at someone who worked with him."

"Don't be ridiculous. We didn't always agree with his decisions, but nobody in RPD would've killed him over one."

I put my hands up in surrender. "Hey, did you know Tony Scavuto had a cabin on the lake?"

"I heard about it last year. Why do you ask?"

"Olinski told me this morning they can't find him. I thought he might be there, and they didn't know about it."

"I'll mention it when I see him. Thanks."

"Sure. Perhaps now you'll believe me when I say I won't interfere in your investigation."

Eric shook his head, hiding a smile behind his hand. "Not convinced I'm ready to go that far, but I'll keep it in mind."

I flapped a hand in the direction of the steps. "Go to work. I'll talk to you later."

He waved and trotted up to the door.

Savannah tugged on her leash, staring longingly at the tree.

"Oh, no you don't. We're going home, double-quick. The sky's going to open up any minute now, and you know how much you hate to get wet."

She wagged her tail and proceeded to stop and sniff every blade of grass on the way. The humidity climbed to a hundred percent, and my slick fingers dropped the keys twice in their attempt to unlock the door. I'd faced more formidable challenges, however. I would succeed, no matter the cost.

Victorious on the third try, we ducked inside, and I basked in the cool air from the ceiling vent. While I chilled on the outside, a ball of ice formed in my midsection, courtesy of my combatant emotions. It seemed Zach wasn't the only one with the urge to find Chief Vick's killer. The inquisitive part of me, eager to take on the challenge of another mystery, battled my pragmatic side. For now, pragmatism had the edge. I'd heard prison food was terrible.

I loaded Chapter Fifteen on my laptop screen and transferred my brainpower to the fictional whodunit before me. The only safe way to bring my two sides together. About the time the delete key obliterated the two sentences written before the last round of interruptions, my phone rang. My mother. I needed to put it on silent while working, which would require remembering every time, however. Not one of my strengths. Regardless, my mother might've recovered from her snit. I swiped.

"Hi, Mom. You feel any better?"

"Better than what?"

Guess not. I took a deep breath. "You seemed unhappy this morning. Are you ready to share yet?"

"Nothing to share. What's new with you?"

All right, subject changed. "Did you hear about Chief Vick?"

"Everyone's talking about it. I can't believe he died."

"It was awful. The image is stuck in my head."

She cleared her throat. "I went to school with him, you know. Him and Anne-Marie."

Perhaps that explained why she was so weird today. They're the same age. The chief's death must be a reminder of her own mortality. Although, he didn't quite die of natural causes. "No wonder you're upset."

"That has nothing to do with it. I'm not upset."

"Okay, no problem."

Her voice wavered. "He was different back then. Easygoing. Fabulous sense of humor. He received invitations to every party. Something happened to him after his father died senior year. We all thought Toby would recover, but he never did."

Toby? Nobody referred to Chief Vick by that name. Not even his wife. At least, not in public, anyway.

"I actually considered going out with him at one point. He kept asking, but he'd dated Anne-Marie for years, and she was my friend."

My jaw fell. "You mean he hit on you while still dating her? Doesn't sound like a guy worth going out with to me."

"Well, it wasn't quite like that. They were on again, off again all through high school, and they both went out with other people when they took breaks. Honestly, I was surprised they got married."

"Plus, they've stayed together all these years."

"Also a surprise."

"Why?"

She cleared her throat again. "He always had a roaming eye. I'm sure I'm not the only one he tried to date on the side back then. Even when they weren't on a break. Anne-Marie pretended she didn't know, but I don't see how she couldn't. Everyone else did."

Perhaps the mayor was the final insult for her. Sounded like motive to me. Assuming she knew about the affair. And the affair actually happened. "Do you think she killed him?"

"Don't you start that detective stuff again!" An edge crept into her voice. "Stay out of it. Don't forget what you put me through last time."

Way to make everything about you, Mom. "I'm not investigating. We're having a conversation. Besides, I do write murder mysteries. Considering all the angles is natural for me."

"Well, let's talk about something else, then."

I sighed. "Okay, what would you like to talk about?"

"On second thought, I'm tired. I think I'll take a nap."

I put down the phone, ready for a snooze myself. Too bad Savannah had stretched out on the couch for a run through dreamland. No room for me. What would I do when she attained full size? Might need a sectional. I scooted her over and squeezed in. She grumbled but dozed back off within seconds.

Sleep eluded me, however. Mom had a right to be concerned. Though the outcome of my last adventure proved positive, things might've easily gone the other way. I'd twice been a whisker away from not making it. A closer shave, and I might not be here.

Also, between me and my nap was the problem she wouldn't discuss. Totally unlike her but beyond my control. She was quite adept at taking care of herself and always reluctant to ask for help. I didn't often worry about my mother. Today was an exception.

CHAPTER SEVEN

Our Monday morning routine a pleasant memory, I relaxed at my desk in the bookstore's back office, coffee in hand, ready to breathe life into the twins' sibling squabble about whether to confront the man they suspected of killing their father. Their voices flew around in my head as Daniel's baritone challenged Dana's contralto for preeminence. *One at a time, guys.*

I missed my table by the window, but my newfound fame since Aletha's death attracted too much attention for me to work in public undisturbed. Plus, my muse was gone. Now, instead of the traffic on Main Street, I stared at a wall full of posters that advertised *The Little Prince*, *To Kill a Mockingbird*, and *Fifty Shades of Grey*. Sometimes I studied a Florida-shaped water stain on the ceiling, desperate to put the words together, but mostly I fixed my gaze on Savannah, asleep on her bed next to my chair. Her ribs' steady rise and fall gave me a point of focus and freed my mind, like a metronome without the annoying tick, tick, tock.

The twins calmed down and conversed rather than continue their free-for-all. They talked, and I typed, backspaced, and typed some more. The discussion culminated precisely where I needed: a direct confrontation with Peter. Perfect. Well, for a first draft, anyway.

Eric, in jeans and a plain red T-shirt today, appeared in the doorway and interrupted my moment of self-satisfaction. "Hey, got a minute?"

I saved my work and closed the laptop to give him my undivided attention. "Sure, what's up?" Savannah hopped out of bed and trotted over to help Eric find a seat by squeezing between his feet.

He scratched her neck and cleared a stack of book catalogues off a chair in front of my battleship-gray metal desk that filled most of the office. "I wanted to see how you're doing. Make sure you're all right." His usually pallid face bore a touch of color to underscore the freckles as if he'd spent yesterday at the beach with too little sunscreen.

"I'm so-so. Trying to concentrate on my writing and stay out of trouble for a change."

Eric picked at a fingernail. "Probably a safe idea. The mayor appointed Olinski acting chief of police this morning. Havermayer took over as lead detective on the case. She's not one of your biggest fans."

Chief Olinski had a ring to it. Like the bells of Notre Dame with Quasimodo on the ropes. "No kidding. I won't waste ink autographing my book for her." I leaned back in my chair, fingers interlocked across my stomach. "How's the investigation going?"

"I can't talk to you about it."

I clenched then relaxed my jaw. "I understand, but did you at least find out where Tony's cabin is?"

"I told Blink what you said, but I'm not sure if he followed up or not."

"I'd consider not calling him Blink if I were you. He's the chief, now. He probably won't appreciate you addressing him by his rookie nickname."

"Possibly, but he's only the acting chief, so he might not care. He'll always be Blink to me."

"He's the senior detective. Doesn't that make him the most likely candidate to take over the job?"

Eric shrugged. "On paper, in our department, yes, but they might hire someone from the outside. Somebody with more experience."

"Like you thought Chief Vick would do with Smith's vacated slot? What do you think will happen now?"

"I hoped Olinski would make the decision. Except . . ." He turned away.

"What?"

"A bottle of cyanide from a previous case disappeared from the property room last Thursday. They think that might be what poisoned the chief. The weird thing is my signature is on the sign-in sheet, but I didn't go in there that day. Someone else signed my name, but I can't prove it."

"You still convinced nobody inside the department could've had anything to do with the chief's death? Who else would be able to frame you like this?"

He rubbed Savannah's chest. "I don't know, but there's a big difference between stealing evidence out of the prop room and murdering a guy because he said 'no' to a leave request."

"I hope you're right. Either way, Olinski will never believe you stole anything. And he'll certainly never believe you murdered Chief Vick."

Eric covered his face with his hands. "Unfortunately,

Havermayer is in charge of the investigation now. Plus, I was in a position to take the bottle and glasses Saturday night. All of which makes me a suspect."

I leaned forward on the desk. "You could've taken them off the table, but how would you have carried them out of the room unnoticed? Even Havermayer can't believe that happened. And she'll believe just about anything, it seems." No way was Eric involved with the chief's death. He was one of the good guys. "Don't worry, they'll sort it out. You'll find something that points to the real killer."

"Not me. Olinski suspended me."

His sunken cheeks accentuated the shadows under his eyes and suggested a sleepless night. He slumped in his chair, hands in his lap, eyes downcast. A marionette with severed strings.

A sinkhole opened behind my breastbone. "What can I do to help?"

"Nothing. All I can do is wait and hope Havermayer finds out who really stole the evidence. As well as who killed the chief, because I didn't."

"Of course not. Who else has access to the property room? Any way someone from outside the department can enter?"

He shook his head. "Not likely. The duty sergeant sits by the door to the basement where the property room is, and there are cameras everywhere."

Frustration grew in the pit of my stomach. There was no way Eric did what they were accusing him of. There had to be another answer.

"You must let me do something. Tell me about the investigation."

"I can't. I won't. The situation's too dangerous for

you to be involved. I couldn't stand it if something happened to you."

Couldn't stand it? What did that mean? "But you're my friend."

He rubbed his hands down the front of his jeans. "That's kind of what I came here to talk to you about."

Uh-oh. What'd I do now? I sat back in my chair. "Okay."

"I've had a lot of time to think the past few days." He cleared his throat. "It's a cliché, but life's too short. YOLO, right?"

You only live once. True, certainly, but what was his point? I nodded.

"We're friends, but do you think we might be something more, someday?"

Right again, Brittany. The one time I needed her to be wrong. I fought back the panic rising into my throat. When Scott left for that job in Paris, it almost destroyed me. We were supposed to get married. Have babies and grow old together. He was the only man I'd ever considered having children with. As badly as that relationship ended, the last one was even worse. A total disaster.

Did I dare take that chance again? No. At least not now.

So, how to let Eric down without losing him as a friend or adding to his troubles? "I can't predict the future." I tried to catch his eye, but he evaded me like a bank robber on the lam. "But I'm not ready to consider a relationship with anyone yet. It's only been a few months since . . . well, you know."

He nodded, pressed his lips together, and relaxed a tiny bit. "You're right. I'm sorry I said anything." He

71

rose to his feet. "I'll let you go back to playing with the twins."

"Before you go, I need to ask you something."

Eric returned to his chair.

"I spoke to Zach Vick yesterday, and he said something about somebody leaving the police department. Did you know about that?"

"No." He leaned forward, elbows on his knees. "Did he say under what circumstances?"

"No, he said his father told him a job would open up by the time he graduated from the academy in September."

"We hired Leonard as an extra last year because Larry was retiring. After Olinski promotes someone into Larry's position, we're still fully staffed. I haven't heard about anyone resigning. There's nobody else near retirement age either. Unless he planned to push someone out to create a spot for his son."

I clasped my hands behind my head. "Would he do something like that? And who would he get rid of?"

"Anything's possible, but Chief Vick wouldn't tell me his plans even if I was the target." He shared a half-hearted grin. "Especially if I was the target."

"Why would he want to fire you? You're a great cop! An efficient, professional officer."

"Thanks, but if the chief agreed, he would've promoted me. Instead, he held the job open, and now we're trying to investigate a homicide while short a detective."

"Well, maybe now he's gone you'll have a fair chance."

"Humph. Assuming I'm cleared of his murder."

I drained the last of my coffee, peering at him over the cup's rim. "Are you guilty?"

A hint of a smile appeared at the corners of his mouth. "Seriously? You need to ask?"

"We better work on proving it then."

The words clattered around my skull as Eric left. Interfering might land me in jail. Particularly with Havermayer in charge. But how could I allow them to accuse my friend of a murder he didn't commit? I'd walked in those shoes, and they're way too tight. No way I could justify staying out of it now. The heck with Olinski and Havermayer. My friend's future was at stake. Eric seemed content to leave his fate to the whims of others, so why not mine? My whims were just as good as anyone else's. To be fair, he believed in the system he'd served for years. I, however, didn't share his confidence. Too many people in it with preconceived ideas.

What about his feelings about our relationship? Did I share those? Honestly, I'd never given it any meaningful thought. Brittany had broached the subject a few times, but I always shrugged her off. Why was I so quick to dismiss the idea of dating Eric? When I was ready, of course. What did Brittany see that I didn't?

The world saw a tall, skinny, pasty-faced, freckled redhead. On the outside. On the inside? A reliable, trustworthy, eager-to-help person who would never consider hurting a human being on purpose. Unfortunately, that described Savannah, too.

Either way, I meant what I said about it being too soon. Pieces of my heart, soul, and pride littered the road behind me. The empty shell needed to refill itself before I could consider offering any part of me to someone else again. Better to worry about the most urgent thing: keeping Eric out of jail.

Enough. Right now, I had to tackle the stack of bills in my inbox. I'd cut expenses as much as possible, and the bookstore had made incremental gains in the last couple of months. It was progress, but not enough. Lacey's salary covered her childcare and not much more. Charlie worked for a percentage of the coffee bar sales. I couldn't ask them to work under those conditions for much longer. Our only way forward was to generate a dedicated clientele. It was hard to compete with all the online bookselling sites, though. We'd have to find a way. There had to still be people like me who'd rather hold a book in their hands than stare at a screen. We just had to bring them in.

My pile of checks grew as the balance in the account fell. The next payment from the Your Life contest, which provided the money for Aletha to open Ravenous Readers, wouldn't come in until February. The last check went into expanded displays and inventory to fill them. And paying the never-ending flow of bills. The pen slid in my slick fingers. I owed it to Aletha to make it through. She'd entrusted her baby to me, and I would raise that baby to adulthood, no matter what.

I closed the business-sized checkbook with a thump and rested my forehead on the cover. No paycheck for me again this week. Thankfully, the burst of publicity after Aletha's death had led to an explosion in *Double Trouble* sales. I was less thankful for the increased pressure to finish the second book from my publisher, who wanted to cash in while the boom lasted. Not that I blamed them.

Chores complete, I called Brittany at the library. Finding Tony had just jumped to the top of my priority list. It shouldn't be too hard. They found Nemo, didn't they? "Hey, you busy?"

"A little bit. What do you need?"

What do I need? She must still be mad about our argument the other night. She'd get over it, though. We'd had quarrels before. "I heard Tony bought a cabin by the lake last year."

"Yeah, someone told me about it."

Did everybody know but me? "Did you happen to hear where it was?"

She breathed into the phone. "Somewhere around my parents' house, but I'm not positive. Definitely on that side of the lake, though."

"Any chance you can unearth it?"

Silence.

"Britt?"

She sighed. "I guess I could check the county clerk's database. Why do you want to know?"

"The detectives can't find him. I think he might be hiding out there."

"Why would he be hiding?"

"That's what I want to find out."

"Poking your nose in police business again?"

Yup. Still mad. "They think Eric had something to do with the chief's death. I have to help him."

Brittany said she'd text me back, so I headed up front to observe the morning rush. Lacey and Charlie huddled at the coffee counter over a piece of paper she quickly folded and put in the back pocket of her khakis as I approached with Savannah on my heels. He greeted me with an ear-splitting grin. "Hi, Boss. Interesting chat with Eric?"

"I guess." My gaze flitted back and forth between the two. "What's going on here?"

His eyebrows shot up. The picture of innocence. "Oh nothing. Shooting the breeze, as they say."

"Yeah, right." I turned to Lacey. "Well?"

Her face turned the shade of a fire engine. "Well, what?"

Super. They were like two five-year-olds caught snitching cookies. "What was that paper you stuck in your pocket?"

"The design for our windows, but I'm not ready to show you yet."

Better be the Mona Lisa reading *War and Peace* for all the fuss she made. "No problem."

She shot me a sidelong glance. "So, how's Eric?"

Charlie leaned forward on the counter with his chin in his hand. "Yeah, how's Eric?"

Oh, brother. "He's fine and nothing is going on between us. We're only friends."

"Methinks the lady doth protest too much," Charlie quoted.

"Nonsense. And leave Shakespeare out of this." I scratched Savannah behind her ears. "Eric's been suspended, which is why he wanted to talk to me."

Lacey's jaw dropped. "Why?"

I outlined the situation for them. "Now, he needs my help, but I'm not sure what I can do. Havermayer's in charge and I'm not one of her favorite people. Not even in the top ten."

Charlie smirked. "I don't think she has a top ten. Or a top *one* for that matter."

"True," Lacey said. "We'll have to work around her. How can we help?"

"As soon as I come up with an idea, I'll fill you in."

CHAPTER EIGHT

I threw my empty cup in the trash, and my phone buzzed with a text from Brittany:

25472 Partridge Rd off SR-32-83.

I thanked her and plugged the address into my navigation program. The route snaked up the screen, and the female robot voice told me to turn right on Main Street. "Lacey, would you mind keeping an eye on Savannah for me? It's too hot to leave her in the car if I have to get out, and I want to look for Tony."

She nodded and waved, so I bolted out the door, then trotted the three blocks to my Dodge, still parked in front of my apartment building. The car door had barely closed behind me when I started the engine and backed out onto the street, which was clear except for a red pickup truck about a block back.

Several turns later, the vehicle still followed. The hair on the back of my neck went on alert. It had to be a coincidence. Somebody else headed to the lake. Still, it wouldn't hurt to be sure. At the next street, I turned right into a housing development, drove up a few hundred feet, and parked. The truck would almost certainly fly right by in my rearview mirror.

My heart raced as I gripped the steering wheel, waiting for confirmation I was letting my imagination run away with me. Except the vehicle made the turn and crept up the road toward me. I got out of the car, and the red, older-model Toyota Tacoma stopped beside me, Zach Vick behind the wheel.

He rolled down his window as I approached.

"Zach, what are you doing here? Why are you following me?"

He scraped a hand through his ebony hair. "Who says I'm following you?"

Kids. "Why are you here then?"

"I'm visiting a friend."

"Really? Which house is his?"

His eyebrows lowered, and pure hate flew from his eyes at me. "Fine, I'm following you. I told you I would find my father's killer."

I took a deep breath to bring my temper under control. The guy had just lost his father and wasn't thinking straight. "I get that, Zach, but why me? You don't think I killed him, do you?"

"Well, no, but you're good at figuring these things out. Nobody will tell me anything. I have to do something, and you have a knack for getting people to talk."

"I understand how you feel. It's frustrating when nobody will tell you what's going on. But it isn't safe for you to be in the middle of a homicide investigation. The best thing you can do is go home and be there for your mother. She needs you. She's hurting, too."

I couldn't help my mother grieve when my father died suddenly in a plane crash. Perhaps our relationship would've developed into something more reasonable if I could have. A lot to ask of a six-year-old, though.

He stared out the windshield, jaw working.

I tried a different tack. "You want to be a police officer, right?"

He nodded without looking at me.

"Well, how would you feel if you were trying to solve a case and some civilian kept getting in the way? You wouldn't like it much, would you?"

"I'm not a civilian." He jerked his head in my direction.

Here we go again. "I appreciate what you're saying. Your father taught you a lot about police procedure, including how to think like a cop. That's great. It'll help you when you get to the academy. But you're not there, yet. As far as the Riddleton Police Department is concerned, you're still a civilian, and they can't see you any other way until you graduate. Does that make sense?"

Zach grudgingly nodded. "I guess. But they're wrong."

"Maybe so, but that's the way it is. Go home and let the professionals do their jobs." Jeez, now I sounded like Olinski.

Without another word, he put the Toyota in gear, did a U-turn around me, and took off.

His left turn signal was blinking when I pulled in behind him to resume my journey. A break in vehicle flow allowed him to make his left and me my right. Lunchtime and business traffic clogged the two-lane road, and the forty-minute trip took over an hour— almost twice as long as I expected. Robot Woman finally instructed me to make a left on SR-32-83. I'd white-knuckled the steering wheel avoiding the lunatics determined to play bumper cars, so I forced my fingers to relax, scanned the street signs, and listened for Partridge Road.

She told me to hang another left a hundred feet past where I'd seen the sign—too late to make the turn. I turned around to the tune of "recalculating." By the time RW completed her calculations, I was where I needed to be.

A potholed dirt road greeted me, barely wide enough for two vehicles to pass. I topped out at fifteen miles per hour to keep my suspension intact. Untrimmed tree branches scratched the passenger side of my car, and I suspected I might regret not having comprehensive insurance once again. I checked for traffic and drifted toward the middle.

When RW announced I'd arrived at my destination, I hit the brakes. There was nothing but hardwoods interspersed with pines on either side of the road. The red dot on the blue track in the center of my phone screen blinked. *Ridiculous.*

No way any local had a cabin here, let alone city-slicker Tony. RW was a hundred feet off when I made the last turn. Why not this one, too? I parked as far to the right as possible without sliding into the ten-foot deep, kudzu-filled ditch and climbed out. A stroll back the way I came allowed me to check every direction for any indication someone might live there.

Sure enough, about a hundred feet back, I removed a pile of pine cones to reveal a small wooden board around six inches off the ground. A few more cones and 25472 appeared in faded blue paint. Beside the sign, a narrow track covered with once-flattened yellow grass disappeared into the trees.

I trotted toward my car, stepped on a branch,

twisted my ankle, and did a hopping pirouette, pinwheeling my arms.

Way to go, Jen.

Face burning, I tested my injured appendage, slowly adding weight until the joint held me. Not too bad. I hobbled to the car like I'd just spent twelve hours on a horse, but it would do. At least nobody saw me.

Backing up until I spotted the board, I rolled onto the track, which extended into infinity. The woods eventually opened into a hard-packed clearing the size of a circus ring. A dusty white SUV sat in front of a weathered log cabin. A decade's worth of grime covered the structure's windows, and the screen door hung crooked on its hinges. Subtract the vehicle parked by the dilapidated wooden steps, and I'd swear the place hadn't seen a human in fifty years.

Adjacent to the lodge stood an outhouse, a quarter-moon surrounded by stars etched into the door. Make that a hundred years abandoned. I eased out of the driver's seat and shuffled toward the smaller structure, keeping my eye on the larger one. Still nothing.

The door screeched open on rusted hinges, and a cloud of dust from the roof materialized around my head. I waved it away and sneezed twice. When the air cleared, I spotted an oversized metal container with attached coiled piping shaped like a giant slinky. Empty glass jugs lined the walls, along with a tattered cardboard box of corks in the corner.

An unmistakable click turned me into stone.

"Put your hands up and turn around, slowly." The voice was deep and familiar.

Fingertips near my ears, I rotated to confront a double-barrel shotgun pointed at me by Tony, whose haggard face and puffy eyes indicated little sleep since the fundraiser.

"It's only me, Tony."

He lowered the weapon and wiped the sweat off his forehead, leaving a streak of grime in its place. "Jeez, Jen, I could've blown your head off. What are you doing here? How did you find me?"

I allowed myself to breathe. "Olinski told me he couldn't locate you. When I discovered you bought this place, I thought you might be hiding out here."

"I came to clear my head after everything that happened. Why would I be hiding?"

"The detectives are looking for you. I wanted to find you first."

"Why are they looking for me?"

"Chief Vick died yesterday morning. I told Olinski you said it was cyanide. I'm sorry."

His shoulders sagged, and he gestured toward the cabin with his free hand. "Come on in. I'll make some coffee."

I followed him up the rickety steps, placing each foot only where Tony trod to avoid crashing through the rotten wood. No broken bones on my schedule for today. Stepping into the room obliterated my expectation that the inside of the building would mirror the out. The log walls were stained deep chocolate, and the floors boasted the glint of several coats of polyurethane. Oriental rugs protected most of the visible floor space.

A small, brown-leather sofa faced the fireplace, and a wingback chair sat on either side, each with a rough-hewn table beside it. The kitchen had modern appliances, which included a dishwasher, and bright yellow curtains framed the windows.

Tony set the coffeemaker into action. "Well, this is my hideout. What do you think?"

"I love it. How far is the lake from here?"

"About a quarter mile down the road. The boat put-in is right beyond the Partridge place."

"Leonard lives up here?"

He shook his head. "Leonard's house is in town, but some members of his family still stay up here. This whole area used to be Partridge land. I think his cousin, Greg, lives in the house up the way."

"Huh. I had no idea Leonard came from money."

"Not exactly. They snatched up all the acreage so they could run moonshine in the twenties. When Prohibition ended, the income dried up, and they had to sell off the property piecemeal. Nothing left except Greg's place since I bought this one."

I accepted a hot mug from him and added cream and sugar. "I guess the still in your outbuilding is a remnant of the old days, then?"

He stirred the same into his cup and studied the swirls as if they held the meaning of life. "Yeah, I'm keeping it as a souvenir. I think it's kinda cool, don't you?"

"Definitely super cool. Does it work?"

"I've never tried it. The chief sure worried about it, though. He used to come out here every so often to make sure I wasn't cooking my own booze to serve at the restaurant. As if I would. I told him he was crazy, but he wouldn't let up on me getting rid of it."

How much dust had to be on the thing for the man to figure out Tony didn't use it? Even I could tell nobody had touched the still in years, if not decades.

I followed him to one of the chairs by the hearth. "Will you come back and talk to the police?"

He occupied the opposite chair. "Why do you care? This has nothing to do with you."

How could I explain this without giving away Eric's secret? He never told me not to tell anyone, but missing evidence seemed like police business to me. "You're right. It has nothing to do with me, and I'd like to keep it that way."

"What does that mean?"

"Havermayer's already trying to find an excuse to pin the chief's death on me. The way I figure it, the quicker the detective clears the obvious suspects like you and— in her mind—me, the quicker she'll find the real culprit."

He studied me over the rim of his coffee cup as he sipped.

"At least consider coming in and talking to her. If you do, it might help throw suspicion off you."

"I suppose I should. They probably do consider me a suspect by now."

"Not necessarily, although you did predict cyanide as the murder weapon. You were no closer to him than the rest of us, were you?"

"No, but if the wine I donated to the auction contained the poison, I'm person of interest number one. Only the wine was sealed. You all witnessed the cork pop."

"The glasses and bottle disappeared so they can't test them."

"Great. Now they'll accuse me of taking the evidence."

I patted his warm hand. "I wouldn't worry at this point. I'm sure they're looking at Anne-Marie as the prime suspect. The spouse often is at first."

"I guess, but I doubt they'll spend much time on her. What's her motive?"

Angus's unsubstantiated tale of the chief and the mayor, for one thing. And the possibility her husband had impregnated another woman. Also unsubstantiated. "What reason does anyone need? Things happen in relationships."

"Perhaps." He sipped his coffee. "Although, why not divorce him if they were having problems? No secret fortune in play I'm aware of."

"True. As far as any of us knows. Unless he bought stock in Apple twenty years ago. Or owned a huge life insurance policy or something."

"Possibly, but not likely. How would he justify the amount to the insurance company? People can't just insure themselves for any astronomical sum they want. Except on TV." Tony rolled his mug between his hands. "Okay, if Anne-Marie is out and so am I, who's left?"

"Well, research shows women use poison more often than men. What about Teresa Benedict? She threatened the chief to someone on the phone Saturday morning, but I assumed she didn't mean it. However, somebody told me he planned to run against her in November. Perhaps that's what she meant."

He barked a laugh. "Tobias Vick for mayor? That would be the day. He'd alienated so many people in this town his chances were nonexistent. Certainly, no reason to kill him."

Valid point. The chief had a way of getting under people's skin. Put that into the mix, and the suspect pool would have no room for water. "True. Might be anyone if we go that way."

We stared at the dormant fireplace. Amazing the heat from our combined brains working overtime didn't cause the stacked wood to spontaneously ignite.

"Tony, what about Xavier Benedict? There's a rumor going around Chief Vick and Teresa had an affair. What if he heard it?"

Tony pinched his lips together. "I can't see him resorting to murder to solve a marital problem. And even if he would, he'd need more than a rumor to go on."

"What if he had more? What if Teresa had been acting strangely or disappearing at all hours? He might act on it then."

"Possible, but either way he couldn't have poisoned the chief. He was at a dental convention in Atlanta all week. He didn't get back until Saturday afternoon. I heard him griping about missing the 10k at the fundraiser."

"I wonder if Havermayer checked it out."

"I guess that depends if she heard the rumor, too."

She was up on all the rumors about Aletha's husband and me. Why not this one too? "Do you know where he stayed in Atlanta?"

"Not a clue. Sorry." He shook his head. "I've been through this before. Cyanide killed the manager of my restaurant in Chicago. The police will have their sights set on me."

My heart leaped. "Oh, no!"

"I was never a significant suspect. Her boyfriend murdered her. But since it's the second time something like this happened, they're going to scrutinize me a lot harder. I held the bottle in my hands, and no doubt, I'm familiar with how cyanide works. I can't prove my innocence, but then again, I don't have to. They have to prove me guilty, but I need your help."

"What can I do?"

He sighed. "Get the cops off my case for starters. Aren't you friends with the red-headed kid? Talk to him. Tell him I didn't do anything."

Well, that's a switch. First, he told me to mind my own business, and now he wanted my help. I tugged at the neck of my T-shirt. "The detectives would be foolish to think you'd copy the exact same method." Unless someone deliberately used the same method to frame him. "Either way, I can't interfere in another investigation, Tony. They'll lock me up and bury me under the cement floor."

"Not likely, but that's exactly what they'll do to me if they can."

"Why would you want to kill him?"

"No reason. I didn't like him much, but neither did anyone else. Besides, I wouldn't be dumb enough to murder him in my own restaurant with a bottle of wine I provided. And how did the poison end up in the wine in the first place?"

"Well, they can't be sure the wine was poisoned. It might've been on the glass, but they can't test anything, so now the medical examiner has the ball. We'll have to wait and see."

His chin hit his chest. "The detectives won't search for someone else if the wine turns out to be the murder weapon." He took my hand. "Please help me. You have experience with these things."

"Yeah, experience that almost got me killed. Twice. And arrested once. Olinski already warned me off."

He had no right to put me in this position. I wrote mysteries; I didn't investigate them. No way I would stick my nose into this one. Havermayer would slice my schnozz right off. The blade on her saber had a razor-thin edge.

Except, I'd already decided to help Eric. Maybe by helping Eric, I could help Tony, too. "I'm not sure what I can do, but I'll try."

"Thank you. That's all I ask."

I nodded and left, carefully keeping to the steps' solid parts. As I opened my car door, a black Chevy Suburban came out of the trees, followed by a trail of dust, Havermayer in the driver's seat.

Perfect.

Deep breath in, slow breath out.

She was out of the car before the engine stopped ticking. "What are you doing here?"

I raised my hands in a gesture of surrender, though her weapon remained in its holster. "I'm checking on my friend. No law against that last I heard."

"No, but interfering in my investigation is. You should've come to me as soon as you found him."

"I wasn't sure Tony was here until I arrived. Plus Eric told me he'd mentioned the cabin to Olinski. How was I supposed to know he wouldn't follow up? Besides, I don't work for you."

Her glare cut through me. "He did his job. Now I'll do mine and you better stay out of my way. I won't put up with your crap like Olinski did. You show up one more place you're not meant to be, I'll lock you up and throw away the key. You understand?"

I gave her an eye roll. "Yes, ma'am."

Havermayer stormed up the stairs, misjudged their stability, and tumbled over the side into the dirt. She brushed her pants off and examined a tear in the elbow of her suit jacket as I turned down the trail, trying not to laugh until I was out of sight.

CHAPTER NINE

Havermayer's mishap kept me entertained most of the way home. Every time the picture of Detective Starchy brushing dirt off her pants popped into my head, I smiled. Couldn't have happened to a nicer person, as my mother liked to say. Poor Tony. She was already mad about having to track him down. The fall from the steps would've only increased her ire.

I coasted into a spot in front of the bookstore and cut the engine. The Havermayer high had worn off, and I rested my forehead against the steering wheel, my arms heavy in my lap. My mind wouldn't settle, though. Tony's story about his murdered manager ran on a loop. My resolve to stay out of his situation became more onerous to maintain by the second, but Havermayer's warning hovered over me like a storm cloud.

Road dust covered my Dodge. The passenger side had light scratches from the tree limbs, which might be buffed out if I had any clue how. Or the time and energy. Maybe tomorrow.

The bells jingled as I entered the store. Savannah ran toward me, ears flopping along with the rhythm of her gangly legs. Charlie had already cleaned and closed the coffee bar and left for the day.

Lacey smiled at me from the cash register, which spit out reports nobody would ever pay attention to. "I was wondering if I was taking Savannah home with me tonight. Not that the kids would mind. They love having her around."

"Sorry. I didn't realize it was so late."

"Did you find Tony?"

"I did, but first I found Zach."

"The chief's son? Where'd you find him?"

"Trying to follow me to the lake. For someone who thinks he's ready to be a cop, he wasn't very adept at it. I spotted him right away."

She shook her head. "Guys that age think they know everything."

Guys of all ages. "I talked to him for a few minutes and sent him home. I feel sorry for him. It's tough to lose your father when you're young."

"You did, didn't you?"

"Yes, but it's not the same. I missed my dad, but by the time I was old enough to understand what it meant to not have a father, my mother had remarried."

Lacey removed the last report from the printer, folded them, and grabbed the stapler. "Which didn't work out too well."

I scratched Savannah's neck. She turned her head and raised her chin to ensure I didn't miss any vital spots. "Actually, it wasn't too bad in the beginning. He didn't welcome me with open arms, but he didn't mistreat me, either. My mother was home with me, and as far as he was concerned, I was her problem. It was only when he got hurt and couldn't work anymore we started having difficulties. He was angry and frustrated and took it out on me. Plus Mom had to find a job, so I lost my protector at the same time."

"It's a shame that happened to you. And your mother. I couldn't imagine losing my husband and bouncing back the way she did. She's a hero."

My mother a hero? Maybe something to think about later. "Anyway, after I sent Zach on his way, I found Tony at his cabin." I filled her in on Tony's story, finishing with: "When Havermayer fell off the steps, I had to speed away so she wouldn't see me laughing. She probably would've given me a ticket for disrespecting an officer or something."

"I'm sorry I missed all the excitement. Seeing her dirty would make my day."

"Just be glad you didn't hear what came before. She was her cheery best. Ripped me up one side and down the other."

"You don't seem any the worse for it. Besides, you should be used to her diatribes by now."

"As much as anyone can be, I guess."

Lacey gathered her things and moved toward the door. "Tony owns a still, huh? Think he's supplementing his vodka with moonshine?"

"Not with that old thing. Definitely Prohibition era. Nobody's touched it in years."

I stopped scratching, and Savannah poked my hand with her cold, wet nose. "You ready to head home, little girl? I'll bet you're hungry."

She ran to the door, ears perked, tail wagging. "I guess that's a 'yes.'"

Lacey chuckled and flipped off the lights. "Looks like it."

I dashed back to the office to pick up my laptop. Might be able to do a little writing before I collapsed for the night. I'd need a healthy dose of caffeine first, though. With luck, I had a Mountain Dew in the fridge. *Have stimulants, will travel.*

As I loaded Savannah into the car, my stomach reminded me I hadn't eaten since breakfast. A stop at the diner worked its way into our schedule. Familiar vehicles lined the street in front of the restaurant, so I could safely bring the puppy in. Mondays weren't particularly busy diner days, anyway.

Angus was cashing out a customer, so I made my way to the end of the counter. "Hi, Marcus!"

He turned, spatula in hand, and a grin split his face. "Hey, Jen, how ya doin'?"

"Doing well. You and the kids all right?"

"We're fine. The girls love it here. And Angus is real good to me."

"He's a great guy. Can you rustle me up a cheeseburger and fries to go, please? And a plain hamburger, no bun, for my furry friend here?"

"Sure thing." He laid two patties on the grill and deposited a basket of wedged potatoes into the amber oil.

Angus came over. "What're you up to tonight, Jen?"

"Not much. Just grabbing some dinner on the way home."

"Marcus got you fixed up?"

"Always. Can you add a chocolate shake to the order, please?"

He jutted his chin in the direction of the dining room. "I think your friend over there might need something stronger."

I followed his line of sight to a corner booth where Eric pushed food around his plate with one hand while the other supported his head. "How's he doing?"

Angus leaned on the counter. "I can't tell. He's not talking much. Putting up a brave front. I suspect inside is a whole different matter, though."

An understatement if I'd ever heard one. "Thanks. I'll go check on him." I turned back. "I heard Xavier Benedict was at a dental convention all last week. You know anything about it?"

"Only that I hadn't seen him, and now I know why."

"So, you have no idea where he stayed while he was there?"

"No. Why?"

"Just wondering."

He grinned. "You think he had something to do with the chief's death, don't you?"

I shrugged. "I'm just trying to narrow down the possibilities."

"I thought you weren't going to get involved."

"So did I."

Savannah dragged me to Eric's table, tail spinning at the sight of one of her favorite people. One of mine, too, although my tail didn't wag as effusively.

He put down his fork and smiled when she planted her front paws on the bench beside him. "Where did you come from?"

I lowered myself into the booth across from him. "Didn't your mother ever tell you?"

"Tell me what?"

"Where puppies come from."

His grin broadened. "Of course, she did. The stork brings them, right?"

We laughed, and he studied my face, his green eyes glistening. Heat filled my cheeks, and I transferred my gaze to the dog, who had climbed up to lean against his shoulder. "Is she bothering you?"

Savannah stuck her tongue in his ear, and he jerked away. "No, but I could've lived without that."

I retrieved the pup and positioned her on my side of the table between me and the wall. "That should keep her out of trouble for a minute." The meatloaf, mashed potatoes, and green beans in front of Eric were untouched, and only one bite was taken out of his dinner roll. I gestured to his meal. "Angus having a bad day?"

"No, the food's terrific. I'm not very hungry."

"Want to talk?"

"Nothing to talk about, really. I'm waiting for the higher-ups to figure out I'm not a thief or a murderer."

"Come on, be serious. Nobody believes that. Certainly not anyone who knows you."

He picked up his fork again and shoved a green bean into his potatoes. "I wish I could be sure. They won't talk to me. I understand it's because of the open investigation, but it still stings. They're supposed to be my friends."

"They are your friends. Trust them." Empty platitudes. I didn't trust them; why did I expect him to? "Were you able to learn anything at all?"

"Not much. Olinski showed me the signature on the property room log. It looked like mine, but no way to prove otherwise without closer examination."

"Is he having the log inspected?"

"He didn't say."

Figures. "Sounds like we need to take a look, then. Can you take a picture without anyone knowing?"

Eric crossed his arms. "Are you kidding? Impossible. I can't enter the building without anyone knowing."

"Why?"

"Well, for starters, the first thing you encounter when you come in the door is the duty sergeant's desk, which is occupied twenty-four seven."

My mental motor hummed. "What about the property room? Is it occupied twenty-four seven also?"

"No, only during day watch. The rest of the time the door's locked, the key kept in the sergeant's desk drawer." He studied me through narrowed eyelids. "Why? What are you thinking?"

"If you didn't sign the log, then someone else signed your name. The only way to get away with that is if nobody else is around."

"You think someone snuck in at night, took the evidence, and forged my name? That's crazy! Besides, there are cameras everywhere. A Ninja wouldn't be able to make it past them all."

I leaned forward, arms folded on the table. "What did the video show?"

"The back of a guy in uniform, wearing a standard-issue jacket with the collar pulled up, and a baseball cap. Could've been me. Could've been Olinski for all we could tell. We don't exactly own a top-of-the-line system."

"All right. Either way, though, it had to be someone with access to the key."

Eric ran a hand over his orange buzz cut. "You think the duty sergeant might be involved somehow?"

"That or someone took the key out of the drawer."

"The drawer's supposed to be locked, but sometimes he forgets. Why would someone do that to me?"

"We'll know that when we figure out who the forger

is. Unfortunately, the only way to tell who did it is to take a peek at the signature. Perhaps we'll find a telltale sign of the forger's handwriting."

Eric tossed a piece of his meatloaf to Savannah, who swallowed without chewing and waited expectantly for more. "And how do you propose we check?"

"The same way it was signed to begin with. We go in there in the middle of the night and snap a picture so we can analyze the handwriting."

"That's a ridiculous idea."

"What's a ridiculous idea?" Angus asked as he set the bag with my burger and fries in front of me and slumped onto the bench next to Eric, who scooted over to make room.

"Jen wants to break into the police department to take a photo of the evidence log."

Angus's guffaw shifted the table an inch in my direction.

I pushed it back. "What's so funny? We need to clear Eric's name."

He regained his control. "Okay, what's the plan?"

"I haven't gotten that far yet. My first idea is to hang around until the sergeant takes a break and snag the key out of his desk. Should be easy, right?"

Eric propped his elbows on either side of his plate. "How would you explain why you're loitering in the station? Sarge is bound to be suspicious."

"I need some time to think. I'll come up with something."

"It's a loony idea, Jen." Eric sat back. "It'll never work. You should let it go."

Angus put a hand up. "Wait a minute. The concept might not be so foolish. You only have one patrol car on the road at night, right?"

Eric nodded.

Angus continued, "What if the sergeant needs to respond to a call? That would keep him away from the desk long enough for Jen to do her thing."

"True, but he'll lock the front door when he leaves. And what about the cameras?"

I tapped a drumbeat on the table. "Any way to turn them off?"

"Not without cutting the power to the whole building."

"Hey, hold on," Angus said. "I saw a movie once where a guy wanted to rob a museum, and he fooled the security guard by running a pre-recorded loop of the empty room on the feed. Can we do something like that?"

Eric snickered. "Sure, if we knew how. Do you?"

Angus shook his head.

I leaned forward. "I don't either, but I might know somebody who does."

"Who?"

"Never mind. Just leave that part to me."

Angus frowned. "But we still have the problem of the locked door."

I touched Eric's hand. "Don't you have a key?"

He nodded. We bounced ideas off each other and made a plan. Tomorrow night Angus would phone the station at closing time and report a suspicious person outside the diner. According to Eric, the patrol car would be at the farthest point in its route, so the sergeant would be required to respond. I'd hide in the bookstore with Eric's key in my pocket, ready to roll as soon as the place was empty. Then sneak in, do what I had to, and escape while Angus kept the sergeant busy. *Piece of cake.*

I collected my shake and paid for my meal, then loaded my dog into the car for the two-block drive home, which I spent pushing her snout out of the food bag. When we hit the top of the stairs, Brittany came out of her apartment in a sleeveless sundress, flyaway hair sprayed solidly into place. Olinski followed.

Savannah lunged at her most-favored person, and I tightened my grip on her leash. "Where are you guys headed tonight?"

She edged toward the steps to stay out of the line of fire. "Olinski's taking me to Sutton for Chinese. Want us to bring you something back?"

I nodded to the bag clutched to my side. "No, thanks. I'm fine."

Olinski studied the shine on his dress shoes.

"How are you enjoying your new job, Chief?"

He picked at the cuticle on his thumb. "Acting chief, and I'm still getting the hang of it."

Why was he so uncomfortable? Surely, he didn't still have feelings for me after all these years. Was he overwhelmed? "You'll do great. You think the council will give it to you permanently?"

"No telling."

Brittany smiled at him. "We better head out. I'll talk to you later, okay?"

Guess it would have to be. At least Brittany was civil this time. "Sure. Have fun."

I tossed my dinner on the kitchen counter with an unexpected emptiness in my chest. Brittany'd had boyfriends before; why did this one bother me so much? With no chance of resuming my relationship with Olinski, why shouldn't she go out with him? We broke up ten, no eleven, years ago. This was the first time I'd seen her happy since her fiancé Frankie disappeared. Was I that selfish?

Still, I missed my friend. Before Olinski, we'd have spent this evening eating takeout and watching a movie we'd seen a thousand times. Chattering about my visit with Tony and my plans to help Eric tomorrow night. She would've insisted on accompanying me, and I'd argue. There seemed to be a fifty-fifty split on winning and losing those arguments. But in the end, she was always there for me. Time for me to be there for my best friend.

I'm happy for her. I'm happy for her. I'm happy for her.

Deep breath in, slow breath out.

Savannah's burger ended up in pieces in her dish. For about five seconds. I replaced it with puppy food, collapsed on the couch, dinner plate in hand, and flipped on the TV. As usual, a hundred and fifty channels with nothing interesting on. I selected a rerun of *The Andy Griffith Show*, which always reminded me of Eric. Could I see myself in a relationship with Opie Taylor? But he wasn't Opie; he just looked like him. He was a catch. A man any woman would be lucky to have.

I'm shallow and selfish.

Terrific.

I swallowed the last of my milkshake and, determined to write tonight, chased it with a Mountain Dew. Stuffed like a turducken, I balanced my computer on my lap, wedged under my bloated belly.

Tony's story ran laps around my head while I stared at the flashing cursor. Havermayer's warning matched stride for stride. Still, a little research couldn't hurt. Might make an interesting plot for book three. If I ever had a reason to write book three.

I typed "restaurant manager murdered in Chicago" into my search engine and retrieved a surprising number of results. Chicago didn't appear to be a healthy place for restaurant managers. Unfortunately, I forgot to ask Tony the name of his restaurant or the manager. I narrowed it down to five possibilities. Something to give my research guru Brittany a place to start, at least.

Curiosity semi-satisfied, I dove headfirst into the fictional mystery of the Davenport twins. The only case in Riddleton I could solve without risking the wrath of Detective Havermayer. And the only one I already knew the answer to.

CHAPTER TEN

Tuesday morning, while Savannah slept off her break-fast on the couch, I sat at my cluttered desk and glared at my laptop screen. After working through most of the night, fatigue won out around four. Then, Savannah woke me at six for her morning constitutional. The vet told me dogs thrived on a schedule, but I never dreamed a German shepherd would be so punctual. Or so unwilling to compromise.

For some strange reason, our plan to break into the police department had energized me and jump-started my creativity again. Perhaps immersion in my writing helped me avoid facing the reality that tonight's adventure might land me in jail before the sun came up. The opportunity to exonerate Eric was worth the risk, though.

However, now the mental dam blocked the river of words and left me floundering in the resulting lake. I took a deep breath, flooded my brain with oxygen, and got down to work, fingers poised over the keyboard.

The phone rang. It was my diminutive, blue-haired agent slash friend, Ruth Silverman. She hadn't called in a while. I guess my regular progress reports had kept her satisfied. "Hi, Ruth, what's up?"

Her Eastern European accent, which originated only she knew where, blasted across the line. "I shouldn't call and check on my favorite author? It's my job, yah?"

Mom, is that you? "Your favorite author? You say that to all the girls."

"Yah! And, the boys, too."

My chuckle harmonized with her cackle. "I'll bet. How's life in New York?"

"Not bad. Although, my old bones have had enough of this fakakta weather. Freezing in the winter, suffocating in the summer. I might retire to warm, sunny Florida."

"In the winter, perhaps. Sizzling and oppressive this time of year."

"Which is what they make the air conditioning for. And they have it in the whole house! Not just sticking out of the window in one or two rooms."

Was she for real? What would I do? I'd never find another agent to put up with me. "Who are you kidding? You love the city."

"True. But there are times . . . What's new with you?"

"Working hard. Finished chapter twenty a little while ago. The excitement is about to start." As soon as I figured out what it would be.

"Can't wait to read what you've come up with." She hesitated. "I hear that kleyntshik town of yours had another murder."

My new word of the day. Ruth liked to drop the occasional Yiddish bomb on me. "What does kleyntshik mean?"

"Tiny. As in little bitty. So, what about the murder? The chief of police, yah?"

"Yes, he was poisoned. How did you find out so fast?"

"The internet. How does anyone learn anything anymore?"

And in this case, the information she had was actually accurate. I regaled her with all the events since Saturday night. "The worst part is, my buddy Eric's been suspended from his job."

"Which has what to do with you?"

"He helped me when I was in trouble. I owe him the same in return, don't you think?"

"What I think doesn't matter. Your editor thinks you need to finish this book. Let the police take care of your friend."

My grip tightened on the phone. "Who do you think suspended him? He's a cop and they think he stole evidence and used it to kill his boss."

"Did he?"

Deep breath in, slow breath out.

"No, he didn't."

"Are you sure?"

I hated when she turned things around on me. However, as usual, she was right. "I guess I can't be positive." I shook my head. "But I know that Eric wouldn't do what he's accused of. I want to help him."

She blew a sigh into my ear. "Fine. Obviously, you won't be able to concentrate until this mess is cleaned up."

"Not true. I wrote two chapters last night. If anything, this real-life mystery is helping center my brain."

Another chortle. "Keep fooling yourself. Your friend is a police officer. Have you spoken to anyone he works with about his situation?"

Havermayer's glower exploded into my mind. "No.

The detective on the case isn't one of my fans. In fact, she hates me."

"What about the other one? Your ex-boyfriend."

"He's the new acting chief. The one who suspended Eric."

"Ach, that's it, then. Might as well give up."

My mouth fell open while my voice climbed an octave. "What? No way. Not gonna happen." I smiled. Ruth was a shrewd little devil. She had the answer but expected me to figure out what to do for myself. A discussion with Olinski and Havermayer was impossible. What about all the other people who worked for RPD? "I might talk to Eric's partner, Leonard. He would have a better idea of who might have set Eric up like this."

"So be it. I'll give you until the end of the week to conclude this mishegas. Afterward, you finish the book. Understood?"

"Understood."

I put down the phone and picked up my coffee cup. There was nothing left but a brown ring around the bottom and dried lip drips down the side. Time for another refill. Savannah lifted her head, her sleepy eyes blinking. "Sorry to disturb you, princess. No excitement here. Go back to sleep."

She yawned, displayed all forty-two razor-sharp teeth, and rested her chin on her paws. Until my hand brushed the treat bag on the counter. The pup jumped to her unsteady feet. Her front paw slipped off the couch, and she tumbled to the carpet, banging the coffee table on the way down. She shook off the embarrassment and sat, accusations plain on her face.

I interrupted my giggles long enough to say, "Hey, I

didn't do it!" I held up the bag that caused the commotion. "How about a treat to make everything all better?"

Her ears perked up, and she trotted into the kitchen to sit at my feet. If only people forgave so quickly. I offered my palm but yanked it back when she made a grab for the bacon-flavored snack. "Uh-uh. Gentle."

She puffed and shook while a bubble of saliva formed in the corner of her mouth, and her tail swept the floor. I should tie a rag to the end. Then she could dust, too. I presented the delicacy again. She nibbled it out of my hand, leaving a streak of drool in its place. *Yum.*

A shower, toasted bagel with cream cheese, and another cup of coffee later, I saddled up my puppy for a canter to the park. Another couple of months or so before her joints could withstand the pounding of an extended run without damage. Plenty of time for me to move my brain in the same direction. Saturday morning with the Riddleton Runners—Eric, Angus, and Lacey—was about all I could manage right now.

We headed out, and Savannah tripped on the first step. I grabbed her by the scruff so she didn't tumble down. Another growth spurt. At long last, I understood why kids were so clumsy. They never knew where their hands and feet were from one minute to the next. Tricky way to live.

The stroll down Park Street was a scene from Picasso's red, white, and blue period. Flags and bunting everywhere. A few A-frame houses even had flashing lights around the windows and doorframes. At least nobody had broken out the fireworks yet. Savannah's first Independence Day would be a challenge. Loud noises and bright lights. Children running around with sparklers. I suspected we'd both be spending the evening hiding under the bed.

Rather than enter the park at the end of the street, we took a left on Second Street and circled down Walnut past the senior center. Our thirty-minute stroll ended at the bookstore. On the other side of the yet un-decorated window, Lacey vacuumed between the tables, her long, brown ponytail swinging in rhythm. There was no sign of Charlie, but since we didn't open for forty-five minutes, he wouldn't be late for another fifteen. Not that I cared one way or the other.

I opened the door, and Savannah charged to tackle her favorite human treat dispenser. Strangely, she didn't view the vacuum cleaner as an enemy that must be destroyed. Maybe that was a good sign. She might not freak out at the fireworks. She circled the vacuum at a safe distance and poked Lacey in the leg from behind with her nose.

She hit the power switch. "Good morning."

My ears adjusted to the silence as I made for the coffee bar to start a fresh pot. "So far, but it's early yet."

She scratched Savannah under the chin and led her to the counter where the super snacks lay hidden. "Our shipment's late again." She pointed to the area by the front window. "Your display's a little bleak."

In the local authors' section, a cardboard cutout of me stood behind a table littered with copies of *Double Trouble*, despite my vociferous objections. I never should've agreed to Lacey's insistence on autonomy. "Doesn't seem too bad. Although, I still think they'd look better on a shelf with everyone else's."

"Nonsense. You love the attention."

"Yeah, right. I became a writer because I love attention. People aren't my strong suit. My characters don't talk back. Much. And when they do, I delete them."

Lacey cranked up the vacuum cleaner again, and Savannah attached herself to my left knee with a full-body lean. Still no barking or growling, though. A fair compromise as long as I didn't end up on my bottom.

Charlie swaggered in the front door decked out in his Zorro outfit—black leather pants topped with a pink, balloon-sleeved satin shirt. Still no cape, mask, or sword. Might have to give him those for Christmas. Plus, a black hat with a feather. Then take a picture, and his cutout could replace mine. No doubt it would draw a lot of interest.

"Hey, Charlie, nice outfit."

He placed his hands on his hips and tipped up his chin in a conqueror's pose. "Thanks. I was feeling adventurous today."

"Glad to hear it because I need your help."

I explained the evening's plan and the solution to the camera issue. "Can you do it?"

"Sure, no problem."

"Great. I'll call you at nine thirty."

"Sounds good."

"Thank you."

I poured myself a coffee and wandered back to my office so Charlie could set up without navigating around me. When I plopped into my chair, Eric's key in my pocket dug into my thigh. I extracted it and turned the bit of brass over in my hand. Just an ordinary key.

Tonight, I would use that key to break into the Riddleton Police Department. The first time I'd considered doing anything flat-out illegal besides exceeding the speed limit.

Why did this bother me so much? Fear of getting caught? I'd never been one to religiously follow the rules. But there was a big difference between breaking the rules and breaking the law. A big difference in the consequences, too. Maybe I did have a slight case of nerves. Especially since I wouldn't be the only one in trouble if they nabbed me in the act. Or perhaps Havermayer had made herself at home in my head, which was her goal all along. Nope. Nobody lives rent-free in my head but me.

I wouldn't allow the specter of Detective Havermayer to stop me from taking a picture of that signature to prove Eric didn't steal the cyanide from the property room. My resolve solidified as it occurred to me I hadn't seen my dog in a while.

I located Savannah in the stockroom, executing a grid search for edibles. Not sure why I bothered. Nothing in the store would hurt her, and she wasn't the destructive type. Chalk it up to parental paranoia since she was the closest thing to a child I'd ever have.

Lacey, who'd ditched the ponytail for a loose, more professional style, found me bent over, rubbing Savannah's belly. She handed me a notebook. "This is what I came up with for the front windows. What do you think?"

On one side of the door, she'd drawn George Washington comfy in a wingback chair next to a fire-place reading Thomas Paine's *Common Sense* to a group of British soldiers sitting rapt at his feet. On the other side, an angry King George III on his throne, waving a sword at his generals. The door in between depicted an

... George's side.

"Lacey, this is brilliant!" I handed her notebook back. "People are going to love it."

"People like the town council, you mean?"

I shook my head. "People like potential customers."

"Yeah, right. You just want a ride in that Mustang convertible."

"That, too. But you'll be right there with me."

Lacey poked her head out the door of the stockroom. "Hey, Charlie, time to go to Bob's. We open in five minutes."

"Oops, I almost forgot. Be right back."

While Lacey worked on her sketch and Charlie collected the sweets from Bob's, I drifted back to the children's section to set up for Story Time. Aletha had believed the key to success was through the children. Bring the youngsters in, and their parents would follow. After fifteen months, the jury was still out on whether it would work.

I arranged the chairs in a semicircle and placed a paper crown on each seat for the kids to color then wear home. The last box of crayons landed atop its crown as Charlie returned from the bakery.

When Savannah took off at the sound of his entrance, I followed quickly, lest she get under Charlie's feet and make him drop his load. Pastries safely on the counter, I helped him line the display trays. "How're things over at Bob's?"

Charlie clicked a full tray of chocolate chip muffins into its slot. "Busy. I had to wait for Greg Partridge to finish ordering enough donuts for a small army. One at a time! I guess he wants to be ready for the revolution."

I chuckled. "Well, you know the war *is* only a few days away."

"While I was waiting I tuned in to all the gossip. Angus will be upset he missed it. I won't tell him, though."

Charlie spent too much time in the diner. "Anything worthwhile?"

"Everyone's talking about Chief Vick."

"What're they saying?"

"Oh, the usual speculation about what happened. They're all puzzling out how he was poisoned."

"Did they draw any conclusions?"

Lacey unpacked the croissants. "I'm sure they pulled all kinds of theories out of their imaginations. No mystery the Riddleton rumor mill can't solve."

Charlie set the last blueberry muffin into place. "Actually, they've narrowed it down to the wine or his glass. Plus, they're concerned about the cyanide that disappeared from the police station. Uncomfortable about the possibility a cop might be involved."

She waved a cinnamon raisin. "How did that information get out?"

Charlie shrugged. "Who knows? It's Riddleton."

I took the blueberry muffins and swung them in beside the chocolate chips. "Either way, that's ridiculous. No way someone used that evidence to poison the chief. Somebody has to be trying to throw us off the track."

"Can they determine if the missing cyanide is the same kind that killed Chief Vick?" Charlie asked.

Lacey looked up. "Perhaps the medical examiner might compare what she finds in the autopsy with the lab reports from the case the cyanide was involved in last year."

I drummed my fingers on the counter. "Possibly, but

h[...] [...]the new ML. I can't
go waltzing into her office and demand information."

"What if she invited you?" Charlie tilted his head
toward the door. "She was going into Angus's when I
was on my way back from Bob's. I'll bet she's still there."

My stomach stirred. Time for an early lunch? "Guess
I'll go over and introduce myself. How will I recognize
her?"

He flashed his perfect teeth. "She'll be the only one
with a British accent."

"How do you know all this?" Lacey asked.

"How do you think?"

Lacey and I chorused, "Angus!"

CHAPTER ELEVEN

I mentally rehearsed my introduction on the way to the diner. Only one block to make my spiel perfect so I didn't come across as a necrophiliac. I wanted to befriend the new ME, not her current patient. *Chief Vick*. A chill sauntered down my spine.

Laughter echoed in the almost-empty restaurant. Angus was ringing up a to-go order for Greg Partridge, and Marcus chatted with a dark-skinned, thirtyish woman who was perched on a stool, clothed in pale-green scrubs and spotless white deck shoes.

Greg left. Angus waved me over, poured another coffee, and set the cup on the counter next to the woman I assumed was the new medical examiner. "Jen, have you met Dr. Kensington yet?"

"No, but I've been looking forward to the opportunity." I stuck out my hand. "Jen Dawson. Wonderful to finally meet you."

She beamed and gave my hand one firm pump. "Ingrid Kensington. I'm happy to make your acquaintance, too. I loved your book."

Yup, definitely British, her accent a salve for my American eardrums. Like an *Endeavor* marathon on PBS.

"Thank you. I'm surprised you read murder mysteries, given what you do for a living, Doctor."

"Ingrid, please. Only the traditional ones like *Double Trouble*. Great twists and turns, by the way. I loved all the fake hints, too. In real life, I can't follow the clues and figure out who the killer is. In fact, other than the autopsy findings, I don't even know what the clues are. Where's the fun in that?"

I added cream and sugar to transform my coffee from dark brown and bitter to beige and sweet. "I love a puzzle, too. That's why I write mysteries."

Angus delivered a fresh cup of tea to Ingrid. "Jen, you ready for lunch yet?"

"It's a little early. How about something simple, like a BLT?"

"Coming right up."

Marcus peeled away from the counter to lay the bacon on the grill, humming under his breath. Someone had a crush on the new ME. Good for him. If he was lucky, the down-to-earth doctor would share his interest. He'd worked hard to turn his life around. He deserved someone who would appreciate him. Not like his tweaker ex-wife.

"How's your new book progressing?" Ingrid asked.

I practiced my poker face. "I made some advances this morning. Shouldn't be too much longer." Perhaps a fib. Perhaps not.

Covertly keeping an eye on Ingrid, Marcus set my plate in front of me. The aroma sent my salivary glands into overdrive. I bit into the lightly toasted sandwich, the creamy mayonnaise blending the cool lettuce and tomato and the warm bacon together. Perfect.

Ingrid's phone chimed. Her lips were constrained in a thin line as she read.

113

She emitted a sigh. "Time for work. The body has arrived."

I laid my lunch down. "Chief Vick?"

She nodded and stood.

Not likely she'd tell me what she finds unless . . . I crossed my fingers under the counter. "My book might contain an autopsy scene. Would you consider allowing me to observe? I want the story as realistic as possible." Definitely a fib. But a necessary one.

"Are you sure you want to? A postmortem can be gruesome for the uninitiated."

"I understand, but with my luck one of my readers will be an expert and broadcast my ignorance all over the internet. I'd rather do my research and be prepared."

Ingrid tilted her head and stared directly into my eyes. "All right, luv. If you think it'll be useful, you can have a go." She jutted her chin toward my plate. "I suggest you skip the rest of your sandwich, though."

I reluctantly pushed my food away.

At the register, I nodded and gave Marcus a thumbs-up.

"What's that for?" he asked.

A head tilt in Ingrid's direction answered his question.

His lips twitched. "No idea what you mean."

"Sure you don't."

I followed Ingrid out the door and ran straight into Zach Vick. "Hi, Zach. How are you?"

He glanced between Ingrid and me. "Fine. What're you up to?"

Should I tell the truth? No, no need to upset him. "Nothing much. Just finished lunch."

He smirked. "Kind of early, isn't it?"

It seemed like he already knew his father's body was

114

at the morgue. Better to keep up the pretense, though. "I was hungry."

"Sure you were." He turned to Ingrid. "I want to watch the autopsy."

She laid her hand on his arm. "That's not a good idea, Zach."

"Why not?"

His petulance reminded me of his youth. A little boy in a grown-up suit about to enter the police academy. Frightening.

"You don't want to remember your father like that," Ingrid replied. "It's a horrible thing to see. It'll stay with you forever."

Anger flashed in his eyes. "I don't care. I want to know what killed my father."

"You will. I promise. Even if I have to tell you myself, but I'm sure I won't. Detective Havermayer will keep you and your mother informed."

"She better." He pushed past us into the diner.

Ingrid peered at me, eyebrows raised.

I shrugged.

We headed down Pine Street for the march to her office on the corner of Riddleton Road and Park. On the way, she told me since our tiny town didn't house enough potential patients to attract the interest of many doctors, the state of South Carolina paid for her medical training. In return, she only had to practice in Riddleton for five years. I'd move across the ocean for a sweet deal like that, too.

"My true passion is pathology, though. I was thrilled when the county agreed to allow me to operate a satellite morgue to handle local cases," she said as we rounded the corner onto Riddleton Road. "They even built it for me because I was already committed."

"A substantial investment for a relatively short period of time."

She laughed. "I suspect they want to convince me to stay. Won't take much, I don't think. So far, I like it here."

We entered through the front door into what would soon be her medical office waiting room. Brown and beige paisley carpet peeked out from under beige-speckled painters' drop cloths, and I assumed the sheet-covered mound in the middle of the room contained beige furniture. Maybe brown. "When do you think you'll be ready to start seeing patients?" I asked, careful not to inhale too deeply lest the paint fumes give me a buzz.

Ingrid glanced at the edge where the immaculate white ceiling met the bare moldings. "A couple of weeks, I think. Should be anyway. If everyone meets their deadlines. However, the exterior signs are already a week late, and the painters were supposed to be finished yesterday." She peered through the hole cut into the wall for the reception area and shook her head. "But, other than that, we're right on schedule," she said with a chuckle.

She led me past the exam rooms to a door at the end of the hall with a sign: "Authorized Personnel Only." On the other side, a covered outdoor walkway carried us to another building, which housed a white and stainless-steel world straight out of a science fiction novel. A room filled with gadgets, which most likely functioned in ways I couldn't begin to guess.

Ingrid handed me a paper gown, mask, and latex gloves. Did she expect me to participate? I fumbled with the bundle, dropped it on the floor, and shivered in the chill. Clearly, the AC wasn't behind schedule.

"You're fortunate this is my first customer. Otherwise, the odor in here would make you chunder for sure."

Chunder? Hard to believe we supposedly spoke the same language. "What's—"

"Vomit," she said with a laugh. "Sorry. I only meant the chief's been well refrigerated, so a little decomposition is all we have to deal with. Also he's my first, so the place doesn't stink yet. You're lucky."

I'd take her word for it. While I figured out the jumble of disposable clothing, Ingrid opened one of the drawers along the back wall. Inside, Chief Vick lay under a sheet on a wheeled, steel slab with collapsible legs. I picked up the corner for a quick peek. He didn't appear genuine. Only a perfect representation, like a wax figure in Madame Tussauds.

I took an involuntary deep breath. Together we hoisted until the supports locked and maneuvered the table to the center of the cement floor, which sloped slightly on all sides toward a drain in the middle. Handy for cleanup, although I hesitated to imagine the gore sluicing through those little square holes after a busy day.

Ingrid removed the sheet. Pink blotches covered Chief Vick's face and lips, his fingernails a muted indigo. My stomach lurched. Queasy already, and the autopsy hadn't started yet. Not an encouraging sign.

I crossed and uncrossed my arms, hands searching for a place to hide while she weighed, measured, and photographed the body, dictating her findings into a microphone. Afterward, she used an industrial-sized magnifier to examine his left arm.

"What are you doing?"

"Looking for injection sites. We still don't understand how the cyanide got into his system."

117

"I thought the police decided the poison was in the wine."

She nudged the glass across his furry chest. "I do my job; they do theirs. They have the luxury of making assumptions. I deal in facts. Whatever I find is the evidence they'll use in court to make the case. Their suppositions can only point them down potential avenues to investigate."

Duh. Someday, I'd learn to think before speaking. An issue my mother always said would be my downfall. All the more reason not to take that particular class. "Makes sense."

When she finished the external exam, she said, "Well, time to open him up. Sure you want to do this, luv?"

Excellent question. My stomach remained confused, but my curiosity was piqued. "Sure, why not?" My legs took two steps back without any prompting from me.

"Smashing." Ingrid opened a metal cabinet on the wall, retrieved two gas masks, and handed me one. "Here you go."

My eyebrows shot up as I eyed the rubber contraption complete with goggles and filters, I presumed, on either side of where my mouth would go. "Are you kidding me?"

"Nope. The body is full of cyanide fumes. I'm not interested in having two patients today." Her eyes crinkled above the paper face mask. "I imagine you wouldn't care to be the second?"

"No, my schedule's booked until next Tuesday."

She helped me into my protective mask, then donned hers with expert hands. Two characters decked out in get-ups straight from the movie *The Fly*. After wheeling over a table full of surgical-style instruments, she seized a scalpel and suspended it over the chief's left clavicle. "You ready?"

I strained to decipher her muffled words and gave her an agreeable nod.

Her strokes were swift and sure. In less than a minute, humming under her breath, she'd added the "Y" incision I'd seen so often on TV. The reason she'd told me to skip lunch became apparent when she used the spreaders to crack open the chest. I managed to keep the one bite I'd swallowed in its proper place. A full stomach would've filled my mask. Strange, since writing a scene like this wouldn't bother me at all.

Ingrid removed, washed, weighed, and measured the internal organs one by one. She flipped over a kidney. "Hey, have a gander at this brick-red discoloration! One of the telltale signs of cyanide poisoning."

"Which the police already suspected."

She laid the organ on the scale. "Yeah, but I've never seen it outside of a textbook before. Isn't it exciting? Now we grasp how he was poisoned. No injection sites on the skin, clear lungs, and affected kidneys, so he must've ingested it. I'll do a wash for stomach contents, but I suspect the evidence is long gone, except what's right here in this kidney."

I caught a little of her enthusiasm. Funny how someone might find so much satisfaction in rooting around inside a dead body. Only a unique person would want to do that for a living. Her bedside manner better be a little more restrained when her patients still had breath in their lungs, though. Especially in a backwater like Riddleton. "Guess the detectives need that wine bottle and the glasses now. Something to compare your findings to."

"No doubt."

It took another hour for Ingrid to complete her tasks, during which I learned more about the human body and how it functions than I ever wanted to. Whoever said, "True beauty is on the inside," had never witnessed an autopsy. However, I'd remained upright and kept my lunch in my gut where it belonged. I considered the event a success.

After thanking Ingrid for an experience I had no desire to ever repeat, and armed with conclusive proof the chief had swallowed the poison, I set out for the library to talk to Brittany about Tony's escapades in Chicago. The Riddleton Public Library was on Pine Street past Main, behind the Piggly Wiggly, across from the post office. A three-block walk back the way I'd come.

I strolled past the weather-beaten picnic table listing against the aged pine, which gave the road its name, and mounted the steps into the sun-bleached brick building. The narrow entry passage gave my pupils a workout as I passed from bright sunlight through the dim hallway and into the fluorescent lights of the reading room.

To my right, the stacks lined with books of all shapes and sizes stretched from one end of the room to the other. The center of the area was occupied by tables and chairs filled with readers. To the left was a half-moon-shaped desk, where Brittany conducted her daily business. Currently, she was checking out brightly colored young adult novels to three chatterbox pre-teen girls. Better her than me.

Brittany's intractable blond hair fell into her face, and she brushed a lock back impatiently. Some things would never change. When the kids ran out the door,

I ambled forward and leaned on the counter. Fingers crossed, she'd recovered from her snit. "Busy day?"

She edged her glasses back up. "The usual. What're you up to?"

So far, so good. "Not too much. Just met the new medical examiner."

"What's she like?"

"She's cool, actually. Not snooty like some doctors. She let me witness Chief Vick's autopsy."

Brittany's mouth fell open, and she crinkled her nose. "Yuck! Why would you want to?"

I straightened up and massaged my lower back. "I wanted to know what she found. I didn't think she'd tell me otherwise."

"Probably not, but what difference does it make? Besides, I thought you were staying out of it."

"I was, but Eric's been suspended because they think he might've had something to do with the chief's death. I want to help him."

She folded her arms across her chest. "So you can have side-by-side cells?"

"Funny. You don't think he's involved any more than I do. Now, we need proof. Your research skills will come in handy. Tony Scavuto was tangled up in a similar murder in his restaurant in Chicago and says he was never a significant suspect. I'm not sure I believe him. Can you look into it for me?"

Her face darkened into a scowl. "You must be joking." She waved an arm over the room. "Look at this place. I'm swamped."

Uh-oh. I'd upset her again. It seemed easier to do lately than ever before. "Don't most libraries have volunteers for occasions like this?"

"The bigger ones, sure. It's not like Riddleton is overrun with people who can or want to help out at the library. Between the recent publicity about libraries closing across the country and the need for computers for almost everything, twice as many people come in here every day now as before. And the people who use our computers are the ones who know the least about them, so I spend half my day teaching them how to navigate a simple search engine. I can't keep up."

I put up my hands. "Okay, I understand. Sorry I asked."

Her glare sent me scuttling out of the building.

CHAPTER TWELVE

I headed for the bookstore with my proverbial tail between my legs. Brittany's outburst was completely unexpected. A sure sign of trouble in the works. My ignorance of the reason was more an indication of my oblivion than my innocence. She wasn't prone to holding grudges, so it had to be more than just our argument the other night.

Her words resonated, however, and by the time Savannah tackled me at the door, I'd come up with an idea to ease her workload. Lacey had transferred the outline of her drawing to the right-side window, and I herded the puppy in that direction.

"It's starting to take shape. I think it'll be terrific when you're done."

"Thanks. I hope you're right. The project's more of a challenge than I realized. I've never worked backward before. Kind of like drawing something to be seen in a mirror, but I can't do it on the outside of the window. The elements would destroy all my hard work."

"We certainly don't want that. Too much can happen between now and the parade."

"Exactly." She put the last dab on King George's nose. "You think we have a chance?"

"As much as anyone else. Although, I suspect the judges might lean toward naming Anne-Marie the winner in deference to Chief Vick. Not to mention her history of success. Some people might complain about it, but I think it would be a kindhearted decision under the circumstances. The contest should be about community involvement and patriotism, anyway."

Lacey laughed. "I can think of some people who might do a whole lot more than gripe, but I'm with you. She should lead the parade."

Savannah dropped her stuffed bone on my foot, and I threw it up the aisle for her to chase. "I stopped by the library on my way here and it was busy. Britt was overwhelmed."

"Was her hair flying out everywhere like she'd just stuck her finger in a socket?"

"No, not more than usual."

"Then she wasn't overwhelmed. Yet. That's the indication she's ready to scream."

How did Lacey understand my best friend better than I did? "Guess I never noticed. Anyway, I had an idea that might help us and her. What do you think about offering free Wi-Fi? It might bring people in the door, at least, and take some of the pressure off Brittany."

She studied me, waving the brush like a torch. "I like it. The more time people spend in here, the greater the likelihood they might make a purchase."

"And the place won't look deserted all the time. Customers seem to like places where other people already are."

"The herd mentality. If someone else thinks a place is worthwhile, it must be."

"Precisely."

She went back to her artwork. I retrieved Savannah's leash from behind the counter and hooked her up. One hand on the doorknob, I turned to Lacey. "I'm headed out. You need anything before I go?"

"Nope. We're good. Have a good night. I'll see you tomorrow."

With good fortune, she would. Not through the Plexiglass visitor's booth at the Sutton County Detention Center, either. The diner closed at ten tonight, leaving me with roughly six hours to kill before Angus made his call to draw the duty sergeant away from his desk. Plenty of time for Savannah to examine every leaf and fire hydrant between the store and home.

When we finally made it back to the apartment, I tossed my keys on the table and filled Savannah's bowl with kibble. While she gobbled her dinner, I scavenged the cabinets for mine, but truth be told, my appetite didn't exist. Scrambled eggs and toast would probably do the trick. A meal I could make that would still be edible by the time I finished.

I went on the hunt for supplies. Eggs, butter, and cheese in the refrigerator, salt, pepper, and minced onion in the cabinet. Then beat it all together like the chef at the Ritz. Who said I couldn't cook? A few minutes later, I had a fair representation of breakfast for dinner. Nothing better to my mind.

As the seconds ticked closer to D-hour, it felt like ants had invaded my body. I paced, sat down, jumped up, and paced some more. Pictures of Chief Vick's death and autopsy ran through my mind like a slideshow of the world's goriest summer vacation, punctuated by the realization my trip to the police station tonight might end up being my downfall. Still, no time for second thoughts. I picked up my laptop and parked myself on the couch.

Chief Vick died from cyanide poisoning. Ingrid, the expert, said so. So, who killed him? The array of suspects I had—Anne-Marie, Mayor Benedict, and her husband, Tony Scavuto, and possibly Eric—made the question impossible to answer at this point. Too many people with motives, and no way to rule anyone out without more information. Perhaps the "how" would lead me to the "who." How did the chief ingest the cyanide?

Based on what I'd read, the poison was fast-acting in a significant dose. Only minutes would've passed between the time he ate or drank it and the time he reacted. When I checked the table the other night after the Benedicts vacated, the chief's dinner plate lay untouched, making the detectives' assumption most likely correct. The poison had to be in the wine or on the glass. Since the bottle and glasses were unaccounted for and couldn't be tested, I'd have to focus on how the murderer would've put cyanide in a sealed bottle.

I asked my buddy Google, and two possibilities came up. Number one: remove the cork, add the substance, and reinsert. Number two: inject through the cork with a long, thin needle. An intact seal covered the cork, which eliminated the first choice. We all watched Tony pull the foil off the bottle and uncork it. Which left me with the second option.

Another trip through the search engine. Six pages of results. I perused the variety of medical, veterinary, and insulin needles on page one. All too short. On to page two. Suggestions on what I might do with a needle. I had suggestions about what they should do with their suggestions. Page three? How to use needles. No help. Time for a different approach.

The needle had to be long enough to penetrate all the way into the liquid. Okay, so try long needles. Results: sewing, weaving, and tapestry. All solid. Long, hollow needles? Nope. The only workable one refilled ink cartridges, but the end wasn't beveled. The thing wouldn't go through the cork without leaving a mine-shaft in its wake. *Where's Brittany when I need her?*

I gave up and turned to the Davenport twins for inspiration. Dana and Daniel chatted with Detective Abernathy about what they'd learned from their confrontation with their father's friend Peter. Must be nice. If I tried that with Havermayer, she'd chop my head off and feed it to the wolves. Not that I'd ever encountered a wolf around here, but she would find at least one, just for me.

There had to be a way to improve my relationship with the detective. After all, she had nothing to justify her animosity toward me. She came in with it the day she and Olinski showed up at my apartment to tell me Aletha had died. They considered me a suspect at the time, but I'd long since proved my innocence. I guess she was one of those people who hated to be wrong. And held a grudge.

A thousand or so words down, and it was time to get ready. I threw on a dark hoodie to make me a little less visible in the dark. My leather biker jacket would've been perfect, but I lost it in the fire at the Cunningham house. And it would have me sweating buckets in no time.

Around nine fifteen, I escorted Savannah on a quick trip around the block, then departed, leaving her happily gnawing on a rawhide chew while I made the short walk to the bookstore. When I hit the bottom of the steps at nine twenty-five, Charlie waited for me, decked out in a balaclava and tracksuit, pants tucked into Converse high tops—all black. A Ninja with a laptop.

"What are you doing here?"

"Thought you might need some help with the bad guys."

I pressed my lips together to hold the laughter in. He was too earnest to risk hurting his feelings. "Have you already recorded the loop?"

"No I'm going to wait until we get to the store so we record as close to the time you're in there as possible."

"That makes sense. Are you sure you want to come along? We could get caught."

He threw his shoulders back and held his chin high. "Caught? No way. *I'm* coming."

"All right, but you have to do exactly what I tell you. Also, no talking."

"You got it, Boss."

The streetlights on Main Street exposed us to view, so we hung a left on Pine Street past the diner to enter the store through the back door. The darkness of an overcast, moonless night enveloped us when we neared the entrance to the alley in the back of the shop.

I drove Charlie back against the brick facade of the town hall as my eyes adjusted to the black. My ears tuned in to the rustle of paper in the slight breeze and the scratches of a stray cat trying to break into one of the trash cans. At least, I hoped it was a cat. A chill ran down my spine, and I raised my hood to keep the hair on the back of my neck at bay.

128

Two cruisers were parked behind the police department, one on each side of the back steps. They'd only be using one at this hour, but which I had no idea. Best to get by them both as quickly as possible. Easier said than done since fear had my feet cemented to the ground, barely able to support my quivering legs.

Deep breath in, slow breath out.

I hadn't actually broken the law yet. I had every right to go to my bookstore, regardless of the time. But someone seeing me meant an end to the plan, along with any chance of proving Eric's innocence. I couldn't take that risk.

I tipped my chin and pulled my shoulders back. I could do this. Stepping out into the dark, Charlie close behind, I hustled past the first car and approached the steps. The station door opened, and a supernova of light exploded out. I grabbed Charlie by the jacket, dove into the corner where the stairs met the wall, and slammed my shoulder into the building, biting my lip against a cry of pain. He landed on top of me with a grunt.

Untangled from him, I shifted for a better view. I slapped a hand over Charlie's mouth as Leonard sauntered onto the landing with a phone to his ear.

He stopped, pulled his cell away, and peered into the darkness. I held the air in my lungs. After a second, he shrugged, closed the door, and resumed his conversation on his way down to the car. As the night once again shielded us, I exhaled. Which way would he turn at the bottom? To the right meant safety, the left almost certain discovery. I willed him to turn right. A test of the power of positive thinking.

We huddled together, my armpits filled with sweat until Leonard made a right and climbed into the front vehicle. Score one for Norman Vincent Peale. As soon as his cruiser cleared the alley, a hand landed on my shoulder. I bit back another scream and turned around, fists ready to strike.

Zach backpedaled, lost his balance, and landed on his butt. "Hey, watch it!"

I reached for him, and Charlie seized me from behind so I wouldn't hit him. I struggled, and his grip tightened until I relaxed. "I'm all right. Let go."

He released me but hovered in grabbing distance.

Zach lay on the ground, wide-eyed.

When my heart rate slowed enough that I could breathe again, I grasped his hand and helped him up. "What are you doing here? You scared the hell out of me."

"Sorry. I saw you come back here and wanted to know why. I thought you might've found a clue or something."

If this kid kept popping up out of nowhere, I wouldn't live to celebrate my thirtieth birthday. "No, we're just going to the bookstore to finish up some work we can't do while the store is open. Nothing exciting." How many fibs was that today? I'd lost count.

"Dressed like that?" He pointed to Charlie. "He looks like he's on his way to a nerdy Halloween party or something."

"Hey!" Charlie said. "No need to be insulting."

Zach put his hands up. "No offense, dude. It's just weird."

I chuckled. "I take it you two have never met?"

They both shook their heads.

I introduced them, and they shook hands. "All right, Zach, we'd better get to work. I'll see you later."

He frowned. "Yeah, see ya."

Charlie and I forced ourselves to stroll to the back door of the bookstore, feeling Zach's eyes on our backs all the way.

Charlie whispered, "You know he's not going anywhere, right?"

"I know. I'm going to need you to distract him while I sneak into the police station."

"Gotcha covered."

Safely tucked into the stockroom, I sank down the wall and landed on the floor to catch my breath and adjust to a different shade of darkness.

Charlie descended beside me. "Whew, that was close," he said. "What a rush!"

I barely heard him over my heart. I didn't dare turn on the lights, even though Zach would find that suspicious. Assuming he was still out there. My phone screen showed 9:35, so I texted Angus that Leonard had left the station a few minutes ago.

"Come on, let's get started." I boosted myself to my feet and followed the bookcases to the office. The store was in semi-darkness, partially illuminated by the street lamps outside. I stayed to the side, hoping nobody would notice us from the street. The last thing I needed was a prowler call. Not my idea of clandestine.

"Thanks for coming, Charlie."

"Of course. Wouldn't be much of a hero if I didn't help a damsel in distress, right?"

I closed the door. If the stars aligned, anyone who saw the light would assume I'd forgotten to turn it off when I left. He opened his laptop, and his fingertips flew across the keys. I hovered over his shoulder until he glared at me. I scurried away.

Surprisingly soon, he said, "I'm in."

"That was fast!"

"I did a dry run this afternoon to make sure there'd be no unexpected issues." He looked up and smiled. "Recording now."

I paced the front of the room.

"Okay, I've set the loop. Hit enter as soon as the sergeant's out of the building and all anyone will see is exactly what's there right now."

"Thank you."

"Text me when you're out so I can reset it before morning. Don't want them seeing what's there right now in the morning."

"No kidding. Make sure you find Zach and keep him busy until I'm inside."

Charlie smiled. "Consider it done."

Xavier Benedict's alibi popped into my mind. "Hey, you want something to do while you're waiting for my text?"

"Sure, whatcha got?"

I filled him in, then let him out the back door and resumed pacing. My table in the corner beckoned me. I sat in the shadows, focused on the nearly deserted street the way I had for so many hours in the past. My left leg bounced under the table, and I wiped my sweaty palms on my thighs. The tattoo of my heart still reverberated off my eardrums.

Deep breath in, slow breath out.

I checked my phone with shaky hands—9:58. Two more minutes until Angus made the call. Two more minutes until D-hour. A couple came out of Antonio's hand in hand. She fixed an adoring gaze on him while he studied the window displays. A match made in heaven.

Eric believed he and I belonged together, but I was comfortable with our friendship. Was I playing it safe, as Brittany insisted? Perhaps. What was wrong with that? What was the problem with protecting myself? I needed to focus on my work and the bookstore. No need to stand in front of that particular firing squad again so soon.

My cell phone jolted me back to reality—Angus texted me he'd called out the sergeant. I slid out of my chair and duck-walked far enough to observe the police department's steps. I held my breath until the man hit the sidewalk and turned toward the diner, unsnapping his holster.

I went back to the table and hit enter on the laptop. *The game is afoot.*

CHAPTER THIRTEEN

I stood on tiptoe and grabbed the bells above the book-store's entrance to silence them. The edges dug into my sweaty palm as my left foot cramped and curled itself into the letter C. I bent my knee and wiggled my toes to provide some relief, but now I balanced on my right leg like a gymnast on the balance beam, using the string attached to a single penny nail as a counterweight.

The tack slid out of the wall, and I went down like a cow in a dissipating tornado. I'd never had any interest in gymnastics as a child. Clearly, my six-year-old self was smarter than me.

I stood, dusted my jeans off, and rushed to open the door, smacking myself in the nose. My eyes filled with tears I brushed away with the sleeve of my hoodie. No time for that. The sting—both physical and emotional—subsided. I'd better give up on my career as a cat burglar. Clearly, clandestine activity wasn't my forte. I widened the crack enough for me to slide through. Time sped by. I had to move.

Deep breath in, slow breath out.

A short sprint later, I stood at the front entrance to the police station and fished Eric's key out of my pocket. The double wooden doors loomed over me, the cloudy glass panes at the top like eyes fixated on my every move. I shook the image out of my head. After another quick glance around to ensure nobody was observing from the street, I inserted the key into the lock and turned. It didn't budge. I wiped my hand on my leg and tried again. No luck. Did Eric give me the wrong one?

After multiple attempts to jiggle and twist and pauses to wipe sweat out of my eyes, the tumblers finally gave, and I ducked inside. The interior was lit like a used car lot, and I blinked and squinted until my eyes adjusted to the glare. The faded gray walls supported photographs of uniformed officers from Riddleton's past. At least there was no "In Memoriam" section. RPD had never lost an officer in the line of duty.

The sergeant's desk blocked the hallway, with an alcove on one side and a break room on the other. The yellowed tile squeaked under my Nikes as I inched down the hall. Despite the artificial illumination and efficient ventilation system, despair thickened the atmosphere like automobile exhaust in a closed garage. A place for the worst moments in people's lives. If I did my job right, I wouldn't join the crowd.

Eric's directions were simple: the key to the property room was in the desk's top-left drawer, the door to the basement was to the right, and my destination was at the bottom of the stairs. Easy-peasy.

I glanced at my cell phone—10:10. We'd estimated Angus would be able to detain the officer for about fifteen minutes. Ten of those remained. I found a ring of approximately a dozen keys, each marked with a different-colored dot, in the designated drawer. No other form of identification. One of them fit the property room lock. Okay, what color would evidence be? Red for blood? Green for money? Maybe white for cocaine. I'd have to try them all.

I closed the door behind me, then turned on my phone flashlight. Each step on the ancient wooden stairs was a firecracker in my ears. Amazing nobody had fallen through them yet. By the time I stood in front of the property room door, a river of sweat flowed down my face. I wiped some off with my shoulder.

Now for the fun part: finding the correct key. The minutes ticked away as I tried them one by one. Red, then yellow, green, blue, and white. No good. Pink, purple, orange, and brown: same result. Only three left. Next up was teal, and the lock turned. My knees buckled.

Shoring up with a lungful of courage, I scooted into the room and flashed the light around. Directly ahead was a divider wall with a glass panel in the middle and an aperture at the bottom. The clock at the rear of the room read ten seventeen. I had three minutes to locate the logbook, snap the picture, and escape unseen.

On the desk behind the partition was an open book with a pen attached, off to one side. That had to be the sign-in log. But could I reach it? The door to the back was locked, and I had no time to hunt for another key. I stuck my arm through the half-moon-shaped hole in the glass. All the way up to my armpit, I barely brushed the edge with my fingertip. Not good enough.

I played the flashlight on the bare gray walls searching for something to use to pull the thing closer. Nothing. I tried reaching the log again. No luck. I needed to explore the rest of the basement and hope Angus could delay the sergeant long enough for me to find a tool that worked.

As I reached for the doorknob, feet clattered quickly down the stairs. I snatched back my hand, pulse throbbing in my ears, then pressed up against the wall next to the doorjamb. The footsteps landed on the concrete floor and paused.

My pulse ramped up even more, and I waited for my heart to burst out of my chest. The thuds covered the sound of my panting. Was I hyperventilating? If I didn't control my breathing, I'd pass out and be discovered.

Deep breath in, slow breath out.
Deep breath in, slow breath out.

The knob turned, and a shadow eased into the room. I stashed my phone in my pocket and positioned my fists in front of my face. I might be caught, but I wouldn't go down without a fight.

A whisper pierced the darkness. "Jen. Jen! Where are you?"

I stayed silent.

"It's me, Eric."

I let the air out of my lungs in a whoosh. "What are you doing here? How did you get in?"

"Spare key. I've been down the street, playing lookout. Sarge is on his way back. What's happening? You should be gone by now."

Suppressing the urge to lash into him about all the issues I'd had, I grabbed his forearm and led him to the desk window. "I had trouble getting in and now I can't reach the logbook. The door to the back part of the room is locked."

He ran a hand over his cropped hair. "Okay, let's see what I can do. My arms are longer than yours."

"Hurry! I don't want to be caught in here."

"Neither do I. It could cost me my job. And my freedom if they decide I'm in here tampering with evidence." He slid his skeleton-thin arm through the slot and grabbed the corner of the log. "I got it."

As soon as he maneuvered the book through the opening, I opened the camera on my phone. "Excellent. Find the page for me."

He flipped through the pages and indicated an entry dated two days before the murder. "There it is."

"Move your finger so I can take the shot."

I snapped two quick pictures, and he popped the logbook back where he found it. "Let's get out of here."

We got as far as the door when footsteps clomped over our heads. Eric tightened his grip on my elbow. "Crap! He's back."

"I'll text Angus and ask him to call him out again."

"Leonard's on his way back to town by now. He'll respond instead."

"All right, we hang out. The sergeant has to use the bathroom sometime. Or he'll go in the break room for lunch. When he does, we'll sneak out the front door."

"I think he eats around twelve, but I'm not sure. It might be a long wait."

I grabbed his shoulders and turned him to face me. "If you have a better idea, I'm listening. Is there another way out of here that doesn't require sneaking past his desk?"

He pointed to a blackened rectangle around two feet long and ten inches high at the top of the wall in the back. "That window's at ground level. Maybe we can squeeze out that way."

"Where does it lead?"

"The alley."

"That works, but do you think we'll fit?"

"It'll be tight. I think we can make it, though."

I wasn't sure I could. Too many chocolate chip muffins. However, what choice did I have? "It's worth a shot. How will we get back there?"

"Did you try all the keys?"

"No, I didn't want to take the time. It took forever finding the key to open this door."

Eric held out his hand, and I gave him the key ring. He flipped through a few he must've known wouldn't work and tried the rest. None of them worked. He stuffed the ring in his pocket. "I guess Sarge carries the key for this door. We're screwed."

"Don't give up yet. There must be other windows down here, right? Where are they?"

Eric snapped his fingers. "There's one in the locker room. We can also use the bench to stand on."

He took my hand and led me through the hall to a room at the other end. "This window leads to Main Street. You okay with that?"

I squeezed his hand. "Do we have another option?"

He squeezed back. "Guess not."

We crept from the dark hallway into the darker room. I played my flashlight around the walls until I found the window. A bank of metallic-gray steel lockers blocked access. No way out unless we moved them.

I turned the light on Eric. "What do you think?"

He took my phone and squeezed between the end of the row and the front wall. Peering behind the lockers, he angled his head to the side. "I think we're in trouble. They're bolted to the wall." He trained the beam near his feet. "And the floor. No way we'll loosen them

139

enough to move without tools, and the equipment room is upstairs." He flopped onto the bench and held his head in his hands.

I hunkered beside him and draped an arm around his bony shoulders. What now? "Looks like we have some time to kill. Got a deck of cards?"

He chuckled. "Nope. Didn't plan on staying long enough."

"Check your locker. You might have something to pass the time."

"Doubtful. Unless you have a uniform fetish. Or a thing for toiletries."

"You never know." I poked him in the ribs. "I can think of some interesting things to do with shaving cream."

Eric jumped up. "Oh, yeah?" He grinned. "I just happen to have some." He opened the door labeled with his name and shined the light inside.

"What the hell?" He turned to me.

I joined him at the locker. On the bottom shelf behind his duty boots was a plastic bag containing a half-full vial of pale-blue liquid. "Is that . . . ?"

"The cyanide missing from the property room. Why is someone trying to frame me?"

I reached toward it, and he grabbed my arm. "Don't touch. That's evidence."

"I know. You told me somebody stole it."

He rotated me to face him. His eyes were wide, and beads of sweat had appeared on his forehead. "No. Now it's evidence against me. It has to be processed."

"Not if nobody else knows about it."

"I need to tell Havermayer. It's relevant to her case."

"Think for a minute. The instant you tell her, she'll arrest you. It will tarnish your name forever. Even if

140

we prove you're innocent. And forget about that promotion."

He backpedaled. "I don't know, Jen. There might be fingerprints or DNA on the bag. That would show I had nothing to do with it."

I closed the locker door. "You really think someone capable of framing you would be dumb enough not to wear gloves? Give us twenty-four hours. If we can't find help for you by then, turn the stuff in as if you just found it."

Heavy footsteps sounded on the stairs, and his gaze met mine. I took the phone and checked the time—11:00. I whispered, "The sergeant's early for his lunch break."

"What can we do? There's no place to hide in here."

No place to hide and no way out. Our only chance was to convince the sergeant we had a good reason for being here. What could we possibly be doing hiding in the locker room in the middle of the night? The last time I faced a situation like this I was making out with Olinski in . . . Oh!

I grabbed Eric. "Kiss me."

"What?"

"Kiss me!" I pushed him against the locker, pressed my body on his, and caressed his lips with mine while running my hands over his chest. My face grew hot, and warmth spread down my figure.

Eric leaned in as if he meant it.

Why didn't I move away?

The door opened, and the overhead lights burst on.

I turned and stood face-to-face with Zach. Air rushed out of my lungs. "How did you get in here?"

He grinned. "I could ask you the same thing, but since I watched you let yourself in, I don't have to.

141

When you didn't come back out, I thought you might need some help."

Charlie and I were going to have a little chat tomorrow. "You saw me? From where?"

"Across the street, by Bob's."

Eric jumped in. "How did you know where we were?"

"I didn't, but since you were involved I figured it had something to do with that missing evidence. This seemed the logical place to start."

I hated to admit it, but the kid might be a good cop one day. "All right, but how did you get past the sergeant?"

"I told him my dad said I could leave some things in a locker down here and I needed them. He let me in. I think he felt sorry for me."

"Okay, fine, but how does that help us?"

"Simple. I'm going back upstairs to tell the sarge I forgot I already picked the stuff up. You're gonna follow me and wait by the door. Then I feel sick and hightail it into the break room to throw up in the sink. The sarge'll come after me to make sure I'm okay, and you run out the front door. Genius, right?"

I had to give it to the kid. It was a great plan. Actually, the only plan we had. "Let's try it."

We tiptoed behind Zach up the stairs. He went out to talk to the duty sergeant, and Eric kept his ear to the door. Voices murmured, but I couldn't make out the words. Then in a loud voice, Zach said, "Oh, crap! I'm gonna be sick."

Two sets of running footsteps followed. Eric cracked the door and peeked. Then he opened the door a little more and stuck his head out. He turned back to me. "All clear. Let's go. Hurry!"

We ran out the door and down the steps to the bookstore. I fumbled for the key, let us in, and closed the door behind us. We stood for a moment, panting and looking at each other.

I busted out laughing.

CHAPTER FOURTEEN

Wednesday morning, my clock radio treated me to an ear-splitting rendition of "My Sharona." I had no clue who Sharona was, but they could have her. I slapped the off button, turned on my back, and got an eyeful of Savannah's snout and a snoot full of dog breath. Respect for personal space wasn't one of her strengths. As I rubbed the water out of my eye, she stuck her tongue up my nose. "All right, that's enough."

I sat up and nudged her away, which she took as a signal for playtime. She seized my blanket, back-pedaled, and flipped ears over tail off the edge of the bed. Laughter-induced tears this time. When I could breathe again, I peered over the side. "You okay, little girl?"

She dropped into a play bow, then took off on a full-speed lap around the apartment.

"I'll take that as a yes."

I threw on sweats, made sure the coffeemaker brewed as scheduled, and leashed Savannah for her morning walk. We made the rounds of grass, trees, and fire hydrants and returned just in time for the final gurgle. I fed Savannah, whose visible ribs broadcasted another growth spurt, and I filled my "Creativity Begins with Coffee" mug.

While my baby wolf devoured her kill, I curled up on the couch and rehashed the events of last night. Eric and I had obtained a picture of the signature on the logbook and escaped from the police station but not unseen. I didn't think Zach would say anything since he was complicit in our escape. And at least Eric remembered to toss the keys under the desk on the way out.

Zach had saved us, but what came before was the problem. I'd shared a hot and heavy lip-lock with Eric. And liked it. Was it possible I had feelings for him after all? Could I even handle another relationship?

Eric wasn't my type. A tall, skinny redhead. Except I hadn't had much luck with the men who were my type. Perhaps, I needed to rethink that concept. What was a type, anyway?

I should judge people for who they are, not how they appear. Knowing what I should do and actually doing it were two different things. However, I should call Eric and check on him. He was still my friend, after all.

I pressed the icon next to his academy photo. Opie wearing his Sunday best.

"Hi, Jen. What's up?"

He's lucky I'm not my mother. Or Ruth. "Nothing, I just wanted to see how you're doing after our adventure last night."

"I'm okay. How are you?"

"Good. It was a little more exciting than I'd anticipated, but it worked out well."

"I hope so."

Time to address the elephant on the line. "Listen, about that kiss . . ."

"It's all right. We don't have to talk about that. I know it didn't mean anything to you."

If only that were true. "It's not that. I'm just not ready."

"I get it. Don't worry, I'm not expecting anything. I appreciate you trying to help me."

"I only hope I can."

We said our goodbyes and I pressed the red icon. None of our feelings mattered if I couldn't help Eric clear his name. The photo I took contained two samples. One from the day in question and one from two days earlier. The signatures should be a close match, but I had no idea how to analyze differences in handwriting.

Should I ask Brittany for help? No, she'd probably bite my head off again. Our relationship was different now. Olinski and the library kept her busy, and I had a store to run and a novel to write. I missed her. However, I had some new friends. Perhaps Lacey or Charlie knew how to compare the samples. Too early for them to be at the bookstore, though. Might as well check out what the twins had to say for themselves in the meantime.

The brown sludge in the bottom of my coffee cup teased me, so I refilled and returned to the desk where Dana and Daniel awaited my brilliance. I hoped they'd brought a book to read. It might be a while.

My word processor produced my latest chapter, and I scrolled down to the end. The Davenports had just left the police station after discussing their conversation with their father's best friend with Detective Abernathy.

Okay, what now?

Dana fished the car keys out of her purse and unlocked the passenger door for her brother. "So, what do you think?"

He rested his arm on the top of the door, propping one foot on the running board. "I don't know. Abernathy said he'd talk to Peter about the meeting he had scheduled with Dad that day, but he didn't seem enthusiastic to me."

"I agree. It was almost like he was patronizing us." She climbed into the driver's seat and buckled her seat belt. "Just telling us what we wanted to hear so we'd leave."

"My thoughts exactly. I think we need to find proof Dad was actually there, and Peter's lying when he says he didn't see him."

"Where should we start?"

Great question. Where do they start? No security cameras in the house, so no video. The housekeeper was off that day, so no witnesses. The outside cameras showed Peter entering the building, but that still doesn't prove he met with Victor.

Think, Jen.

They could search the living room again in case the police missed something Peter had lost. Maybe, but even if they unearthed something, that only proved he was present. They'd have to stumble on a clue that showed Victor was there at the same time. But an item belonging to Victor could've been left anytime.

Hey, what about the note Dana discovered in their father's desk? What if they compared the handwriting to the one she found in Victor's sock drawer? It would match but still wouldn't prove Peter and Victor actually met that day. The clue would, however, give Detective Abernathy a reason to take the twins seriously. Worked for me.

The clock in the lower right corner of my laptop reminded me I needed to go to the bookstore for some real-life handwriting analysis. But first, a shower and clean clothes. My house-only sweats weren't for public view, except for a short stroll with Savannah. When we were out together, she attracted all the attention, which was fine by me.

Showered and clothed in jeans and a Motor Supply Company T-shirt, I leashed Savannah, and we headed out into a sunny blue sky dotted with wispy white clouds. When we strolled into the store, Lacey wielded her favorite duster, and Charlie was setting up the coffee bar.

I hated to interrupt, but I needed help with Tony's issues in Chicago, information on how to compare writing samples, and how the cyanide wound up in the wine bottle. Assuming that's the way the chief was poisoned. The possibility it was in the glass still existed since we'd left the glasses on the table unattended when we went home to shower and change, but it was still more challenging to achieve. Better to go with the obvious choice until I ruled it out.

Charlie lined up the condiments and napkins while I poured him a cup of coffee. "Black, no sugar?"

He glanced up from the box of wooden stir sticks. "Yes, thanks." He turned to face me with a suppressed grin. "Hey, wait a minute. You never get me coffee. What do you need?"

My jaw fell. "What do you mean?"

He let the grin blossom. "Never mind, I'm only kidding." With lowered eyebrows, I pinched my lips together.

"You'd better be." Then my smile matched his. "Actually, since you mentioned it, I do kinda need a favor."

"I knew it!"

I explained what I needed and gave him the CliffsNotes version of what I'd done to this point. "If you can do that for me, I'll owe you one."

"Dinner?"

I moved as if to punch him, and he crossed his arms over his abdomen, paisley satin sleeves billowing with the movement. "Now, don't you start that again."

During the first six months after he moved into the apartment below mine, Charlie incessantly badgered me to have dinner with him. Our one date, as payment for his help identifying Aletha's killer, went much better than anticipated, but definitely just as friends. No chemistry. Another one who wasn't my type.

We agreed to a compromise when I inherited the bookstore, and he became the new barista. He wouldn't ask, and I wouldn't squash him like a palmetto bug. So far, so good.

"Oh, by the way, Charlie, what happened with you and Zach last night?"

He shrugged. "I couldn't find him. His truck was gone, and I checked everywhere and didn't see him, so I assumed he'd gone home. Why?"

"He turned up at the police station last night."

His eyes widened. "Where was he hiding?"

"Across the street, by Bob's."

Charlie's face turned red. "I'm so sorry. I swear I tried to find him."

"I believe you. It turned out well, though. He helped us get out of there when the sergeant came back before we were ready."

"Us?"

"Eric showed up too. It was quite the adventure, but we got what we needed. I appreciate your help with it."

"Anytime."

I leaned on the pastry display case. "Did you have any luck with Xavier's alibi?"

"Yup. There was a dental convention at the Atlanta Convention Center that week and he stayed at the Sheraton."

"Do I want to know how you found that out?"

"Nope, but I don't know how helpful it is. Atlanta's only a couple hundred miles from here. He could've driven back, put the poison in the wine, and still returned in time for the next day's activities."

"True, but it seems unlikely. He'd also have had to break into the restaurant, find the bottle, and escape without anyone knowing he'd ever been there. We'll put him on the back burner for now."

Lacey flipped the closed sign to open and unlocked the front door. Charlie scurried through on his way to the bakery. She came up beside me, her hair tied back off her shoulders. "What's going on?"

When I leaned against the table of the *Double Trouble* display, my cardboard eyes bored into my back. I really wished she would take the spectacle down. "Nothing. I asked Charlie to do some research for me."

"What are you after this time?"

"The details of how Tony's manager in Chicago died."

Savannah charged up with a once-beige stuffed bone hanging out one side of her mouth, chewing the squeaker between her molars. She tossed the plaything at my feet, which interrupted my hands' journey to my ears. Whoever invented squeak toys must've been stone-deaf.

I tossed the slobbery, puppy objet d'art to the Ravenous Kids' section at the back of the store and wiped my hand on my leg. She dashed away and skidded to a stop before one of the child-sized bookcases, barely avoiding a collision. Did German shepherds get rug burns?

Lacey propped herself on the coffee bar while Savannah shook the toy to break its neck. "You know she'll tear the thing to shreds, don't you?"

"Probably. Sooner or later. Then, I'll just get her another one. She loves that thing."

A fallen book on the display table caught Lacey's attention, and she stood it back up. "Goodie." She motioned toward Charlie's laptop. "Why are you looking into Tony?"

Savannah flopped down at my feet, sides heaving. A tired dog is a happy dog. Or so some book said. "He said the manager of his restaurant in Chicago died from cyanide poisoning, but I couldn't find the whole story. With luck, Charlie can."

She propped her chin in her hand. "Wow, that's awful. Could it have been an accident?"

"I don't see how. I doubt they had cyanide in the restaurant. Health codes and all that."

"True. Who did it? Did they investigate Tony?"

"He says they didn't consider him a suspect, but I'm not sure I believe him. Can't say why, but I think the circumstances are more involved than he let on."

Lacey barked a laugh. "They usually are."

"Anyway, I have an investigative project for you, too, if you're interested."

"What's that?" She leaned on the counter.

I produced the picture of the sign-in log. "I need to

151

figure out if these two signatures are the same. Do you know anything about handwriting analysis?"

She took the phone and enlarged the photograph. "I've read a little about the subject. We had a book, but we sold it last week. Which ones are we looking at?"

"Eric's. This is the log he supposedly signed the day the cyanide disappeared from the property room."

She studied me under raised eyebrows. "I'm not going to ask how you got this."

"Good, because I'm not going to tell you."

Lacey spread her thumb and forefinger across the screen and squinted. "This is difficult to see. Email the photo to the store so I can print a hard copy."

"You should probably enlarge it too. We don't want to miss anything."

She returned with a page containing only Eric's signatures and the three in between. Enlargement made the writing a little fuzzy, but we could make out enough for a comparison.

Charlie came through the door with a box full of assorted cookies, muffins, and croissants. I helped him line the trays. The fresh-baked fragrance teased my nose and turned on the garden hose in my mouth.

With the last cinnamon-raisin croissant in place, he typed away on his laptop. To my left, Lacey studied the signatures with a magnifying glass. As usual, everyone was hard at work but me. I rested against the counter next to her while she examined the magnified squiggles.

Charlie tapped me on the shoulder and handed me a chocolate chip muffin on a napkin. "Ready for some news?"

"Absolutely. Whatcha got?" I bit into my treat and chewed slowly while he retrieved his work. A morsel of chocolate melted on my tongue, and I groaned.

"Close your eyes," he said with an impish grin.

Lacey put down the magnifier. "C'mon, quit messing around. What did you find?"

He poked out his lower lip and backed away from his computer. "You guys never let me have any fun."

I joined Lacey's guffaw. "Are you kidding? Do you remember how you were dressed yesterday? Try that any place else and see what happens."

He lowered his eyebrows and forced his lips together. "Do you want to see this or not?"

I studied the screen. A small photograph of a much younger Tony accompanied the headline: *Scavuto Trial Ends in Hung Jury*. Good grief! So much for him not being in the crosshairs. I perused the rest of the summary.

The trial of Antonio Scavuto for the murder of twenty-nine-year-old Melanie Esposito ended today with the panel of eight men and four women unable to reach a unanimous verdict. Assistant District Attorney Jeremy Oglethorpe stated they would not attempt to retry Mr. Scavuto at this time.

CHAPTER FIFTEEN

My breath caught in my throat, and I stared at the words until they melded into a you've-gotta-be-kidding-me stew. Not only was Tony a suspect in his manager's death, but he'd also stood trial for the crime.

Lacey's brows scrunched together. "He said they never suspected him? Stupid man. He had to figure this would come out eventually."

"He literally said he was never considered a suspect. Guess I should wander across the street for a little chat with Mr. Scavuto. The lying sneak!" My jaw clenched.

Charlie brandished an imaginary sword. "Want me to go?" He whipped the weapon back and forth, his other hand on one hip. "He'll tell the truth or else!"

A giggle escaped, despite my irritation. Times like this reminded me why I enjoyed having him around now that he no longer harassed me about going out with him. "No, thank you, I can handle the situation. If I need backup, I'll call you."

His pout almost elicited another laughing spell, but I bit my lip. No reason to hurt his feelings. He only wanted to help. However, I sometimes found it difficult to take such an ostentatious character seriously.

My conversation with my agent about speaking with others from the police department bounced back into my mind. I had someone else to talk to, also. I turned to Lacey. "Have you seen Leonard lately?"

"He came in for coffee yesterday afternoon around three. Weird seeing him without Eric, though. Why do you ask?"

"I need to speak with him about Eric's suspension. Even though the evidence was in his locker. Somebody put it there to frame Eric." I was determined to find out whom.

Charlie mopped cookie crumbs off the counter with a clean, white cloth. "How can you be so sure? Wasn't his signature on the paperwork?"

Ah, the sticky wicket. "Hopefully, our investigation will prove otherwise. Besides, even if Eric was dishonest enough to do such a thing, he's not an idiot. Why would he sign his own name?"

Lacey shook her head. "People who want to cover up a homicide don't always think clearly. Sometimes they do reckless things. Or perhaps that's what he wanted people to think, to make it look too obvious to be true. Give me some time to check out those signatures."

I fought back a flash of anger. "You've been friends with him longer than me. How can you say something like that? Do you honestly believe you run side by side with a murderer every Saturday morning?"

She put her hands up. "I'm only playing devil's advocate. I know he's innocent. He doesn't have the psychological makeup to kill someone. I hope he never has to shoot someone on the job. It would destroy him. Anyway, what would his motive to kill the chief be?"

How about the promotion he didn't get and the stolen win in the 10k? Neither would be worth killing over, but sometimes people snap. Was Eric the kind of person who would snap? No way. "I can't think of any that make sense. I want to talk to Leonard. If I can find him."

The front door opened, and a frazzled Veronica Winslow barreled in, a twin toddler guided with each hand. "Are we too late for Story Time?"

Lacey's eyes widened. "Gosh, is it ten thirty already?"

Veronica smiled, the dark half-moons under her eyes not entirely concealed by her makeup. "A few minutes after, but if you're not reading today, I can take the boys to daycare."

"No, we're fine. I lost track of the time." Lacey offered a hand to one of the three-year-olds. Peter, maybe. Or was it Parker? Either way, the Winslows were clearly Spider-Man fans. "Come on back. We're all set up."

I took hold of the other boy's sticky fingers and followed her to the kids' section, where a semicircle of munchkin-sized chairs waited in the corner, and searched for some clue as to which twin I had. The half-moon faced a golden throne from which Queen Lacey would regale them with tales of adventure.

Savannah trotted along with us, and Veronica trailed behind. "What book's on the menu?" she asked.

Lacey glanced over her shoulder, careful not to step on the tiny toes that skipped beside her. "*The Gruffalo.* Have you read it to them already?" She guided her Winslow twin into a chair while I parked his brother in the seat next door. Savannah stood between them, receiving love pats from both sides.

"No, not yet. In fact, if they like the story, I'll pick up a copy with my gift certificate. I might as well spend it on something since Jen won't finish her next book for me."

I stuck my tongue out at her.

Charlie materialized with two small plates of oatmeal raisin cookies, and Savannah camped at the boys' feet for crumb collection duty. My bookstore ran like an ant colony. Everyone had their jobs.

As Lacey mounted her throne, tome in hand, I said, "I'm headed across the street."

She waved and tucked her smirk behind the picture book. Empathy for Tony, I imagined.

Veronica said, "Lacey, do you mind if I leave the boys here while I run back to the office for a minute?"

"Not at all. Take your time."

Veronica fell into step beside me on our way to the door. "Havermayer mentioned you attended the autopsy yesterday. Was the process as gruesome as people say?"

My belly lurched. "Absolutely."

She nodded. "Was it cyanide poisoning?"

Should I answer her? Ingrid never told me not to discuss what I'd seen, and her findings would soon be public. Besides, Veronica worked at the town hall. She probably knew more than I did about the results and didn't want to let on. "Yes. He ingested it at the dinner, although she couldn't pinpoint the exact time."

"Well, that narrows things down. You think the poison was in the wine?"

"That's the popular opinion. Ingrid couldn't say for sure since his stomach was empty, but how would someone put it in the bottle? I did some research, and the closest thing was an ink needle. But those were flat at the top, so if someone tried to use one, it would've left a crater in the cork obvious to everyone. Certainly to Tony."

She brushed a strand of auburn hair off her forehead. "Unless the company they bought them from messed up and sent the wrong type like they did us last week."

I stopped. "What do you mean?"

"We ordered a box of ink needles like the ones you described, and they delivered a different kind instead. We could probably use them in a pinch, but they're not what we paid for, so I'm sending them back. They're in a cabinet in my office."

"No kidding."

Veronica smirked. "Perhaps the killer purchased from the same website."

"Or used one of yours."

She shook her head. "The box was sealed in shrink wrap when I put it away. If I open it, they won't take it back. The company's supposed to send a return label. Funny how they're not quite as efficient fixing their mistakes as they are making them in the first place."

We gravitated to the sidewalk. "You're probably right about the seal, but would you mind checking for me anyway? Solely to account for all possible weapons, so to speak."

"I'll be happy to. If only to eliminate anyone at the town hall from the suspect list." She waved and turned right down Main Street.

I made a beeline toward Antonio's. Somebody's got some 'splaining to do, as Ricky Ricardo would say to Lucy.

The pavement in front of the restaurant was empty when I yanked on the door handle. The aluminum plate fought back, and my fingers slipped off, stinging. I fished out my phone—10:58. They didn't open for two more minutes. A bit longer for my irritation to sizzle.

Why did Tony lie to me? Shades of when Tim Cunningham lied about his background even though it made him look guilty. Perhaps Tony used the same idiotic reasoning. That still didn't mean he wasn't involved in the chief's death, but I should at least listen to his version of events.

My shoulders relaxed some as the deadbolt turned. A purple-haired, college-aged hostess in a black vest and radiant smile cradled a leather-bound book in one arm and held the door open with the other. "Hi! Welcome to Antonio's. One today?"

Definitely a hospitality major. "Actually, I need to speak with Tony. Is he around?"

"Come on in, and I'll check if he's available."

She laid the menu on the podium and started toward the kitchen. After a few steps, she turned back. "Say, aren't you the mystery writer?"

"Yes," I replied, unconcerned about an inquiry about the second novel. Too young to be in love with Dana and Daniel.

"My mother loved your twins. All she talked about for months. Drove me crazy!"

"I'll bet. Sorry."

She shook her head. "No, don't be. Whenever she raved about your book, she didn't bother me about my grades or my boyfriend." She shot me a sideways grin. "Please tell me the next one's due out soon."

Wonderful. Question by proxy. "I'm getting closer."

She gave me a thumbs-up and hurried through the double doors.

Directly across from my table, a large box with "Partridge" scrawled across the side sat by the front register. Leonard must've been picking up food for the police station. My gaze traveled to where Chief Vick collapsed. The staff had restored the dining room to its typical configuration, the podium and banner gone. My belly twisted, and I swallowed back nausea. Good thing lunch wasn't on my menu.

A flash of purple in my peripheral vision drew my attention away from the scene. Tony followed the hostess out of the kitchen as he wiped his hands on a towel stained with a morning's worth of restaurant remains, wearing a smile that didn't come within a mile of his eyes. "Hi, Jen. What can I do for you?"

"Can I talk to you for a few minutes?"

He glanced around the empty room. "We'll be busy soon. What about?"

"Chicago."

"What about it?"

"You lied to me. You not only were a suspect, you also stood trial for Melanie's murder."

He crossed his arms. "So what? Why's it any of your business anyway?"

Not my business? "You asked for my help, remember? I need to know what I'm working with. Who I'm working for."

"Well, maybe I don't need your help."

"You know that's not true. You're already on Havermayer's radar. You want to go through another murder trial? You might not be so lucky this time."

He sighed and gestured toward a two-seat table. "You want something to eat?"

My stomach lurched again. "No, thank you."

"I'll grab us some coffee."

I lowered myself into a seat, and the room shrank around me, the contents of my lungs leaden. Time to confront another dishonest man. Could any of them be trusted? Eric had never lied to me. At least I hadn't caught him yet.

Deep breath in, slow breath out.

Tony set down two cups filled with dark brown liquid. "Cream and sugar?"

"Please."

He returned with the condiments and landed in the chair opposite me, fatigue and worry etched into his visage. He pulled air in and emptied his lungs bit by bit.

Did he have the same therapist?

"You obviously did some research and now you're wondering why I didn't tell you the whole story. That about sum it up?"

I nodded and waited for him to continue while dumping cream and sugar into my fifth cup of the day. No response. Apparently, he needed a push. "I assume you didn't want me to think you were a serial killer. But you didn't just leave out part of the story. You flat-out lied."

Tony rubbed a hand down his haggard face. After a long breath, he said, "First of all, I didn't kill Melanie Esposito and certainly not Chief Vick. Please believe me."

"I want to. Convince me." I lifted my cup to take a sip, then set it back down. Tony was about to tell me the story of how he *didn't* poison someone in Chicago, just like he *didn't* poison Chief Vick. What if he'd decided to *not* poison me too?

Tony arched an eyebrow. "Something wrong with your coffee?"

You tell me. "No, I just decided I'd had too much today already."

"I can get you something else if you want."

The aroma wafting from the cup set my nerve endings on fire. I clasped my hands together under the table. "No, thanks. I'm fine. Go on with your story."

"Melanie was my cousin's youngest child, but I loved her like a daughter. She spent almost as much time in the restaurant as I did. She bused tables after school then waitressed her way through college. Learned all the positions. Made perfect sense to make her the manager when she graduated. She was a natural. We made more money with her in charge than we ever did when I ran the place. She was everything to me."

He drained his coffee in one long swallow and gestured to the purple person for a refill. She topped off his cup and hurried back to the hostess's podium, although not a single customer had come in since my arrival. Was it a slow day or too much bad publicity over the weekend? No way to tell in a town as small as Riddleton.

He continued his tale. "Things went along great until Mel hired Uly Yates."

My coffee had cooled enough that the scent had dissipated, but my mouth still watered. I tightened my grip on my clasped hands. "Uly? Unusual name."

"Short for Ulysses, I think. Anyway, she hired him as a prep cook, and he did a terrific job. Charming, handsome, a real pro. Everybody loved him, but something seemed off about him to me. Before long, Melanie followed him around like a puppy. I tried to convince her she was moving too fast and needed to step back a little. Get to know him better, but she wouldn't listen. She fell hard for him.

"After a while, Uly decided following other people's orders was beneath his dignity. He pressured Mel to

162

fire the sous chef and put him in the position, despite his lack of experience. The sous chef's work was exemplary. She refused, and things went downhill between them, but she stood firm. Three weeks later, Melanie was dead, and the police arrested me."

My right hand slipped its bonds like a puppy in a collar it hadn't yet grown into and moved toward the coffee cup. I jerked it back. I had to do something about this addiction of mine. "What made them think you were responsible?"

He shook his head. "Mel and I argued about Uly the night before she died. His attitude destroyed the harmony among the staff. He had to go. I should've fired him myself, but I didn't want to undercut her authority. As the manager, employee issues fell under her jurisdiction. Unfortunately, her infatuation blinded her. She wrote off the complaints as jealousy."

"And the poison?"

Tony flattened his lips together. "That was the worst part. The cops came after me because somebody ordered cyanide pills on the dark web, used my name and the restaurant address for delivery, and paid with the business credit card. They placed the order from an internet café where the video cameras were broken. They never established the identity of the person but arrested me anyway.

"Luckily, my lawyer found enough evidence pointing to Uly to create reasonable doubt and hang the jury. That's the only reason I'm still a free man. Although, the prosecutors can change their minds at any time, and I'll end up right back in court. Technically, I'm still out on bail. The judge let me relocate because the district attorney wouldn't commit to a retrial."

I raised my eyebrow. "Wow, what an awful way to exist. Never knowing when the hammer's going to fall."

He studied his fingernails. "Plenty of worse ways to live. At least I can walk down the street without fear of attack with a sharpened spoon." A hint of a smile lightened his words. "But I'd gladly spend the rest of my life in prison if it would bring Melanie back. And I shared a cell with Uly Yates."

Now, I had to decide whether or not to believe him. Someone else could easily have arranged the prodigious evidence against him. The only hiccup was the credit card, which narrowed the choices to Melanie, someone she gave it to or someone who knew where she kept it. The only reasonable option, in either case, was Uly, unless Tony really did do it. "I'll let you go back to work. Thanks for speaking with me."

I walked out on the sidewalk by the still-empty restaurant, grateful I'd escaped without drinking the poisoned coffee, and debated my next move. Tony's far-fetched story was credible from a writer's point of view. If I wanted to set up a character as the perfect patsy, that's exactly how I would proceed. I was no closer to knowing who had killed Melanie Esposito than the jury members. And even less to finding who killed Tobias Vick.

CHAPTER SIXTEEN

I headed to the bookstore, and as I hit the curb on the other side of the street, Veronica came out of the town hall, waving her arms at me. "Jen, wait up!"

We met in the middle of the block, in front of the police station. "Did you find something?"

"More like what I didn't find. Come with me."

Uh-oh. Sounded like she didn't have any luck crossing anyone off the suspect list. I followed her into the impressive stone structure, which housed the Riddleton government. The fluorescent overhead bulbs brightened dark paneling and beige paint, the two separated by a brown-stained dado rail. The corridor led to the mayor's personal workspace. Through the opening, Teresa Benedict sat behind a desk piled high with papers and files, shouting into her headset. Clearly, her favorite way to communicate.

Veronica unlocked her office. Sky-blue paint made the room cheerier than the corridor, and light poured in the eight-paned window behind the clean, organized worktable, taking up most of one side. File cabinets adorned with African violets obscured both sides of the wall around the glossy, white closet. Yellowed, cracked linoleum was the only indicator of the age of the edifice, built in the Forties when the county elevated Riddleton from village to town status.

She unlocked the storage closet and came out with a small cardboard carton surrounded by torn shrink wrap. I glanced at her with a raised eyebrow.

"Open it," she said.

Inside, I found a plastic tray with three slots designed to hold large-bore, beveled needles attached to syringes, only two of which were occupied. "Didn't you say the box was sealed?"

"It was when I stashed it in there last week." She picked up the package. "I put this away with a sticky note saying, 'Do Not Use' so I could return it. The note's gone and so is one of the syringes."

My turn to play devil's advocate. "Perhaps somebody refilled a cartridge."

"They're the wrong kind of needles. I checked the ink level anyway. It's almost empty, the same as when I placed the order."

"What about one of the other printers?"

She shook her head. "There are no others. All print jobs go through this one for security. Nobody here can produce anything I'm not aware of. Not even the mayor herself. Besides, the ink hasn't come in yet. We're out of that, too. Plus my office stays locked when I'm not present."

How did someone enter a secure room, open a locked closet leaving no sign of a break-in, and steal a needle and syringe out of a sealed box? Then possibly use them to inject cyanide into a wine bottle to poison the chief of police. Was it time to start believing in ghosts?

Veronica perched in the chair behind her desk and gestured toward the one in front. "So, what do you think?"

I blew out a breath and flopped into the chair opposite Veronica. "I don't know what to think. Does anyone else have a key to your office?"

"The police department received a set so they can enter in case of an emergency. And the mayor, of course. Nobody else that I know of."

This means Eric's access to those keys might be evidence against him. I was certain he didn't do it. But what about someone else in the department? Did Havermayer even consider one of the chief's employees might be involved? Not likely. Except for Eric, of course.

"Is it possible someone borrowed your keys and returned them without you noticing?"

Veronica sat back in her chair and crossed her legs. "No way. They're always with me. Except when I'm sleeping. I don't think my husband ever met Chief Vick, let alone had a reason to murder him. Besides, you saw my boys. They'd be more likely to throw them out the window and make me hunt in the grass all night. A total giggle-fest for them."

My smile belied the turmoil inside. I eased to my feet, feeling older than when I'd ambled in. "Let me think a while. You do the same, and perhaps—between the two of us—we'll come up with an explanation."

She accompanied me out. I waved and hung a left to the bookstore. As I approached the steps to the police department, a black Suburban and a patrol car pulled into the reserved spaces in front. Leonard opened the door and helped someone out of the back of his sedan. My mouth opened as Detective Havermayer escorted a handcuffed Tony into the building.

I glanced at Leonard, who leaned against his cruiser,

arms crossed, searching for scuffs in the toes of his high-gloss duty boots. "Leonard, what's happening?"

He straightened and wiped a drop of sweat off his broad forehead. "We've arrested Tony for the murder of Chief Vick."

"Are you kidding me? Based on what?"

"You're well aware I can't tell you."

I clenched my teeth. "It's ridiculous. All he did was donate a bottle of wine to the auction. Besides there's still no confirmation the poison was even in the wine. The chief could've ingested it anywhere."

"Anywhere in the restaurant owned by Tony Scavuto. Havermayer is convinced he's involved somehow."

"What's she basing her assumption on? There's no evidence."

His nostrils flared. "I can't give you confidential information about an investigation. Why do you care anyway? You barely know the guy."

"I've seen how the police railroad people." Like me.

"Now, who's making assumptions?"

"Fine. So, what happens now?"

His glare provoked me back into an upright position. "We do our jobs."

The detective can be closed-minded about hers, though. "This is Havermayer's first try as lead detective. She'll do whatever she deems necessary to close the case."

Leonard pressed on his mustache as if the glue had released in the humidity. "Arresting an innocent man doesn't help anyone. Not Havermayer, not the department."

I paced a four-foot box from the edge of the sidewalk to the stairs and back. "Can't we team up on this,

Leonard? You and me? Eric's in Havermayer's sights, too. What if she decides he had something to do with the chief's death? Who'll help him then?"

"Somebody else. I'm still a rookie. I have to toe the line."

"Think about it, at least. He's your partner. Remember, information sharing goes two ways. I may learn things, also."

He studied me with flinty brown eyes. "If you know something, you better tell Havermayer. You want to be arrested, too?"

I shook my head and moved back toward the bookstore.

"Hey, Jen, wait."

I replaced my irritation with a poker face, then turned around.

Leonard waved me back.

"What?"

He glanced around furtively. "I think you're right. We should work together."

My pal paranoia made its second appearance of the day. "Why the sudden change of heart?"

"Eric can't help himself, so we'll investigate for him." He broke into a half-grin. "Besides, somebody's gotta keep you out of trouble."

"I can take care of myself, thanks." My attempt to keep the sarcasm out of my voice didn't succeed.

He blew out a deep breath and rested his hands on his hips. "Yes, you can. I was new for the Cunningham case, so I didn't say much, but I observed everything. Olinski and Havermayer were way off base. You followed your instincts, stood up to everyone, and did what you had to do. I admired your grit."

"Thanks." The hair on the back of my neck danced again. He might only want to con me into talking. Time to test the theory. "Why did Havermayer arrest Tony?"

He flushed and swallowed hard. "She wouldn't tell me."

Finally, the truth. "I guess that's your first assignment. When you find out, call me, and we'll figure out what to do next."

Savannah greeted me at the bookstore door; her bushy tail whipped like a flag in a hurricane. I scratched her neck and dodged kisses until she pranced away to grab a toy from her collection. The afternoon rush—two middle-aged women and a man wrinkled enough to be an American Civil War veteran—was in full swing.

Lacey came up to the register with an armload of books. The prattling ladies trailed behind, Visa cards in hand. They ended up with seven volumes between them. A couple more sales like that, and we might make payroll today. If anyone actually got paid.

After their departure, I sidled up to the glass-topped counter, which enclosed a display of pithy bookmarks and clip-on lights for reading in bed without interrupting partners' snores. "What did they buy?"

"Two young adults and a cozy for one. Two cozies and two cookbooks for the other. Not bad for a Wednesday after lunch."

"I can live with it. And a lot more."

She smiled and nodded. "What've you been up to?"

"I watched Havermayer lead Tony around in handcuffs, talked to people and learned lots of new things, which may or may not be relevant. Starting with Tony's story about what happened in Chicago. Apparently—"

Lacey put her hand up. "Whoa, wait a minute. Tony got arrested? Why?"

"No clue. Leonard's on that job."

"Leonard? How did that happen?"

"I suggested we work together to exonerate Eric. I suspect he has an ulterior motive for agreeing, but I can't imagine what it might be. Perhaps he only wants to help his partner. Regardless, I'll take all available assistance at this point."

Lacey twisted her lips. "I'm not sure, Jen. I'm leaning more toward ulterior motive than Helpful Harry. He's a grievance collector. He remembers every slight, no matter how minor, and keeps score. He's not the helpful type. If he offered his assistance, it's to his advantage in some way. Watch your back."

"I will. Thanks."

"Gotta put my psychology classes to use somehow. Now, tell me what Tony had to say for himself. Did he kill that woman in Chicago?"

I gave her the abbreviated version of his long-winded tale, finishing with: "He insists the boyfriend is guilty, and I'm not convinced he's wrong. It could go either way, depending on your perspective, but I still can't think of a viable motive for Tony to kill his cousin. Still, even if he got away with murder in Chicago, it doesn't mean he killed Chief Vick. Would someone execute a man over a bad Yelp review?"

"Of course not, unless you consider the supposedly rigged Independence Day contest, too. Now, that's worth killing for."

"Only in Riddleton."

The godforsaken squeaky bone landed on my foot, and Savannah wiggled expectantly. "Not now, little girl. I'm tired."

"She knows you're unhappy," Lacey said.

"What do you mean? I'm not unhappy." *Good grief.* I sounded like my mother.

She cocked an eyebrow. "Really? Eric's been implicated in a murder investigation and you're okay with that? Even if you're only friends, as you insist, it's stressful."

"We *are* only friends, and I'm not okay with it. What can I do, though? I want to find the real killer, but I don't have much to work with."

"Perhaps, but I think you care more about him than you want to admit."

I shuffled over to the coffee bar, poured a cup of fresh brew, and offered it to Lacey. She shook her head, so I added my fixings while I pondered her words. Was she right? Did I care more about Eric than I'd allowed myself to believe? Possibly, but I refused to make that mistake again. Although, what would protecting myself cost me in the end?

After blowing the steam off the top, I took a small sip. "I can't risk a relationship with someone again so soon, Lacey."

"You're not the only one who's ever had problems. We all go through stuff. You can't give up on love, though. What kind of life can you have without it?"

"The peaceful kind?"

She laughed and poked me in the arm. "Get real. You're only what, twenty-five?"

"Twenty-nine."

"Still too young to consign yourself to spinsterhood. What is this, eighteen eighty-eight? So, you made some mistakes. Now, you have a better idea of what you're after, right?"

She had a point. "You sound like Brittany."

"She's a wise woman, then."

I scowled. "Well, you need to knock it off or I'll send you back to the library. Britt's been grumpy about you not being around to help out. And everything else these days, it seems."

"I've been worse places," she said with a shrug and a smile, and strolled over to the Confederate cannoneer. He had given up browsing and was asleep on the brown-and-gold-striped couch, a paperback hanging from his limp fingers. She glanced back at me. "Should I wake him up or bring him a blanket?"

"Are you sure he's breathing?"

She rested a hand on his chest. "Yup."

I shook my head. "Leave him be. You don't want to startle him into a heart attack. Not like his snorts will scare off the crowd."

"True." She stood and stretched her arms overhead. "What's up with you and Brittany?"

A chocolate chip muffin called my name, so I reached into the pastry case. "Where's Charlie?"

"We've been so slow in the afternoons we decided he didn't need to be here. I can handle the coffee bar and give him his share of what little we make. It's the least I can do. He's working for practically nothing as it is. Might as well allow him some time off to chase his bad guys, or whatever he does when he's not here."

I swallowed a mouthful of muffin. "What does he do, anyway?"

"I think he spends most of his time on the computer. Playing hero, rescuing damsels in distress from evil ogres."

The bone landed on my shoe again. I threw it, sending the careering puppy into the depths of the stockroom. That should keep her busy for a minute. "Yeah, but how does he support himself? We're not paying enough to cover his commute to work, and he walks here."

"Beats me. He doesn't say much, and I don't pry."

I downed the last of my snack. "I suspect we don't want to know. I always picture him huddled in front of his laptop in the dark with a blanket over his head, hacking into the Treasury Department or something."

Lacey snickered. "I figure his family was happy to provide support just to oust him from their basement. This way, they're not aiding and abetting when he gets caught." She took a turn propelling Savannah and her toy out into the hinterlands. "And don't think I didn't notice that nifty change of subject. Think you're slick, don't you?"

An expression of wide-eyed innocence took over my face. "Who me? What'd I do?"

"Very funny. So, what's the problem with you and Brittany? We kids don't like when Mom and Dad fight."

My shoulders slumped. "It's not a fight. We just don't seem to communicate well lately. I guess every friendship has a hiccup once in a while. Her life is taking her in one direction, and mine's moving in the other. Weird since this is what I'd expected to happen when I left for college and it never did."

She squeezed my arm. "You two seemed fine at the fundraiser the other night."

"True. It was a lovely night until—"

The bells over the door did their thing, and Leonard joined us at the coffee bar and helped himself to a cup. Savannah trotted up to him, sniffed his shoe, then trotted away.

"What's new, ladies?"

I caught and held his gaze. "You tell us. What did you learn about Tony?"

He took a sip of his coffee, swirled the liquid around, and sipped again.

Lacey and I exchanged glances. Was he playing hard to get? Enjoying some kind of power rush since he had information he knew we wanted?

Bunk that. "Come on, Leonard, spill it. What did you find out?"

He smoothed his mustache. "They found the missing wine bottle and one of the glasses in the back seat of Tony's car. That's why Havermayer arrested him."

Lacey and I exchanged glances again, this time with our mouths gaping open.

CHAPTER SEVENTEEN

Leonard gulped his coffee. I followed suit while my brain processed the new information. Tony killed Chief Vick? And kept the evidence in the back of his car? No way he would be that stupid. Why wouldn't he just bury the stuff in the woods near his cabin? "So, what's the working theory here? He's a dumbass?"

He set his cup on the display case, obscuring a cinnamon-raisin croissant. "Actually, he says you were the only one who knew where he was, so you must've planted the stuff."

A guffaw flew out of my mouth before I could stop it. "That's ridiculous. He can't possibly expect anyone to believe him, but he's got nerve. I'll give him that."

Lacey laid a hand on my arm. "Havermayer will. She already wants to suspect you."

"Wonderful. Now she has an excuse. Good thing she can only charge one person at a time."

"Plus, the only fingerprints found on the bottle belonged to Tony and you," Leonard said. "Somewhat damning evidence."

"Not necessarily. We both handled it before the auction. Besides how did they obtain my prints to compare it with?"

"Remember when somebody broke into your apartment after Aletha Cunningham's murder? They had to print you for exclusionary purposes."

A memory I'd tried to forget without success. Except for the fingerprinting part, apparently. "What about the glass?"

"Chief Vick's and Brittany's. They had hers because she had to be excluded from the break-in too."

Detective Starchy was probably at the library right now interrogating Brittany. It'd be just like her to save me for last. More fun letting me sweat. "The killer must've worn gloves. Will they test the contents?"

He shook his head. "They were both emptied and rinsed with something. No contents to test."

Lacey grabbed a cloth and wiped a handprint about my size off the display case. *Oops.* "So, we'll never know if the poison was in the bottle or the glass. Or the asparagus on his dinner plate or the burrito he had for lunch that day," she said.

Leonard nodded and gestured at the snoozing cannoneer. "Who's your friend?"

"Some old guy who wore himself out browsing."

"Want me to roust him for you?"

Lacey shook her head. "Leave him be. He's no bother. If he's still here when I'm ready to leave, I'll wake him up."

"All right, if you're sure." He turned to me. "Where do you want to go from here?"

Canada's cooler this time of year. "Apparently, we have two projects on our agenda now: discover who stole the evidence from the property room and who left the stuff in Tony's car. Assuming it wasn't Tony himself, and I'm not convinced that's a safe assumption. He would

177

understand we'd never believe he was that stupid, which would make it the perfect cover."

"True, but how would he get in the property room? We might be talking about two different people. I'll see what I can find out." He turned toward the door but stopped at the window. "You did a fantastic job on these decorations. I love Washington reading *Common Sense* to the British."

"Thanks," Lacey said. "It was a challenge."

He faced her. "You drew freehand?"

"From a drawing. The fun part was sketching the scene backward on the inside of the glass."

"Wow, you did it backward?"

"She's a regular Ginger Rogers," I said.

They both looked at me like I was crazy. I couldn't prove them wrong. "You've heard the quote, 'She did everything Fred Astaire did, except backward and in high heels.'"

"Whatever you say," Lacey replied with a chuckle. "But, I don't do much of anything in high heels."

Leonard shook his head. "Either way, I'm impressed. I studied art for a while. I had an eye for detail but could never quite master the transfer of what I observed to the paper, so I became a cop. Figured I should use my skills to solve crimes, instead."

I never would've guessed he was an artist. A well-kept secret. From me, anyway. "Perhaps you can show us some of your drawings sometime."

"They're all packed in my parents' attic somewhere. It would take weeks to find them."

When Leonard deposited his empty cup in the trash and left, I turned to Lacey. "Let's take a look at those signatures."

She pulled out the copy of the logbook page and grabbed her magnifying glass. "I studied Eric's real signature and found a couple of things we can compare." She focused on his first name. "Notice how he makes a little loop in the middle of the 'E'?"

I examined the "E," which resembled stacked semi-circles connected by a tiny oblong opening. "Yup."

"Now, check out the one in question. The loop is there and exactly the same. Which isn't impossible, so I'm not sure of the relevance, but nobody signs the same way twice."

"Someone could've traced the signature, then copied it to make the signatures match."

"No way to know. Same thing with the dot over the 'I.' Eric's is like a small slash. A dot run amok, so to speak. The other one is similar, but if you look closely, you'll notice slight hesitation marks, as if somebody tried to make them the exact same length. Again, that doesn't mean the signature's a forgery. If Eric signed the second time to steal evidence, he'd be thinking about what he was about to do, and that might account for the hesitation."

I worked my jaw. "Sounds like anything we find can be written off as coincidence. What's the point of all this?"

Lacey laid the magnifier on the counter. "You have to remember this isn't an exact science, and I'm not an expert. Someone who knows the subject might notice all kinds of things I don't. Not to mention issues that can't be seen in a photograph. The pressure of the pen on the paper, for example."

"That means we need to study the original, which is impossible."

"Right. However, we still don't know for sure Olinski hasn't brought someone in to do that. He might already have the answer."

"Then why hasn't Eric been reinstated?"

"The expert might've been as uncertain as we are. Everything's inconclusive. Close enough to be real, different enough to be a forgery. If the thing's a fake, it's an excellent one."

I threw my hands up and lowered them back to my sides. "Terrific. We're right back where we started."

The cannoneer on the couch stirred, and the paperback in his fingers bounced to the floor near his feet. He leaned down to collect it. Gravity threatened to land him on his head, so I hustled to help him. Easier than levering an old man up off the carpet. I held his arm as he struggled into an upright position. "Are you all right, sir?"

He nodded. "I don't sleep much anymore. Sometimes it catches up with me."

"I understand. The couch is really comfortable. That'll get you every time."

The old man smiled and shuffled to the register. Lacey rang him up and waited while he fished bills out of his wallet with shaky hands. I locked eyes with her. That would be us one day.

Transaction completed, I touched his shoulder. "I'm about to head out. Would you like a ride home?"

"You're a nice young lady."

Lacey smirked at me when I thanked him. I blasted her through narrowed eyelids.

He continued, "I appreciate the offer, but my car is parked outside. I'll be fine."

I'd have to remember to keep Savannah out of the road. Me too, for that matter. I escorted him to his

Chevy Impala—almost as ancient as he was—and cringed as he inched his way into Main Street traffic. Might have to stay off the sidewalk, too.

I stood in front of the store and allowed the sun to warm my face, but the chill inside was purely psychological. My brainstorm had withered into a drizzle. The signature comparison didn't exonerate Eric, and I had no idea how to proceed. I'd asked him to give me twenty-four hours before turning in the evidence found in his locker. Twenty-four hours to save his career, perhaps even his freedom, and I'd failed.

The police station door opened, and I swiveled in that direction. Eric descended the steps, head down, shoulders slumped.

I met him at the bottom. "Hey, are you okay?"

He stopped and refused to meet my eyes. "I showed Olinski the cyanide."

"Why? I thought you agreed to allow me some time to help you?"

Hands jammed in the pockets of his jeans as if they might otherwise escape, he studied his scuffed Skechers. "I had to. I didn't sleep a wink last night."

"In other words, you don't trust me."

Anger jerked his head up. "This isn't about you, Jen. It's about who I am and who I want to be. I'm a cop. I have to tell the truth."

"I only asked you for one day. You couldn't give me that?"

"What did you find so far?"

Busted. "Well, nothing yet, but you didn't know that."

Eric freed his hands and took me by the shoulders. "Everything will be all right. I never touched that bag. They won't find my fingerprints on it."

181

"Olinski's not gonna buy that. Did they stop making gloves in your size?"

He let me go and backed away. "Sounds like you don't trust me, either."

"Glad we found out before it's too late. I can't be in a relationship without trust. Can you?"

He squeezed his brows together. "The problem is you don't trust anyone. The sooner you figure that out, the better off you'll be."

I crossed my arms. "That's not true."

"And denial is your favorite river, right?"

He climbed in his car and drove away.

My hands shook as I lowered them to my sides, and the anger drained away. The sun's rays still brushed my face but with no warmth. What had I just done? Alienated another one of my few friends. First Brittany, now Eric.

Smooth move, Jen.

Time to leave before I did any more damage to myself or anyone else. My twins still loved me; they were the only things I had any control over in my life. Well, to a certain extent, anyway. They still took off on their own periodically, but always to my benefit, which was more than *I* did for me, as a rule.

I called Angus and placed a to-go order while I retrieved my dog and waved goodbye to Lacey. More comfort food for my bruised soul. It'd better soothe my soul because it did nothing for my waistline except make it easier to see.

The diner was busy when I stopped to pick up my dinner, and Angus had no time to talk. Probably a good thing since I couldn't afford to lose another friend today. I grabbed my bagged grilled-cheese sandwich and fries and left a ten-dollar bill by the register.

The parking area in front of my building was almost full, and I glided into the only empty slot next to Charlie's Ford. Whatever he did with his free time, he did seem to spend most of it at home.

I freed a few letters, primarily bills, from their five-by-six-inch prison cell and trudged up the stairs, Savannah at the point. While she swallowed her dinner, I flipped the TV on and channel-surfed, finally settling on a documentary about the Civil War. Maybe the cannoneer from the bookstore would make an appearance.

The Second Battle of Bull Run ended as I swallowed my last French fry. With Northern Virginia in the hands of the Confederacy, I relocated to the desk and opened my laptop. Dana and Daniel were in the middle of a battle of their own. Kidnapped and duct-taped together, blindfolded in unfamiliar woods with the sun going down.

Sweat dripped into Dana's eyes as she fought to break her hands free. "Daniel? Daniel wake up!"

He groaned. "Where are we?"

"I don't know, but we have to get out of here. Are you hurt?"

"I don't think so. Just groggy."

She searched in the dim light for something to cut the tape. A sharp rock peeked out of a pile of leaves near a tree about ten feet away. "I see something, but I need your help."

They pushed with their feet and shifted their upper bodies through the leaves and twigs for an eternity, stopping twice to rest. Finally, the life-saving stone was within reach.

All right. Now Dana would cut through the duct tape that bound her wrists together and free the two of them. Of course, it couldn't possibly be that simple. A few cuts and bruises, the rock would roll away, and they'd chase it in the dark. Then what?

The night was black, and they had to find their way out of a strange place. No cell service, so they couldn't call for help. Wait, maybe one bar to send a text? No. Let them struggle for a while first. Then they could send the text but never be certain it went through. But first, another sibling squabble.

Dana would want to plow ahead, and Daniel would insist they stay put until the sun came up. He proposed the safer plan, but patience was not one of his sister's virtues. The argument would last until they heard something moving among the trees.

My fingers chattered away on the keyboard. Page after page skimmed by as the teenagers fought each other and their inner demons. I lost myself in their world.

Until a crash and a grunt jerked me back to reality. Savannah blinked at me from the floor between the coffee table and the couch. She'd fallen off again, clearing half the table in the process. Tough job being a puppy.

She shook herself and trotted to the door. Reluctantly, I climbed out from behind the desk. The choice was simple: take her for a walk or clean the rug. No choice at all, really. She danced her enthusiasm, risking an accidental puddle. "Hold on, kid. I'm coming."

We made it to the ancient oak in front of the stairs before her bladder released a flood. I scratched her neck with gusto. "Good girl!"

The rest of the trip around the block ensured she

was completely emptied and ready to settle in for the night. Fatigue filled my eyelids with lead. The twins would spend the night in the woods.

I completed my pre-bed ablutions in record time but spotted the mess Savannah's tumble had created. Might as well pick it up so I didn't have to in the morning. I gathered the collection of book notes, old receipts, and unopened mail. An envelope written in block letters with no return address caught my attention. Junk, most likely. At least I could open it without fear of catching a virus unlike the spam on my computer.

The packet contained a single sheet of paper. More block letters.

**CUTE PUPPY.
IT WOULD BE A SHAME IF SOMETHING
HAPPENED TO HER.
BACK OFF!**

CHAPTER EIGHTEEN

After an interminable night spent on the couch with Savannah pressed against my chest, I witnessed the sun's ascent over the horizon through the balcony doors. The center of the living room shimmered in an eerie orange glow. The walls remained in shadow; a villain lurked in every corner. I'd guarded my furry baby throughout the overnight hours but couldn't shake the sensation someone spied on us from every nook and cranny. All because I'd decided to stick my nose into somebody else's business.

Why? Why did I decide to involve myself in another murder investigation, knowing it would put me at risk? Put Savannah at risk. Eric needed help, sure, but he had the entire police department on his side, even if it didn't seem that way. They always took care of their own in the end, right? Plus, he was innocent and had nothing to worry about, anyway.

Tony had also asked for my assistance, but I only agreed because I'd already decided to participate. If I was honest, though, I'd always known I'd jump in. No matter how much I tried to convince myself otherwise.

It's who I am.

That still left the question of why. What did I receive from it, other than danger to myself and anyone around me? Was I a thrill-seeker? No, it was more like a sense of control. Taking matters into my own hands, so to speak. Not allowing others to dictate events around me as they did when I was a kid. Living with Gary was a constant reinforcement of how powerless I was. How little input into my own life I had.

Not anymore.

Except, the note accused me from the table, black block letters a reminder of my inadequacy. My initial reaction to receiving Savannah came back to unsettle me:

How can I take care of a puppy? I had enough trouble with my own upkeep.

I should've listened.

Why would somebody send me a threatening letter? The intention was to scare me off investigating the chief's death, but I hadn't learned anything useful, so what threat did I pose? And to whom? Tony or the mayor? The mayor's husband or Anne-Marie? Could be any one of them, and they all understood I'd never stop looking until I discovered the truth.

This internal conversation resembled a rehash of the one a few months ago when someone ransacked my apartment. "Déjà vu all over again," as Yogi Berra once said.

I squirmed out from under the pup and set the coffee-maker to work. Savannah lifted her head briefly, stretched, and closed her eyes again. If only I could sleep on command the way she did. *Pathetic.* I envied my dog. On second thought, what's not to envy? She lived a rather enjoyable life. Food appeared like manna from heaven, with no preparation or money required.

187

Multiple strolls around town every day. People petted and played with her, asking nothing in return. How could I not be jealous?

I had to take the threat seriously. Holding Savannah all night had temporarily alleviated my fear. I couldn't keep that up forever, though. Sleep was a necessity, even for me. I had to find a safe place for her where nobody would ever look. Only one came to mind. My mother's house. Mom grew to love Savannah while I recovered from my last adventure, though I doubted she'd admit it.

The hunt for my phone began on the table and ended behind a couch cushion.

I pressed the green button. "Hi, Mom. Got a minute?"

"Sure, honey, what's wrong?"

Honey? What a difference a few days made. The last time my mother called me honey, I'd stumbled in front of a speeding car, and a quick-acting neighbor had saved me. I was five years old. Pretty sure she called us both honey that day. "I need a favor. Can you keep Savannah for a day or two?"

Her sharp inhalation came clearly over the airwaves. "The dog? Why?"

Should I risk telling her the truth? If I did, she'd likely launch into a lecture about minding my own business and the dangers of playing detective. The diatribe would include a multitude of insults and admonishments and at least one "I told you so."

The alternative was to make up a persuasive lie. Unfortunately, that needed to be achieved before I called. I could be creative or quick, but not both. A failing my half-completed novel testified to.

I laid out the situation succinctly, with as little detail as possible, and braced for the torrent to follow. What she hit me with turned out to be far worse than anything I could've expected.

A glance at my phone proved the line remained open. "Mom?"

A long, exhaled breath.

"Mom, are you okay?"

"I'm fine. Just doing one of my calming exercises."

Seriously? Where was this woman hidden my whole life? "When did you start doing calming exercises?"

"Your father's doctor recommended them to reduce his stress. I've been helping him."

He's not my father. And what stress? He hadn't left the house in fifteen years. "What's wrong with Gary?"

More silence.

I waited for her to finish counting breaths or whatever it was she did.

"He has cancer."

The sharp intake of air belonged to me this time. "I'm so sorry. Tell me about it."

"He didn't want me to tell you."

"It's not fair to expect you to carry this load by yourself. Talk to me."

"The doctor said he has stage-three colon cancer. The surgery's next week."

Stage three was as bad as it could get without having moved to other parts of the body. I tasted my coffee to quell nascent nausea. "What's his prognosis? Will he be okay?"

She sighed. "They don't think the cancer spread, so we're hopeful. Of course, they won't be sure until they open him up."

"Tell me when, and I'll be there for you. And never mind about Savannah. I'll figure something out."

"No, bring her over. It'll give us something else to focus on. Your father loves her, too. He always asks about her."

Did my stepfather have a soft spot after all? For dogs, maybe. "All right. If you're sure."

"I'm sure."

I said goodbye, rested the phone face-down on the couch, and scratched Savannah behind the ears. She pushed her head against my fingertips. "Well, little girl, I think we finally understand what's wrong with Grandma." She abandoned her ear-scratch and headed for the door. Time for her morning walk.

With Savannah leashed, and my pockets loaded with plastic bags, we descended to the sidewalk below. I had no trouble empathizing with my mother and what she was about to go through. Calling forth empathy for Gary would be a struggle, but I had to try. Cold-hearted wasn't a description I wanted to be applied to me. Besides, he could be okay sometimes, although I still believed his illness might be karma.

He once locked me in my room for six hours because I tripped over his ottoman and spilled beer on his lap. And there was the ranting when I was a minute late coming home from school or didn't move fast enough when he barked an order at me. But the worst part was what he said during those rants. The belittling. The insults. I hated him not only for what he did but for how he made me feel about myself.

However, he also introduced me to the old TV shows and movies I now loved. When my junior-year English teacher asked us to name all five Marx Brothers for extra credit on a test, I was the only one in the class to collect all the points. Thanks to Gary.

After a quick trip around the block with me examining every house and behind every tree, I locked the apartment door behind us. A shoulder bag held Savannah's food, treats, and necessary toys. I inserted the letter and envelope into a Ziploc and stashed it in my pocket.

I loaded my German shepherd into the car and surveyed the area again. No strange people or vehicles in sight. Couldn't tell who might be observing from the buildings, though. Too bad the X-ray vision I ordered hadn't come in yet. So much for two-day delivery.

My Dodge started right up, and I backed slowly out of my parking space. There was still no activity on the street, but I took no chances. Making a right on Park rather than the usual left on Main, I split my attention between the windshield and the rearview mirror. Nobody followed.

Averse to the risk, I made right turns on Riddleton Road, Oak Street, and Main, which took us completely around the block, just in case. Still nothing. The twenty-minute drive to my mother's house took closer to forty as I periodically turned down random streets. It was worth the extra time, though, because I eased into the driveway, confident my puppy would be safe.

Mom insisted on reading the message that caused all the fuss, then her calming exercises failed her. She might've been less upset if they'd threatened me instead of Savannah. Another reason to be jealous of my dog.

She led Savannah into the kitchen and set up her food and water bowls. "Did you learn anything new about Toby's death?"

"Not that I'm aware of, but somebody clearly thinks

I did. I only wish I knew what it might be. Then I'd have some idea of where to turn next."

"You'll figure it out."

Those calming exercises had to be miracle cures. Unless my mother supplemented them with barbiturates. "I hope so."

Handoff completed, I headed back to Riddleton with a few more random turns along the way. No suspicious vehicles joined me. My neck and shoulders relaxed for the first time since I read my mail last night. One less thing to worry about. For now.

Now, what should I do with the note? My first instinct was to call Eric, but he couldn't be involved in any aspect of the investigation. Mainly because we found the evidence missing from the property room in his locker. Besides, after our last encounter, he likely didn't want to hear from me, anyway. A hollow place appeared in my chest. Did I miss him already?

The concept of bringing it directly to Olinski made me uncomfortable now that he was acting chief of police. He'd pass the letter down to Havermayer, who'd be angry that I'd gone over her head. That left the detective herself and Leonard. Since Havermayer would probably post Savannah's whereabouts on social media, Leonard would be my go-to person. He was on evenings this week, so it would have to wait until he came on shift this afternoon. In the meantime, I had something else important to do.

I maneuvered into the library parking lot to make things right with Brittany. Our friendship spanned almost twenty-five years. I wouldn't let it go without a fight. Especially since I still had no idea what'd caused the rift to begin with. A silly argument about Olinski couldn't possibly be responsible for all this strife. There had to be another reason.

Pine needles crunched under my feet as I climbed the steps, and my hand hesitated before reaching for the door. Strange. My best friend was on the other side. What was I afraid of?

Losing the most important person in my life since my father died without any idea why.

The dim hallway greeted me, reflecting my emotions. I stopped before entering the brightly lit reading room.

Deep breath in, slow breath out.

I trudged into the light. Brittany wheeled a book-laden cart past the stacks. She turned with a smile, but it faltered when she recognized me.

A hole opened in my gut. "Hey, Britt. How's it going?"

She leaned against the trolley, arms crossed. "Fine. How are you?"

"I'm okay."

"That's good."

"I, um, thought I'd stop by and see how you're doing." I hesitated and glanced over at the empty computer stations. Only one person working. Not bad for this time of the morning. "Looks like you have a little time to yourself today."

She nodded. "Still early. But that's not why you're here, is it?"

I took a deep breath. She wasn't going to make this easy. "I wanted to check on you. Did Havermayer talk to you about your fingerprints on the chief's glass?

"No, but I don't understand why she would. She knows we set up the dining room that day. Of course, my prints are on the wineglass," she said in an even voice.

193

I hopped up on the table closest to her and swung my feet. "She's not famous for being reasonable. Although, maybe she's only unreasonable with me. I've never seen her interact with anyone else."

"Don't be silly. I'm sure she doesn't treat you any differently than she does any other suspect."

"Suspect? Thanks a lot!"

"Relax, I'm messing with you."

"I couldn't tell. We haven't spoken lately."

Brittany shook her head. "It's only been a couple of days, Jen."

I shrugged. "I know, but I miss you."

She snorted. "Yeah, right. Miss having me at your beck and call, you mean."

"That's not true. C'mon, Britt, what's this really all about? I know I'm not the perfect friend, but you can't possibly have just figured that out now."

"No," she said with an eye roll. "I've known since the first grade."

"Uh-uh. You were just mad because I learned how to write before you did. Remember how Miss Tomkins used to make me stick my finger in between the words so I'd stop running them all together?"

"Talk about a run-on sentence."

"No kidding."

She selected a volume from the cart and flipped through the pages. "How's your book coming along?"

I picked a pencil off the table and pretended to throw it at her. "Not you, too!"

"I only wondered if you'd made any progress. We haven't talked about it in a while. We haven't talked about much of anything."

"That's ridiculous. We discussed lots of things before

194

the fundraiser. The whole time we were setting up, remember?"

Brittany looked at me over the tops of her glasses. "Whatever." She shelved the book in the third section. "Was there something in particular you needed?"

What kind of question is that? "No."

"You sure? No research you couldn't manage to do on your own?"

Heat rose into my face, and my ears burned. "No. I thought you might like to know somebody threatened to hurt Savannah if I don't stop looking into the chief's death, but I shouldn't have assumed. Sorry I bothered you."

I turned and strode away.

"Jen, wait!"

My hand shook so hard I scratched the paint next to the car's door lock with the key. I closed my eyes and envisioned the anger draining down my legs into the blacktop. Another trick learned from Dr. Margolis. Calmer, I unlocked the door and sank into the driver's seat.

My brilliant plan had backfired. Not only was I still clueless about why Brittany was upset with me initially, but I'd also made her angrier. Not sure how I accomplished that, either. Nothing I said made anything better. I'd never encountered this Brittany before and had no clue how to deal with her. Perhaps it would be best if I didn't try.

In front of my building, the space I'd vacated a few hours ago remained empty. I eased in. Still, nothing suspicious in the area, though my neck hair stayed unconvinced. I plodded up the steps and let myself into my apartment. An eerie silence assaulted me in place of the leaping puppy I already missed. Almost ten months had passed since I'd returned home to an empty place.

I nuked a cup of coffee and opened my laptop, but a jumble of images flooded my head. Chief Vick's foamy mouth, cyanide in Eric's locker, the kiss, the note threatening Savannah's well-being. I paced the track laid out around my home for occasions when restlessness precluded any other activity.

Thirty-nine steps from the front door, down the hall, around the bedroom, back down the hall into the kitchen, and around the living room to the door. Counting the footfalls banished the pictures and quieted my mind. Except for the letter, which lived entrenched in my psyche.

It would be a shame if something happened to her.

CHAPTER NINETEEN

I leaned against one of the brick pillars that flanked the police station steps and waited for Leonard to show up for his afternoon shift. The letter threatening my dog's safety rested comfortably in my pocket. I, on the other hand, couldn't describe myself as comfortable in any way. My only hope for her safety was for the cops to find the writer before the writer located Savannah.

He came around the corner in jeans and a denim jacket, a black backpack slung over one shoulder, deep in conversation with his cousin, Greg. They stopped in front of the town hall, Leonard scowling when Greg poked him in the chest with his forefinger. He pushed his cousin away.

Greg said, "You better take care of it!" loud enough for me to hear and retreated back the way he came.

Leonard noticed me watching and rearranged his face into a smile. "Hey, Jen. What're you doing here?"

"What was that all about?"

He glanced over his shoulder. "Nothing. Just a family thing."

"Glad I'm not in your family."

"Greg's okay. He just gets worked up about things sometimes. He's mad because I have to work on my uncle's sixtieth birthday next weekend. He wants me to come to the party."

Remind me to never upset Greg. "He must have a heck of a shindig planned. Sure you want to miss it?"

"It doesn't matter what I want. With Eric suspended, we're too shorthanded for me to take off. There's nobody to cover me." He shifted his backpack to the other shoulder. "Anyway, you're not here to discuss my family. What's up?"

"I found this in my mailbox last night." I presented the plastic bag containing the note. "A threat to hurt Savannah if I don't stop looking into the chief's death."

He took the letter and glanced down at my side. "Where is she now?"

I hesitated. Could I safely tell him? The more people who knew her whereabouts, the higher the likelihood the information would leak out. "She's protected."

Leonard smoothed his mustache. "If you tell me where she is, I can keep an eye on her for you. I don't want anything to happen to her, either."

Extra security would be helpful, but my mother's house didn't fall into his jurisdiction. "I appreciate the offer. However, she's not in town."

He nodded. "Smart move."

"If you really want to help, find out who wrote that letter."

"I'll do what I can."

"Thank you."

He trotted up the stairs and ducked inside. I started toward the bookstore. A middle-aged blonde came out with a Ravenous Readers shopping bag in one hand

and her phone in the other. A shopping bag meant multiple books. There might be hope for the place yet.

As I approached the door, a voice recognizable in the football stadium during a Saturday afternoon home game called my name. Detective Havermayer. I waited for her to catch up instead of meeting her halfway. A minor power play, but I took my wins where I could.

"What can I do for you, Detective?"

She tugged on the bottom of her crisp, black suit jacket. "I need to ask you some questions." She gestured at the door. "Care to talk inside where it's cool?"

"I'm okay here. Did Leonard give you my letter?"

"What letter?"

"Someone sent me a threatening note, which I gave to him."

Havermayer adjusted the collar of her blazer then stuffed her hands in her pants pockets, adding to her already substantial hips. "I haven't seen him yet, but I'm sure he'll turn it over for me to look into."

Skepticism became my word for today. She was more likely to carry out the threat than investigate the sender. "I appreciate anything you can do."

"Tony Scavuto says you planted the bottle and glass in the back of his car."

I clenched my jaw. "Some people will say anything to escape trouble."

"He said you were in the yard for several minutes before he came out of the cabin."

"The house looked empty. I thought he might be in the shed, but all I found was an old still. I didn't go anywhere near his car."

She snorted. "So you say."

"I'm telling the truth. If he was so worried about it why didn't he come out when I pulled up?"

"Tony claims you were the only one to find his cabin. Why should I believe you weren't there to plant the evidence?"

I ran a hand through my hair, unconcerned if tufts stuck out in places afterward. "Why would I do it in broad daylight? Besides, you found him too."

Her eyebrows dove toward her nose, lasers shooting out of her eyes. "I had to question him. He's a person of interest in my investigation."

"Okay. When did you find the evidence?"

"On my way out."

After you put it there? "In other words, either one of us could've planted the stuff."

She stepped toward me. "I had nothing to do with it."

I held my ground and tilted my head back to make eye contact with the detective, who stood half a head taller. "Neither did I."

"We'll see about that." Havermayer turned toward the police station, then back again. "In the meantime, watch your back. Tony was released this morning. If he really believes what he's saying, he could come after you."

"Come after me? That's crazy, I didn't plant that evidence in his car."

"He says you did."

"How did he get out of jail, anyway?"

"The evidence is all circumstantial. The judge wouldn't let us hold him on that basis."

"Thanks for the warning. I'll be careful." I pulled the door open and went inside, leaving her alone on the sidewalk.

Lacey assisted a man in the middle-grade section while Charlie handed muffins to two teenaged girls lugging book bags by the handles. If he was still here, the store had been busy all afternoon. He glanced at me and winked. I smiled at him in gratitude for his hard work.

The late shipment of *Double Trouble* had come in, and my display was fully stocked. The cardboard cutout grinned at me. I shook my head, but I'd adapt sooner or later. Unless I got lucky and somebody stole the thing. As a rule, I didn't experience that kind of luck.

I grabbed a towel from behind the counter, wiped down the dirty tables, and straightened the chairs. Might as well make myself useful. The idea of returning home to an empty apartment made my stomach clench. An instant reminder of why my home was unoccupied in the first place. Time to check on Savannah.

My mother answered on the second ring. "Twice in one day is a record for you."

"I wanted to see how you were and make sure Savannah wasn't too much trouble."

"She's no trouble at all. Right now, she's in your father's lap helping him demolish a bag of corn chips and watching *Old Yeller*. I told him he had to cover her eyes when the dog dies. We don't want her to have nightmares."

I chuckled. "Have fun getting her to hold still while you shield her, though. She doesn't like that kind of thing much. Too nosy."

My mother's voice took on a somber tone. "Did you figure out who sent the letter yet?"

"No. I gave it to the police to work on. As soon as I learn something, I'll let you know."

"All right. I have to hang up now. They're almost to the part where he saves them from the hogs. Talk to you later."

She disconnected the call, and Savannah reappeared on my home screen with a chew stick hanging out of her mouth like a cigar. I better find out who mailed that note quickly, or my puppy would be the centerpiece in this year's Connally family Christmas card photo.

Across the street, Antonio's showed little activity. Too early for dinner, too late for lunch. Perhaps Tony had come back from Sutton by now. I needed to confront him about his baseless accusations and make him understand I had nothing to do with his troubles. Even if Havermayer was correct about him possibly attacking me, he wouldn't do something that dumb in front of all his staff. I would be safe as long as we stayed in the dining room.

I strolled to the restaurant, trying to seem casual while my heart raced in the Belmont Stakes, and sweat soaked my T-shirt. Tony would never hurt me, would he?

The door opened with no trouble this time, and I strode into the building. The purple-haired hostess greeted me with a miniature American flag pinned to her vest, and a grin stretched across her face. "How are you? I told my mom I'd met you, and she was thrilled. She gave me her copy of your book for you to sign if you ever came back." Her smile faded a bit. "If that's okay with you, of course."

"Absolutely. I'd be happy to. I'm actually here—"

She gestured toward the empty dining room. "Take a seat anywhere and I'll be right back."

The purple person disappeared. I approached the nearest table, and she returned before my bottom made complete contact with the chair. She should join the runners. She'd give Eric and Lacey some competition.

She handed me a dog-eared paperback of *Double Trouble* and a pen.

I flipped to the title page. "What's your mother's name?"

She bounced on her tiptoes. "Christina. She's gonna be so happy!"

"I'm glad." I scribbled something and returned the book.

"But, not as happy as she'll be when the next one comes out."

"It's on the way. I promise." Before she could inquire about book three, I asked, "Is Tony around?"

She shook her head. "I'm sorry. I guess you haven't heard. They arrested him for Chief Vick's murder. But he didn't do it."

"They released him hours ago. I thought he might want to check on the restaurant before he did anything else."

"He hasn't been here. Hasn't called either."

Odd. If I'd been gone a while, checking on my business would be a priority. "Well, if he calls or shows up, would you tell him I'm looking for him?"

"Sure thing."

As I retreated into the sunshine, it occurred to me that after a day spent in jail, a shower and clean clothes would top my must-do list. Tony rented a small house on the edge of town, but I had no idea where. I went back to the bookstore.

Lacey finished ringing up the middle-grade guy, and Charlie handed a cup of something or other to a leggy college girl in ripped jeans and a Metallica T-shirt.

The teenagers huddled in front of the Romance section, making the place seem like a real bookstore. Aletha would be proud.

I nodded to middle-grade man as I passed him on the way to the register. "That looked like time well spent."

"Definitely," Lacey said. "He has two young daughters and a teenaged son. The future of our business."

"I know I don't say this enough, or at all, but you're doing a terrific job."

Her cheeks reddened. "Thank you. What've you been up to?"

I told her about Tony's accusation and the note.

"Oh, no! Is she okay?"

"She's fine, but I'm not sure I trust the police to do anything."

"You're gonna investigate yourself, aren't you? Even though they might hurt Savannah if you do."

"*Because* they might hurt Savannah. Havermayer has more important issues to deal with than my puppy's safety. More important to her, anyway. I'm not leaving Savannah's future in the hands of someone who hates me."

"I get it. How can I help?"

"Right now, I want to track down Tony. Do you know where he lives?"

"Over on Walnut, I think, but I don't know which house. Isn't he in jail?"

"They let him out."

"Oh. You think he might've been the one to write the note?"

"It's possible, but either way I have to convince him I didn't put the bottle and glass in his car. Maybe we can put our heads together and figure out who did."

"You'd better get going then. It'll be dark soon."

"I'll let you know what I find." Walnut Street was about two miles long. Too far for me to walk since the temperature was still in the nineties. The humid air soaked me on the way home to retrieve my car. I climbed into my Dart and covered the three blocks back to Walnut, my only option being to drive up and down searching for Tony's white SUV. The good news? There were no garages attached to the Forties-era houses. He had to park at the curb.

After the right on Walnut from Main, I cruised slowly past flags, bunting, a million red, white, and blue lights, and every make and model vehicle imaginable, except a white SUV. Up one side to the dead end, around, and back down the other. I completed the circle back to Main Street. I'd either missed it in the approaching dusk or Tony didn't go home.

Fiddlesticks.

Where could he be? Another futile pass by the restaurant verified the continued absence of his car. The only other place he might be was his cabin. Should I risk the trip out in the dark? Perhaps. I had to convince him I had nothing to do with what the police found in his back seat. Also, I still hadn't ruled out the possibility he sent the letter, which was already in the mail when Havermayer arrested him.

A confrontation with Tony alone in the middle of nowhere might not be wise. Havermayer wouldn't think so. But she didn't trust anybody. Besides, if he genuinely believed I set him up for the chief's murder, what would stop him from coming after me at home? I was just as alone there as at his hideaway. Perhaps the purpose of the note was to get Savannah out of the way so I'd

205

have no protection. No, it was better for me to take charge of the situation.

I woke Robot Woman and told her where to take me. Rush-hour traffic congested the two-lane road, and I spent a bunch of time trapped behind people waiting to make left turns into subdivisions. No room for turn lanes, apparently.

RW finally prompted me to hang the left on SR-32-83. Now I blocked traffic. Nothing I could do about it, though. Sixteen cars and two trucks passed until I made the turn and peered into the encroaching dark.

Creeping down the road at the speed limit, I slowed at each street on my left to read the sign. My imagination provided commentary from the driver of the car behind me. My thick skin came in handy, for once.

I flipped on my signal and slammed on the brakes when Partridge Road came into view, then braced myself for a rear-end collision. Brake pads squealed, but no contact ensued. I blew out a hard breath and relaxed my shoulders. Only three cars to wait for before the street cleared.

The black night encompassed the narrow dirt road. I activated my high beams and inched ahead, desperate to remember how far down Tony's place was. Navigating potholes like a trainee on an obstacle course, I managed to avoid about a third of them, then pulled over and parked around the halfway point. No way the small wooden sign would stand out in the gloom. I had to walk. No guarantee I'd notice it that way, either.

I fished a small flashlight out of the glove compartment and shifted the switch. Nothing happened. Dead batteries. I had another one buried in the trunk, but it would require a miracle of water-into-wine proportions to locate it. Besides, I'd likely encounter exhausted batteries in that one, too. The light on my phone would have to do.

A kudzu-filled ditch yawned on my right. How deep was the trench? Not interested in learning the hard way, I shuffled along. About a hundred yards down, I found the placard. Well, a pile of pine cones, anyway. When I cleared them away, the faded blue paint reflected 25472 beside the grassy track. Funny how the board ended up covered again after I'd exposed it last time. Was Tony trying to make his hiding place more secure?

Leaving my cell behind as a beacon, I somehow stumbled back to my car without damaging any part of my body. Maybe I had a miracle in me after all. I turned at the signal, retrieved my cell phone, and crawled down the path into the empty clearing. The cabin appeared deserted, with no vehicle in front. Tony didn't come here.

The still in the outhouse tempted me to take another peek, but it was too late, too dark, and I was too tired. When I turned onto the dirt road again, headlights appeared in my rearview mirror. They'd better not be in a hurry. My vision barely covered ten feet ahead of me, and I couldn't safely creep along any faster. Unfortunately, the lane wouldn't accommodate two vehicles side by side under the current conditions.

I'd progressed almost halfway to my previous parking place when the lights filled my car's interior. I flipped the mirror up to cut the glare and drifted as far to the right as I dared. The vehicle behind didn't pass but followed me over instead. I tightened my grip on the wheel.

I tapped the brakes. The driver didn't take the hint. I held my breath; my abdomen clenched. What was this idiot doing?

Speeding up didn't help, either. The headlights did the same, then swerved slightly toward the center and clipped my driver's side bumper. The steering wheel slipped in my fingers, forcing me off the side of the road into the ditch. A flash of brown roared past and out of sight.

My Dodge bounced through a sea of kudzu. The airbag exploded into my face, and pain seared through my head. Something warm and wet flowed over my chin and down my neck. The car landed near vertical, leaving me suspended over the dashboard by my seat belt.

What the hell do I do now?

CHAPTER TWENTY

My Dart stood nose down. The seat belt constricted my chest and my breath hitched in shallow gasps. My airbag-battered face collected the rush of blood squeezed from my body. I had to free myself before I passed out.

I stared into the steering wheel, my extended chin falling just short of the horn. Fortunately, the airbag had deflated automatically. Otherwise, I'd be suffocating too. I arched my head back to look out the windshield and found only thick, green foliage and drifting steam in the headlights. The engine still hummed, but since I couldn't reach the pedals, it did me no good. I turned it off.

Gingerly, I turned my head from one side to the other and tested my limbs. My arms and legs moved, but my sticky face burned. My nose throbbed, and my vision was obscured by my rapidly swelling cheeks.

I fumbled for the belt-release button. The red plastic didn't budge. Eric once told me to keep a knife in the car for such an emergency, but of course, I didn't listen. Not that it would've mattered. I couldn't reach the glove compartment anyway.

Fear overwhelmed pain, and I fought back panic. Staying calm was my only hope for escape. That and

911, but my phone had sailed off the seat. Why didn't I put it in the holder? Fog rolled into my brain. I struggled to think. An effort to take a deep breath resulted in stabbing pain in my right side. Add a broken rib or two to the injury list. The slight influx of oxygen cleared my head a little, though. For a minute.

Could the seat belt be unlocked from this position? *Think, Jen.*

The mist skulked back in, and ideas and images tangled together like a string of Christmas lights I'd just hauled down from the attic. *Tony.* Maybe he would find me on his way to the cabin. Was my Dodge visible from the road? Perhaps the silver paint would reflect in his headlights. There was no guarantee he would come up here, though. I might have better luck with one of the Partridges. At least they lived out here all the time. Or would the driver of the brown truck come back to finish the job?

I risked taking another full breath in and bit my lip against the backlash. An instant of clarity produced the answer. I must lessen the weight on the belt. How, when I hung like a freshly slaughtered pig?

Shoving hard off the wheel was the only way, but the mass shift might send the car end over end to the bottom of the ditch. Assuming it wasn't there already, in which case, it would tip over and land on the roof, squashing me into a pancake.

The alternative was to hang here, fighting for each breath until somebody stumbled across me in the daylight. Would I survive that long with all brain cells still functioning?

I stuffed the deflated airbag between the wheel and the dashboard. While my left hand gripped the wheel, my right reached for the release. With a lion's roar, I shoved down hard, doing a one-handed push-up into the back of the seat, and pressed the button with my other thumb. No luck. I pushed harder and arched my back to create more distance between me and the strap. My torso sang a funeral dirge.

The belt popped free, and I plunged nose first to the steering wheel. A lightning bolt of pain shot through my head, and a thunderous scream tore into my eardrums. The car plummeted farther down the embankment. I covered my head with my arms, which wouldn't protect me at all when it capsized. What felt like a lifetime later, my vehicle stopped its forward motion but teetered precariously on the front bumper.

Crap.

A few slow breaths helped clear my mind and push back the free-floating panic in my chest. I had to reach my phone and call for help, but the night obscured its exact location. No matter where it had landed, I couldn't get to it without adding more weight to the worst place imaginable: the front of the car.

I was wedged between the steering wheel and the door, my grasp of the wheel the only thing keeping me off the floorboard. Since I'd stayed awake last night with Savannah, the likelihood of dozing off and losing my grip approached a hundred percent. The adrenaline had me buzzing at the moment, but it would be a long night. The buzz was bound to wear off sometime, and sleep wouldn't be far behind when it did.

The door handle hovered beside my head. Did I dare reach for it? The simplest solution would be to open the door and jump out. But my legs were wedged under the dashboard. To jump, I'd have to push off the floor.

The weight shift caused by the open door and the push-off would almost certainly tip the vehicle over. Could I stand the agony that was sure to ensue? More importantly, could I make it out in time?

My only hope was to retrieve the cell phone. The driver's seat stuck out like a shelf. If I climbed on the back, I might be able to cross over to the passenger side. Adding my right hand to my left on the wheel, I pulled my upper body up, ignoring the squeals from my ribs. The Dodge creaked. I froze.

After an hour-long minute, the Dart settled, and I hooked my feet around the seat back. The only task that remained was to release my hold and grab it. My brain sent the message.

No response.

I willed my hand to let go of the steering wheel and grasp the side of the seat.

But it wouldn't move. I had two choices: climb on the seat or fall to the floor and possibly die. I opted for the former. Now I had to convince the rest of my appendages to cooperate. One more try.

This time, my hand obeyed, grabbing the edge. I hoisted myself on top of the seat back, adrenaline the only thing between me and agony. With my belly draped across the seat, my arms dangled on one side and my legs on the other. The car rocked. I trapped air in my lungs and waited.

Steady again, I wormed my way into the same position on the passenger side. My cell had wedged itself into the corner by the door. I could get close enough to reach if I maneuvered into the right spot. I hugged the seat back, wrapped my feet around it, then enfolded the seat with my legs. Almost there.

Sweat stung my eyes. I wiped them with my forearm and inched ahead, halting after each three-inch gain. When the phone appeared within reach, I extended my right arm. My Dodge groaned and swayed, and my heart leaped into my throat. This was the end. There was no way it wouldn't go over this time. Moisture poured down my face, thinning the sticky blood.

The rocking stopped. Somehow the vehicle didn't fall. I expelled the ensnared air from my lungs, stretched out my arm again, and made contact. My sweat-soaked fingers slipped off the phone. Another attempt, and I snagged the cell between my thumb and pinky. I scooted back to a safer position and lit up the screen—10:22 sprawled across the center. The battery icon in the upper right corner showed half-full, and I had three signal strength bars. Perfect. I'd be on my way home in a flash.

I pressed the green button and dialed 911.

A deep voice answered, "911. What's your emergency?"

"My car's been run off the road and is standing on the front bumper in a ravine. I can't move or it'll fall over."

"All right, ma'am. Stay calm. What's your name?"

Stay calm? Sure, buddy. "Jen Dawson."

"Where are you?"

"I'm on Partridge Road near the lake."

No response.

"Hello? Are you there?" Nothing. I checked my phone. The screen was dead-battery black. What happened? The battery was half-full. Perhaps the accident had damaged it. Did he hear enough to send help? More significantly, did I dare stick around to find out? One strong gust of wind, and it wouldn't matter either way.

I calculated the nearest rescue team was probably ten minutes away. I switched the key to accessory, and the clock came on—10:25. If the dispatcher heard the whole message, they should be here by ten thirty-five at the latest. If . . .

The seconds ticked away. I tried to relax, but residual adrenaline had my legs itching to flee. Nowhere to run and nothing to take my mind off my predicament. Darkness enveloped the vehicle, fueling my imagination. What kind of animals roamed out there? No bears or wild hogs, for sure. Possums maybe. They could be mean. Cottonmouths, especially this close to water. My brain conjured an image of wriggly, venomous snakes all over my car.

I breathed as deeply as my damaged ribs would allow. *There are no snakes.*

Ten minutes disappeared with no indication of lights or sirens, even in the distance. I was alone, unsure how to get out of this mess. What would Dana and Daniel do? How would I maneuver them to safety?

The back seat was directly behind me. If I threw myself against it, the force of my additional hundred and thirty pounds might tip my Dodge onto its wheels again. However, the push off the front might send the vehicle the other way.

I edged backward off my perch, sore ribs shooting pain up my spine. When my feet made contact with the seat bottom, I allowed my body to fall back. The ultimate trust exercise. My head bounced off the seat, and I grabbed the console to stop a forward slide. The car rocked.

Forward and back.

Forward and back.

On the third rearward tilt, I planted my toes and used my legs to propel myself backward. The automobile fell. The thud of the back tires against the earth threw me into the back of the seat. I felt agonizing pain in my midsection, and I couldn't move air in or out. After all my effort and all the pain, I'd suffocate while on solid ground. I froze in place until the agony diminished, and my diaphragm relaxed. I pulled in as much air as possible without starting the cycle again.

The car remained slightly tilted, but with all four wheels where they were supposed to be. I could live with that. A peek out each back window did nothing to help me decide which would be the safest exit. The darkness was impenetrable. My imagination provided the wildlife lurking within.

I squeezed between the seats to collect the keys and my phone for whatever good either would do me in this situation. The door opened onto a sea of kudzu, and I studied it long enough to establish nothing rustled through the vines.

I lowered myself into the morass. My feet slid under me, and I skidded to the bottom of the ditch on my back. Stinging pain fired through my chest and face. I panted it into a manageable ache. The remains of Sunday's rain lingered under the greenery, and I helped soak it up with my jeans.

My Nikes sank two inches into the mud when I stood. There was no sign of any critters, so I took a tentative step toward the road, gripping my car for support. I had no idea how far away the road might be. I'd been too busy holding on to keep track while the car tobogganed down. I gripped the mirrors and door handles to haul myself upright, arms trembling, my ribs more painful with each breath. No matter, though. I had to climb out of the trench.

When I reached the rear bumper, I took a breather. A half-moon had risen, and the end of my struggle appeared about fifteen feet ahead. A surge of energy jolted me forward. Fistfuls of slick kudzu kept me moving in the right direction. My throbbing legs propelled me over the top; I collapsed on the asphalt and rolled over onto my back. Sirens wailed in the distance, and flashing red lights lit the sky. I closed my eyes.

CHAPTER TWENTY-ONE

I stared up at the mottled half-moon as a fire truck pulled up beside me, followed by an ambulance and a police car. I guess my message got through, so what took them so long? Two light blue uniform shirts appeared by my side.

One paramedic stuck two fingers against my neck. "Ma'am, can you hear me?"

Ma'am? The guy must be twelve. I focused on him, nodded, then instantly regretted the movement. The adrenaline had worn off, and the pain ran amok. "Yes."

The other checked my blood pressure while the first placed a plastic collar under my chin. "What's your name?" the collar man asked.

The cuff squeezed all the fluid out of my upper arm. I winced. "Jen Dawson."

"Do you know where you are, Jen?"

"Partridge Road, and yes, I know the year, and who the president is."

He leaned over me and pressed his fingers into my shoulders. "Oh yeah? Prove it," he replied with an impish grin.

He thought he was cute. I'd fix that. "Eighteen seventy-eight. Rutherford B. Hayes. Am I right?"

"On the money. Well done." Running his hands along my extremities, he asked, "Do you have any pain anywhere?"

Everywhere. "Ribs, mostly. Neck, and shoulders, too."

He gently explored my abdomen. "I'll bet that nose isn't too peachy, either."

"Saving the best for last."

He flashed a light over each eye. "Were you thrown from the vehicle?"

"No. I rode it all the way down. Like the Fury roller coaster at Carowinds, only no picture at the end."

"My kids love that place. Especially the part where you can stand with one foot in North Carolina, and the other in South Carolina. My five-year-old thinks that's just the coolest thing."

The fire truck pulled away, and somewhere behind me, a deputy called for a tow on his radio. I handed my car keys to one of the paramedics to give to the deputy. Then the paramedics strapped me to a backboard, placed me on a wheeled stretcher, and loaded the whole package into the ambulance. I closed my eyes against the bright lights and concentrated on the orange insides of my eyelids instead of my inflamed, throbbing face. Then a sudden sharp pain in my left arm made them fly open again.

"Ouch!"

The paramedic taped a needle into place in the crook of my elbow and adjusted a bag of clear fluid. "Is there anyone you'd like me to call for you?"

Yes, but who? My mother would freak out, so forget that. Brittany and Eric were both mad at me. Still, Brittany was my best friend, and she'd be even madder if I didn't tell her what happened. "Brittany Dunlop."

I gave him the phone number, the only one I remembered besides my own.

He made the call while the ambulance rocked its way to the Sutton Medical Center and backed into the bay. This was the third time I'd made a trip like this in less than a year. I really had to find a safer place to live.

They parked me in a curtained cubicle and hoisted me to the ER bed. A nurse took my vital signs, helped me into a flapping gown, and bagged my soaked, muddy clothes. A woman came in with a compartmented wire basket loaded with tubes of various colors, needles, and tourniquets to draw my blood. Two full tubes—one purple-topped, one gray—later, I asked the vampire lady, "What are those for?"

"Some tests the doctor ordered."

Before I could reply, she disappeared through the screen.

I dozed for a while, until a short, stout man in a white coat entered through the curtains, introduced himself, and poked around on my ribcage. He found every tender spot with ease.

"Okay, Ms. Dawson, I don't think anything is broken, but I'll send you down to X-ray to be sure. When you get back, we'll set that nose for you."

"My nose is broken?"

"It can happen with an airbag injury. You should be fine once we put the bone back in place, and the swelling will go down in a few days."

I suspected it actually broke when I landed face-first on the steering wheel. Not sharing that particular adventure if I could help it, though. "Thank you, Doctor."

When the nurse showed up with the wheelchair, I didn't bother to argue, I just grabbed the back of my gown and settled in for the ride. The halls were quiet at this hour. There was no traffic jam at the elevator, and we had the metal box to ourselves. I was thrilled not to run into anybody I knew. The last thing I needed after a night like this was a rousing chorus of "Not again, Jen!"

The X-ray room was chilly, and I stretched out on the even chillier table. I rubbed my arms to stay warm, ribs protesting until the tech instructed me to keep my hands down by my sides. Three snapshots later—one chest, one neck, and one nose—I was headed back to my cubicle in the ER. When I came through the curtain, I found Eric, in jeans, and an Atlanta Hawks T-shirt, in the chair by the bed.

He winced when I cruised in. "Holy cow, Jen! Are you all right?"

After our argument, he was the last person I expected to see. He really did care about me. "It's not as bad as it seems. How did you find me?" I asked, sounding like I'd caught the Jolly Green Giant's head cold.

"I heard the call on my scanner."

I climbed back into bed, my arm pressed against my ribs. "Since when do you have a police scanner?"

"My uncle gave it to me for my birthday last year. Guess he thought I didn't spend enough time at work already. It's come in handy the past few days, though. Made me feel like I was still part of the department."

"You *are* still part of the department."

He lowered his chin and studied his fingernails. "For now, perhaps, but I'm not sure how much longer. Olinski was irate about the cyanide in my locker. I was right, though. My fingerprints were nowhere to be found."

We both understood the lack of prints didn't prove anything. "Did they find anybody else's on the bag?"

"Only Olinski's and the property room officer's. Olinski's the detective who turned the evidence in to begin with, so his were no surprise." He took my hand. "Never mind about all that. Tell me what happened."

The nurse came in and removed my plastic collar. Just as well. It clashed with my gown. Plus, I didn't have earrings to match. "The X-rays showed your neck's fine. Ribs too. They're only badly bruised. Seat belts'll do that to you. Your nose, however, is broken, as we suspected. The doctor will be in shortly to put it right again."

Eric waited for the nurse to leave, then asked, "You want to tell me what happened?"

"I went out to see if Tony was at his cabin. He wasn't there, so I left. Headlights roared up behind me, and next thing I know, something crashes into me, and I'm sliding off the side of the road."

"Did you recognize the vehicle or the driver?"

"I couldn't see anything. It was pitch-black. A flash of brown went by as I lost control. Might've been a truck, but I can't be sure."

He leaned toward me. "What makes you think it was a truck?"

"The headlights came straight in my back window, blinding me."

A navy-blue-clad deputy came in, produced the standard cop notebook, asked all the same questions Eric did, and received all the same answers. "Ms. Dawson, are you certain another vehicle hit your car? We haven't found any evidence to support that theory."

I lowered my eyebrows. "Glass broke, my car lurched, then veered into a ditch. What else could've happened? I wasn't drunk."

He nodded, face expressionless. "Your blood tests confirm that. Do you have any medical conditions that might've caused you to lose consciousness? Were you tired enough to fall asleep?"

Gritting my teeth sent a flash of pain through my face. "No, and no. Somebody hit me. A brown truck."

"All right, ma'am. Thank you for your time. Someone will be in touch."

Someone will be in touch. Right. I wouldn't hold my breath. I didn't look that good in blue. I turned to Eric. "He thinks I'm crazy, and simply drove off the side of the road."

"He doesn't think you're crazy. He wants to establish what caused the accident."

"I told him what happened. He doesn't believe me."

"If it helps any, I believe you."

I tamped down my irritation. It wasn't his fault. There was no reason to take it out on him. "Thank you. Why do you think it took so long to rescue me, anyway?"

He smiled. "Your call got cut off, and all dispatch heard was Partridge. West Blackburn has a Partridge Drive. Since there's nothing substantial on the road where you were, they assumed you were in West Blackburn. Only after nobody could find you on that street did they realize where you had to be."

"Couldn't they triangulate the cell towers or something? They do it all the time on TV."

"It takes longer in real life than it does on TV. You weren't on the phone long enough." Eric pulled up a

222

chair and took my hand. "Listen, I need to talk to you about the other day. I understand why you're upset with me for telling Olinski about the evidence."

I swallowed the lump in my throat to make room for the crow I was about to eat. "I was wrong. I shouldn't have asked you not to tell anyone. But I only wanted to help you."

"Your heart's always in the right place, but sometimes your methods are a little out there. I just couldn't do what you wanted me to do. It wasn't right."

"I know. I'm sorry. Can we be friends again?"

Disappointment flashed over his face, which he quickly covered with a smile. "Of course. You're not getting rid of me that easy."

"I'm glad." His distress tugged at me, but all I had to offer was friendship. For now, anyway. Although, he was here, holding my hand when I needed him. And he believed me. Didn't that count for something?

The nurse trundled a cart topped with an instrument tray borrowed from *The Dentist*'s set through the curtains. "You ready for your nose job?"

I eyed the tray of torture devices. Maybe not. "Will I look like Emma Stone when you're done?"

She scrunched up her face. "Well, perhaps more like WC Fields. At least until the swelling goes down. After that, you'll look like you again." She snagged a bottle of nasal spray off the tray. "This is lidocaine for the pain. It'll keep you numb for a half hour or so."

Two squirts in each nostril, and I felt like I no longer had a nose. For the first time in hours, my face wasn't ready to explode. My neck muscles relaxed as my head hit the pillow. As long as I didn't breathe too deeply, I could pretend tonight had never happened.

When the doctor came in to set the break, the nurse lowered the head of the bed. Eric went to the vending machine to get coffee, but I suspected he didn't want to be around for the procedure. My hero. Couldn't blame him, though. Neither did I.

The doctor selected a gadget that must've once belonged to a Lilliputian gynecologist. I braced myself, but when he stuck the speculum up my nostril, I had no pain. He peered up both sides, then gently massaged the top of my nose. The bone popped back into place, and I could breathe again. Until he stuffed a spongy thing up each side.

"Okay," he said. "Everything looks fine. You need to take it easy, and leave the packing in for a week or so." He placed an adhesive strip across the bridge of my nose. "The nurse will be back with your discharge instructions."

"Dank ooh." Wonderful. I'd spend the next week sounding like a two-year-old. Good thing I was a writer. Talking was optional.

Eric came back in now that the hard part was over. I'd never pictured him as squeamish. Guess being a small-town cop didn't expose him to many gory crime scenes. Probably for the best. They'd spend as much time resuscitating him as gathering evidence.

He settled back into the chair by the bed. "How are you?"

"I'm okay. No pain for the bobent."

He laughed. "No, I'll bet not."

I stuck my tongue out at him.

"As soon as you're ready, I'll take you home."

"What about clothes and my car?"

He patted my hand. "It's being taken care of."

"By who?"

The curtain parted, and Brittany entered the cubicle with a shopping bag. "Olinski went to the scene to make arrangements."

I struggled to focus. "Danks for cobing."

Her lips lifted at the corners, and she covered her mouth. "My best friend is in the hospital. Again. Where else would I be?"

"I didn't dink you liked be anybore."

She glanced at Eric, then turned back to me. "That's silly. Don't worry about it now; we'll talk tomorrow."

Eric stood. "I can go, if you want to talk."

Sweet guy. I grabbed his sleeve. "No, wait. You don't have to go."

The nurse came in with my discharge instructions: rest, no heavy lifting, no strenuous activity, ibuprofen for pain, ice every one to two hours for twenty minutes, and hot, steamy showers. I could handle the rest and the showers. Not sure about everything in between, though.

I signed my life away, and, with a friend on either side, the nurse whizzed me out the door.

CHAPTER TWENTY-TWO

"Aaak!"

The unrecognizable figure in the mirror screamed along with me. My hair stood out all over my head. Black circles cradled my puffy eyes, and my swollen nose was the centerpiece of my bloated face. WC Fields? Uh-uh. The zombie apocalypse had begun with me as the leader of the band.

Brittany tapped on the bathroom door. "Are you okay?"

I opened up. "That depends on your perspective."

Her mouth fell open. "Wow. I see what you mean. Maybe I shouldn't have let you go to sleep when we got home. Does it feel as bad as it looks?"

"A little sore, but bearable."

"Go ahead, and take your shower. I'll start the coffee and make breakfast."

"Thanks. And thanks for hanging with me last night."

"Of course. That's my job, right? Who else is gonna keep you together?"

True. Brittany had saved me from myself more times than I wanted to admit. I couldn't imagine where my life would be right now without her love and support.

I needed to give more back. Perhaps that's why she worked so hard to push me away sometimes.

I turned on the hot water. Steam billowed over the top of the shower curtain and fogged up the mirror. I added a little cold to make the temperature tolerable, and I stepped in the tub. Streams of liquid pelted my neck and shoulders for a poor person's massage. My knotted muscles fought back. I turned my head from side to side, determined they wouldn't win this war.

A purple stripe ran from my left shoulder to my right hip, connected to another running right to left from the lap belt. Seat belts may save lives, but they don't do much for curb appeal in the aftermath. My sore ribs made it difficult to take a deep breath or turn from side to side. But it was a minor inconvenience considering how bad it would be if they were actually broken.

By the time I'd shampooed and soaped, I could move freely, apart from my torso, and the only public reminder of my adventure stared back at me while I combed my hair. When I came out of the bathroom wrapped in my baby-blue bathrobe, Brittany handed me a cup, two ibuprofen, and an ice pack. She'd make somebody an awesome wife one day. If I ever gave her a divorce.

I washed the pills down with a mouthful of coffee and clapped a hand over my mouth to keep the scalding liquid from spewing back out again. I should've done a temperature check first. The sizzle of bacon floated out of the kitchen and made my saliva flow and stomach grumble. Too bad it would contain all the flavor of cardboard between my sponge-stuffed nose and burned tongue.

Brittany relocated the crispy strips to a paper towel, then said, "How do you want your eggs?"

227

"Over medium, please. Want me to do the toast?"

She glared at me over the tops of her glasses. "No. I want you to ice your face. The instructions said every one to two hours. You've only iced once since we arrived home."

"We didn't get here until a little while ago, and I was asleep for most of the time."

"Jennifer Dawson put the cold pack on that mug of yours, this instant!"

I started to wrinkle my nose at her, but a stab of pain changed my mind. "Can't be too important, you didn't use my middle name."

"I'm saving it for your tombstone." She waved her spatula at me. "Now, cooperate, please."

"Yes, Mother."

The toast popped, and Brittany scraped butter across the surface. "Speaking of your mother, did you call her yet?"

I hadn't even considered it. "I'll try in a little while. I should probably go over there, but she'll freak if she sees me like this and I didn't warn her first."

Brittany's lips twitched. "Not a die-hard *Walking Dead* fan?"

"Ha ha." I returned the ice pack to the freezer and refilled my cup. "You want more coffee?"

She carried the full dishes to the table. "Please."

We ate in silence, broken only by the clatter of forks against plates and the occasional slurp. As I wiped up the last of the yolk with my last bite of toast, I asked, "So, what did you want to talk to me about last night?"

"Nothing important, but I need you to tell me why you think I don't like you anymore."

I leaned back and bit my lower lip. "It was the medication talking. I didn't mean what I said."

"Circumstances have a way of bringing out the truth."

"Spare me the psychobabble. Dr. Margolis gives me enough of that already."

She studied me, her cup not entirely hiding a hint of a grin. "I'll bet he does."

"Very funny." I shrugged and dipped my head. "But you might be right. There was some reality in what I said. I know you like me, but you've been a little distant lately. Sometimes it seems like space has grown between us. I'm sure my imagination is working overtime, though."

Brittany set her coffee down and gathered toast remnants off the tabletop with her fingertip.

Perhaps not my imagination, after all. I picked at the cuticle on my left thumb.

"No, it's not your imagination."

My heart jumped into my throat. I swallowed hard. "What's wrong, Britt?"

She sighed. "I guess it feels like you don't need me the way you once did."

Huh. Our last argument was when I asked her to help me with research. Perhaps she didn't want to admit to herself what really bothered her. "That's crazy."

"You sure? We used to talk to each other about everything. You didn't even tell me you were looking for Tony last night, let alone ask me to come with you. I worry about you." She shot me a sidelong glance. "You have a tendency to get yourself into trouble."

"I do not. It just seems to find me."

She looked at me over the top of her glasses.

"Okay, fine. But you haven't exactly blown up my phone, either." I took a deep breath. "Maybe you're right. I have been avoiding you."

"Why?"

"You don't have time for me anymore. And you've been so sensitive. Everything I say sets you off. I don't like when we fight."

Brittany touched my hand across the table. "Jen, I always have time for you, but I understand why you believe that. Honestly, I think I avoided you too, because I thought you were upset about my dating Olinski. Plus, now you have all these other people to turn to when you need something. I guess I was jealous. Then, I got angry when you asked for help because I figured you'd already tried everyone else first."

"I suppose I should admit to being a tiny bit jealous about Olinski. Honestly, I'm not jealous about you taking him away from me; it's the other way around. He's taking you away from me. I want you to be happy, though. You deserve that. I'm an idiot."

Her cackle broke the tension. "No more than usual. Don't worry, I'm used to it." Her eyes darkened. "I'm glad we had this talk. I've missed you."

"Me, too. You know I'm always here for you. Even if it doesn't seem like it sometimes. I love you." I glanced at the kitchen clock. Eight thirty-five. "Hey, isn't it time for you to leave for work?"

Her gaze followed mine. "Crap. I gotta go." She jumped up and headed for the door. "Don't forget to ice your nose. I'll call you later."

I drained the last of my coffee and gathered the dirty plates. A two-ton weight had fallen off my shoulders. Feeling energized, I washed the dishes, which was a significant accomplishment. For me, anyway.

The arctic torture pack was frozen again, so I stretched out on the couch and chilled my face. I enjoyed fitting my whole body on the furniture again, but I missed

Savannah. Her absence left a hole in my heart, though she was happy and healthy and would be home as soon as I chased down the creep who'd threatened her.

When the ice melted, I returned the pack to the freezer and grabbed my laptop. The inflammation had gone down slightly, and the tops of my cheeks no longer cushioned everything I saw. I suspected that wouldn't last long, however. I swallowed another round of ibuprofen and went to work.

The twins had floundered around in the woods for hours, much closer to safety than they realized. The sun finally peeked through the trees.

Daniel sat in the leaves, leaning against the tree's base with his head in his hands. "Anything?"

Dana paced up and down the clearing, holding her phone in the air, searching for cell service. "Not even a flicker. We're in a dead zone."

He nodded and climbed to his feet. "Okay. At least we have an idea what direction we're going in now."

"True. Too bad we have no clue if it's the right way." She took a few steps toward a gigantic oak, one of the few hardwoods in the predominantly pine forest. "If I scale that tree, I might be able to pick up a bar or two."

Daniel followed her gaze. The lowest limb was four feet above her head. "Okay, but how will you climb up there? The branch is too high."

"Not if you boost me." She trotted to the base of the tree. "C'mon give me a leg up. This is our only chance to find our way home, and to catch the guy who left us here."

Now I had decisions to make. When Dana gets up in the tree, does she receive a cell signal? If so, how high up does she have to go? Once she has a signal, is it strong enough to make a 911 call? Or must she risk texting their housekeeper Mrs. Barlow and hope the message goes through? After that, does Dana climb down unharmed, or does the thin branch break, and she drops to the ground? If she falls, is she seriously injured or just banged up? Whoever invented the algorithm for writers' plot questions would become an overnight billionaire.

I was still chewing on question number one when the phone rang. I glanced at the screen. My agent twice in one week? Sounded like trouble to me. I swiped and trotted out my chipper, everything-is-wonderful voice. "Hi, Ruth. What a lovely surprise! How are you?"

"Very well, thank you, except I recently developed a headache."

"I'm sorry to hear that. Are you taking something?"

She put the call on speaker, and her voice took on a tinny tone. "Not yet. I'm hoping it'll go away on its own after this conversation."

Uh-oh. "What's going on? I've been working hard, I promise."

"I know you have, bubbele, but on what? Are you working on your manuscript or trying to find a killer?"

"Can't I do both?"

Her silence served as my answer. Something had changed since the last time we spoke. "Tell me what's happened, Ruth."

"I had a call from your editor this morning, Jen. Her boss is frustrated and running out of patience. They want the second book, or you will be in breach of contract."

My heart hammered, and my chest tightened. I pulled air through my narrowed windpipe. "How long do I have?"

"August fifteenth. Written, edited, and polished."

"What if I can't do it?"

She sighed. "They cancel the contract, and you return the advance you received for the second title."

No problem, except the money was long gone. "Guess I'd better put my fingers into overdrive."

"I'm sorry, Jennifer, you've already missed three deadlines. I understand what's happened to you, but I can only do so much. Your future is in your hands, now."

"I get it." I ended the call and laid the phone on my desk. My stomach hosted an Irish step-dancing troupe.

Deep breath in, slow breath out.

Could I finish the first draft in a month? Was it possible? Sure, for some writers. I wasn't one of them. It'd taken years to write and rewrite *Double Trouble*. There was no way I could recreate the magic in the few weeks I had left.

I understood what the publisher expected when I agreed to the deal. What was I thinking? Clearly, in retrospect, I was overwhelmed by the realization my dream was about to come true. In all the time I'd spent honing my craft to find an agent, I never once considered what would happen to my writing routine if a publisher picked up the series.

Maybe I should give up. I had a bestselling novel. Which is one more than most writers ever have. There was nothing wrong with being a one-hit wonder and having nothing left to prove. I had the bookstore and friends. I maintained a reasonable relationship with my family for the first time since I was a kid. Plus, I had Savannah. What more could one person expect?

I stared at the narrative on my laptop screen. The twins were lost in the woods with no food, no water, and no hope of rescue. Could I just leave them there forever? Didn't I owe them more than that? The kids had been good to me.

Nonsense. They were fictional characters born in my head five years ago. Only words on a page. They didn't take a single breath without me. They didn't exist.

Really? Who got me out of the car last night? My bookstore or my friends? My family? No. Dana and Daniel. Figments of my imagination, sure, but they were real to me. They deserved better than to be left in the woods to die. A thousand words a day from here on out will leave me enough time for a rewrite, maybe two. I could do that. I *would* do that.

Okay, so how far must Dana climb up the tree to receive a cell signal?

CHAPTER TWENTY-THREE

After three hours of typing and deleting, I finally led the twins out of the woods. Dana never did find a cell signal, but she climbed high enough to determine which way they wanted to travel. She tumbled from the tree on the way down but only injured her arm, which broke her fall. Now they stood on the side of the road, and I was fried. If only I could find the solution to my problems by simply climbing a tree.

I crawled on the couch for another round of ibuprofen and ice. The swelling had reduced to the point I no longer resembled a zombie. More like a losing MMA fighter. There were no beauty pageants in my immediate future, so no worries for now.

I still needed to call my mother, though. That conversation would be anything but okay.

Perhaps a nap, instead. My phone went off, Brittany's college graduation picture on the screen. So much for that theory. "Hey, Britt, what's up?"

"I just wanted to check in. You getting some rest?"

I barked a laugh. "Not a chance. Ruth called. To top it all off, my publisher wants to dump me. Can't say I blame them, though. The deadline for this book was months ago. It's not their fault Scott discarded me for a job in Paris, and then, Aletha was murdered, and I almost died catching her killer." I left out the part about Brittany's fiancé going missing in Afghanistan. No need to scrape off that scab.

"I'm sorry, Jen."

"They've been patient, considering, but they have a machine to operate, and I'm jamming the gears. I still have six weeks to finish up, including revisions. They gave me until the fifteenth. Can't say how good the product might be, though."

She blew air into the phone. "Can you do it?"

"I'll let you know next month."

"How can I help?"

Write half the remaining chapters for me? Not her strength. "Feel like doing some reading? If you'll skim over what I have so far, the revisions will be easier."

"Sure. Email it to me."

"Thanks."

"You're welcome. By the way, Olinski wanted me to tell you they parked your car at the bookstore and left the keys with Lacey. Apparently, you're the luckiest person I've ever met. Not only did you walk away from the accident practically unscathed, but so did your vehicle. Other than a few dents, and scratches, it's running fine."

My jaw fell. "You're kidding."

"Nope. You're a genuine rabbit's foot."

"Too bad I won't fit in your pocket."

"Did you phone your mother yet?"

I lowered my eyebrows and groaned. "You mean my other mother?"

"Your birth mother. I'm your adoptive one, remember?"

"Yup. Which means you made a choice, so quit complaining."

"Never. Now, I have work to do. Make the call!"

I hung up and pressed the icon for my mother. Because it was time to inform her about what'd happened, not because Brittany told me to.

"Hi, Mom! How's Savannah?"

"She's fine, and so am I. Thanks for asking."

Oops. "Sorry. I miss my girl, that's all."

"I miss you, too, dear."

I checked my phone screen. "Mom." Since when did my mother make jokes? Savannah must be rubbing off on her. "Listen, I need to tell you something."

A long pause, then: "The last time you said that to me someone had tried to kill you. What is it this time?"

"Well, somebody ran me off the road last night. I'm fine. Nothing to worry about. I didn't want you to hear it from anybody else."

"Are you sure you're all right? Where were you?"

"Really, I'm okay. I was visiting a friend out by the lake." No way would I tell her I'd been injured during another investigation.

"Seriously, though, how are you? Do you know who did it?"

"Just a little banged up. It was someone in a brown truck, I think. I couldn't see anything else."

She paused again. "I hesitated to mention this, but a guy's been hanging around here."

My pulse picked up speed. "What guy?"

"Some man was sitting in a pickup in front of the house next door when I took out the trash this morning and relocated to the other side when I checked the mail later on. Pretty sure I've never seen him before today. He's wearing one of those sweat-shirts with a hood, though."

"In July? He must be nuts. What kind of pickup?"

"I'm not sure. Something big, and red."

Who drove a red truck? Could be anyone. Might not even be a man at all. "You guys stay inside. Savannah too. I'll be there as soon as I can. If he gets too close to the house, call 911, okay?"

"I'm sure that's not necessary. We're fine."

"I know, Mom, but he's after the dog. If I pick her up, he'll leave you alone."

She sighed. "But then he'll come after you."

"He's after me, anyway. At least you'll be safe. I'll stop by the police station on my way home, and put them on alert. They'll make extra patrols or something. Don't worry, we'll be fine."

"You should stay here where we can take care of you."

No way. I'd never spend another night in that house. "None of us will be protected if I'm there. That's what I'm trying to tell you. I'll see you soon."

My hand trembled as I set my phone on the table. There was still no word from anyone about the origin of the note. Who could've sent it? Tony's name came to mind. He was in jail when I received it, but it'd been mailed a day or two earlier. The judge had released him, and now he'd disappeared. Perhaps he was busy attempting to kill me and stalk my dog.

But why would he ask for my help and then attack me for helping? It made no sense. Then again, according to Havermayer he believed I'd planted incriminating evidence in his car. I hadn't heard it directly from him, though. I wouldn't put it past the detective to throw

238

something out there just to see how I'd react. She'd done it before.

Who else might've murdered Chief Vick? His wife, but no clues pointed in her direction. Except, I still hadn't followed up on Lacey's lunch-with-the-pregnant-lady story. I needed to ask Angus about that.

Eric still couldn't account for the evidence from the case last year, which had disappeared, and landed in his locker. The mayor had access to the ink needle, but what motive did she have? The "woman scorned" theory was viable but a little extreme. Would the chief really have stood a chance against her in the next election? I seriously doubted it, and I suspect Teresa did, too. Of course, Xavier Benedict hadn't been ruled out yet, either. No matter how unlikely his involvement was, Atlanta wasn't far enough away to clear him completely.

I replaced my sweats with jeans and a short-sleeved button-down. No way I was pulling anything over my head if I could help it. Removing my T-shirt had generated enough pain to be a reminder for at least a day or two.

A call to Angus set lunch in motion. Then I searched the junk drawer next to the sink for my spare house key so I could lock up when I left. Good thing Brittany had one to let us in last night. Too bad she didn't think of leaving it here for me. After pawing through three different kinds of batteries, two other keys that unlocked hell if I had any clue what, and a length of rope coiled into a ball, I found the backup wedged into a corner.

One slow step at a time, I proceeded down to the sidewalk, arriving at the bottom of the stairs without jarring my nose. The rest of the walk would be easy if I didn't stumble or trip over anything. However, nobody had ever called me Grace. I ventured into the sunny, blue-skied afternoon with caution.

Locals packed the diner. Friday lunch came in second only to Sunday as the busiest time of the week. Angus stood behind the counter near the cash register, conducting another performance of the Dandy Diner Symphony. At the far end, Marcus presided over a grill loaded with burgers, spatula in one hand, cheese slice in the other.

During a momentary pause, Angus turned in my direction. His jaw dropped. "What happened to you?"

I was surprised he hadn't already heard. A broken link in the gossip chain? "I lost a fight with an airbag, but don't worry, it was a bloody mess by the time I got through with it."

His lips lifted into a smirk. "I'll bet. Too bad the blood belonged to you."

"Minor detail." I grabbed a plastic bag next to the register. "This one mine?"

"Yup. Tell me what happened."

I gave him a quick rundown while I checked the order and thumbed through my wallet. "I assume the sheriff's department is trying to find the truck, but no word from anyone yet. The deputy who interviewed me acted as though I was at fault, despite my blood tests all coming back negative."

"Let me see what I can find out for you."

"You have friends in that area?"

He nudged me with his elbow. "I have spies everywhere."

"Speaking of which, I heard Anne-Marie Vick had lunch with a young pregnant woman the Friday before Chief Vick died. And Anne-Marie was very upset.

240

Scuttlebutt has it the chief might've been the father of her baby."

Angus laughed. "I hate to say it, but the grapevine has it wrong this time. That young lady was Anne-Marie's niece. She was angry because her brother threatened to disown the poor kid because she let her deadbeat boyfriend impregnate her."

That takes care of one motive, at least. It doesn't entirely let Anne-Marie off the hook, but her remaining motive was too small to amount to much. Throw it back.

I said goodbye to Angus and munched fries on my way to the bookstore, ignoring objections from my nose, and dropped the bag when my car came into view. The front bumper was flattened, the hood crumpled but still closed. At least the windshield remained intact. I retrieved my lunch and surveyed the rest of the damage. Scratches down both sides, some left from my first visit to Tony's cabin. The rear end was undamaged except for the shattered driver's side taillight. That alone seemed like proof someone hit me. How else could I break a taillight when the car landed front end down?

I squatted for a closer look. On the quarter panel beside the smashed headlight was a tiny smear of brown paint, most likely invisible in the dark. I pulled out my phone, snapped pictures of my vindication, and sent them to Olinski. Take that, Deputy!

The bookstore entertained two customers when I arrived—a woman browsed the gardening shelves, and a man flipped through a thriller—and I headed toward the back, head down, to avoid frightening them off. On the other hand, perhaps I should hang out in the para-normal section as a display for the latest zombie offering.

Lacey rolled a cartload of books out of the stockroom. "Jen! How are you? Brittany told us what happened. Are you okay?"

"Contrary to what your eyes tell you, I'm fine. Just a little knocked around."

"So, you think somebody ran you off the road?"

I showed her the pictures. "Here's the proof. Someone tried to scare me off. I'm getting close to something, but I have no idea what."

She squeezed my arm. "You shouldn't be out and about."

"I need to collect Savannah. My mother has a mystery man prowling outside her house."

Her eyes widened. "Could it be whoever threatened you?"

"I'm not taking any chances."

"Let me pick her up for you. You go home, and be safe."

I shook my head. "Thanks, but I don't want to involve anyone else if I can help it. As long as this lunatic is still out there, everyone around me is at risk."

"I can take care of myself."

"Sure, you can, but you have a family to think about. Where are my keys?"

"On your desk."

I collected them and went out to the car. The Dodge started up as if nothing had happened, and I made a beeline to Mom's, devouring my burger on the way. No need for subterfuge, the letter writer already had a bead on my puppy. I needed to bring her home where she'd be safe. Where we'd both be safe.

There was no sign of a red truck when I turned into my mother's driveway. Did he get tired and give up? Or did he somehow know I was coming? Impossible.

Unless he had someone observing me while he kept an eye on Savannah. Nope. Paranoia strikes again.

My mother freaked when she saw my face, as I'd suspected she would. It took five minutes to convince her I wasn't about to keel over dead. Savannah charged when I entered the living room, and I calmed her with one hand while blocking my face with the other. No protection for my ribcage, though.

Gary sat in his chair, glaring at the television. When I called his name, he clenched his jaw and changed the channel.

Mom gathered Savannah's things. The pile appeared suspiciously larger than when I'd brought her over. I angled my head toward my stepfather and sent a questioning glance to my mother.

"He's upset because you're taking Savannah home."

The man who refused to let me have a dog when I was a kid? "Since he seems to have mellowed on the subject, perhaps you should get him a dog of his own."

She pursed her lips. "Perhaps I should."

Savannah secured in the back seat, I laid out her share of lunch, which she wolfed down before I could occupy the driver's seat. A few miles back toward Riddleton, I caught a glimpse of a red truck parked in an opening in the woods that lined the road. Was it the mystery man? A heck of a coincidence if it wasn't. There was only one way to find out.

I pulled over, locked Savannah in the car, and worked my way back to the pickup, tree by tree. When the driver came into view, his hood was down, and I froze, flushing with anger. Zach Vick. Was he Savannah's stalker? He had to be. Why else would he be hiding in the trees three miles from my mother's house?

When I stepped out from behind a pine, Zach turned, and his eyes widened. He reached for the ignition, and I sprinted toward the truck, holding my nose with one hand and my ribs with the other, gritting my teeth against the pain. Jerking the passenger door open, I climbed in. "What are you doing here?"

He smirked. "What happened to your face?"

"I had a run-in with an airbag. What are you doing here?"

"Answering a text from my mother. See?" He held up his phone.

I ignored it. "Hidden in the woods on the side of the road?"

"Not hidden, obviously. You found me."

Time to start over. "Why have you been stalking my mother's house?"

He studied his well-chewed fingernails. "I'm not getting anywhere trying to find my father's killer. Nobody will talk to me, and I don't know what to do."

A burst of maturity? That had to be difficult for him to admit after insisting he was "almost a cop" the other day. Not the time for an "I told you so," though. "I understand, but why are you shadowing my mother?"

"I had no idea it was your mother's house. I followed you yesterday, and saw you leave your dog here. Leonard told me about the letter, so I thought if I took her and then helped you search for her you'd help me discover who murdered my father. But they never left her alone."

So much for maturity. "Listen, Zach, I get why you're determined to do this, but every cop on the force is working on it." I laid a hand on his shoulder. "They'll find whoever did it. Go home and be with your mother. She needs you right now."

He nodded, still staring at his hands.

"You know, if you get caught doing stuff like this you'll get kicked out of the police academy before your class even starts." I opened the door and stepped out. "How exactly did you follow me anyway? I used every trick I knew."

A grin spread across his face. "I guess my dad taught me a few tricks you didn't know."

Shaking my head, I trotted back to my car for the trip home, which was much faster now that I had no need to worry about who might be behind me. Safely back in our apartment, the pup stretched out on the couch and thumped up a dust storm as I unloaded her belongings. I really should vacuum the thing. Put it on the schedule for August sixteenth. My novel was the only thing on the agenda between now and the fifteenth.

I held my girl in my lap for a few minutes before heading to my desk. How did she worm her way into my heart so quickly? She was only a dog, after all. Yeah, right. No such thing as *only* a dog. For the first time in my life, I understood what it meant to have something more important to worry about than myself.

It took me almost an hour to relocate the twins back home. They contemplated their next move in their father's office. Time for them to find the giveaway clue. But not right now. My face and ribs ached, and I needed a break. I swallowed a couple of ibuprofen and retrieved the ice pack from the freezer.

"Shove over, little girl. I want to lie down."

Savannah grudgingly made some space, although not nearly as much as I required. The discomfort was worth it, though. I'd missed her. The ice numbed my face, and the pills kicked in, dulling the pain in my ribs. My leaden eyelids closed, and I dropped into oblivion.

When I woke up, Savannah sat by the door, staring longingly at her leash. I levered myself off the couch and took a step toward her. She turned her head toward me then back to the brown nylon tether draped over the doorknob.

"Great idea, kid. Let's go for a walk."

She jumped to her feet, wagging. Her ears perked, and she repeatedly licked her nose, brush-like tail hammering the wall. Which would give first, the tail or the Sheetrock? My security deposit hoped it wouldn't be the wall, but my wallet couldn't withstand a broken tail.

The prancing began when I grabbed the leash, and the battle ensued. "Savannah, drop it."

The corners of her mouth turned up slightly. Stupid dog was laughing at me. I truly needed to check into a trainer. Releasing my end took away all the fun out of the tug-of-war, and she sat, lead draped around her bottom teeth. She worked the nylon off with her tongue and spit it out.

"Now, are you ready to cooperate?" I put my hand up in front of her face. "Stay."

Her butt wriggled, but she remained in position while I clipped the tether to her collar. "Good girl!" There might be hope for us yet.

Down the stairs we went, off for another adventure. For Savannah. I wanted the peace of the outdoors, otherwise known as Mother Nature's balm for a troubled mind. We quickly traversed the two blocks to the park, Savannah seeming to have figured out our destination. Uncharacteristically, she made no stops along the way.

She must've intuited I had nowhere else to be. If I'd been in a hurry, she would've taken thirty minutes to make the ten-minute trip.

When we passed through the gate with patriotic bunting wrapped around the wrought iron, we turned toward the baseball fields. There were no games on Friday afternoon, so there would likely be few people around. We lucked out, though. There were none at all. I unclipped Savannah's lead, daring the "All Dogs Must Be Leashed" sign to do something about it. Everyone needed a little freedom to run now and then.

Savannah sniffed and peed, sniffed and pooped, then sniffed and peed again. I tore a bag off the roll by the side of the path and retrieved her leavings. Before I could drop the collection in the trash, a squirrel with more guts than brains darted past Savannah toward a tree. Too tempted to resist, she took off after it. I took off after her, face and torso screaming in protest. "Savannah, wait!"

The squirrel abruptly changed direction and headed for a different pine. Savannah tried the same maneuver, but her legs slipped out from under her, and she ended up sliding across the pine needles used for mulch like a runaway sled on ice. The squirrel stopped under the target tree and sat on its haunches, mouth open, flashing its long, pointy incisors. I could swear it mocked her.

The dog shook herself off and trotted away as if nothing had happened. *Must be nice.* If only I shared her propensity for living in the moment. No concerns about the future or regrets from the past. Just right now. Nothing on my mind but the trees, the musty pine needles, and the joy of spectating while my puppy made a fool of herself.

The silly squirrel lived in the moment, too. The anxiety of the chase gone, it ran for another tree. Of course, Savannah followed, tongue out, sides heaving. I trailed behind, in identical condition. Well, maybe not tongue out, but my mouth opened, desperately trying to keep my lungs filled.

Skittering through the needles, the squirrel leaped, caught hold, and scrambled up the tree. Savannah slammed on the brakes, bounced off the trunk, and landed on her back in a pile at its base. She clambered to her feet and sniffed and scratched at the mound. Something was in there she badly wanted. I meandered over to investigate.

"Whatcha got, little girl?" She ignored me, continuing to poke and scratch. As I approached her position, the heap appeared more extensive than it had initially. What I'd assumed was a random mass of pine needles turned out to be much more. Beneath Savannah's probing nose was a human hand with an ink needle clutched in the fingers.

CHAPTER TWENTY-FOUR

For the second time in less than twenty-four hours, I was surrounded by flashing lights and uniforms. Savannah and I stood outside the crime-scene tape as officers in navy blue swarmed the park like locusts, searching for clues. Havermayer and Dr. Ingrid Kensington, wearing her medical examiner hat, huddled around the tree's base, removing pine needles from the body one at a time lest evidence be missed. Olinski coordinated the uniformed officers.

Leonard approached us with his notebook in hand. "Hey, Jen, you okay? You've been through a rough couple of days." He reached down and barely touched Savannah's head as if he might catch mange or something. She pulled away and snuffled his wrist.

What does okay mean anymore? "I'm all right. Did you find out anything about the letter I received?"

"Havermayer hasn't said anything."

"She probably threw the thing away."

He smoothed his mustache. "She said she'd look into it."

I gestured toward the crowd. "They figure out who that is yet?"

"They haven't completely uncovered him."

"What makes you think the body's male?"

Leonard eyed me from under lowered brows. "I don't. I assumed because of the size of the hand. Could be a woman, I suppose. Nobody's been reported missing, though."

"Tony hasn't been seen since he got out of jail yesterday morning."

"It's not unusual for someone in his situation to stay out of sight for a while."

I nodded toward his notebook. "Are you here to take my statement?"

"If you're ready." He flipped to an open page. "Tell me what happened."

"Not much to tell. I took Savannah to the park for a walk, and let her off the leash for a minute since nobody else was here. A squirrel ran by, and she chased it into the pine needles, which concealed the dead body. I called 911."

"Did you see anything or touch anything?"

"No. When I realized what I was looking at, I pulled Savannah away, and we waited for you guys."

A smile bloomed beneath the closely pruned bush that covered his upper lip. "I must say, for a writer you tell a dull story. Except for the dead body part, of course."

"Gee, thanks. I'll try to make my activities more colorful from now on."

"Did you see anyone else when you arrived or on the way here?"

"Nobody. Not even a car. A little strange now that I think about it. Kind of like the whole town had been abducted by aliens."

He chuckled. "I was only kidding about your story being boring. No need to embellish."

"Actually, I didn't. It was really quiet for a Friday afternoon. Usually, there are more people around. Angus's place had a ton of customers for lunch. Where did all those folks go? They couldn't have vanished."

"Are you pulling my leg?" He drew his eyebrows together. "'Cause if you are, I don't think you're funny."

No surprise. "That's what you get for saying my story is dull."

"Well, let's stick to the facts from now on. Tell me what you saw when you arrived at the park."

"I did. There was nobody here but us and the squirrel. Would you like a description?"

"Of what?"

"The squirrel. It was brown, with a bushy tail—"

He slammed the notebook shut, stuffed it in his uniform pocket, glared, and strode away.

Some people were just too easy to mess with. The man should develop a sense of humor. Leonard approached each situation as a potential threat, which sucked the energy out of his soul.

I sat on the grass next to Savannah. She stretched across my lap, and I rubbed her chest while her tongue dripped on my forearm. Havermayer and Ingrid stood and brushed the dirt off their gloved hands.

When Ingrid glanced in my direction, I waved. She gestured for me to come over, so I scrambled to my feet and ducked under the yellow tape. As they backed away from the body at their feet, Tony Scavuto stared at me through dull, lifeless eyes. My gut churned, and I reeled Savannah in. I stopped three feet away with her on a short leash at my side, careful to focus anywhere but the ground.

Havermayer scowled and headed straight for me. "You can't be here. You're contaminating my crime scene. You and that mutt of yours."

Heat rose from my gut to my face. "Now, just a minute. We're not—"

Ingrid stepped between us and stared down the detective. "First of all, this is my crime scene until I release it to you, Detective. Second, I asked Ms. Dawson to join me. If you have a problem with her presence, you need to address your issues to me." She crossed her arms. "So, do you have a problem?"

Havermayer opened and closed her mouth like a fish flopping on the floor, then marched away, fists clenched at her sides.

Ingrid rolled her eyes, then smiled at me. "Hello, luv. What brings you here? More research for the book?"

Despite my efforts, the question directed my gaze to the gory scene. Tony lay on his left side, hair matted, a bloody, grapefruit-sized rock tucked behind his back. A weapon of convenience, not premeditation. I swallowed back bile. "We found the body."

She squeezed my arm. "Oh, I'm sorry. Nasty business."

"Thank you. Any idea how long he's been dead?"

She pried the ink needle from Tony's fingers and deposited it into a plastic bag. "I won't know for sure until I do the autopsy. Best guess based on rigor mortis and lividity is yesterday evening or early last night."

If that was the case, then it wasn't likely Tony ran me off the road. Even if he did manage to borrow a brown pickup from someone, the timing didn't work. He still could've written the letter, though. If so, Savannah was safe now. I scratched the back of her neck.

"Would you like to attend this autopsy, too? It should be much more interesting than the last one," Ingrid said.

No way was I going to go through that again. "Interesting? How so? It seems straightforward to me."

She gestured toward Tony. "Just a plain old bash on the head, right?"

I nodded but suspected she would prove me wrong.

"Could be. Or maybe he was already dead, and the head injury's postmortem. Not much blood here so one question is if this is the primary crime scene or did someone move him? Or perhaps he died that way, but he was unconscious or drugged first. Or drunk. He might've stumbled and hit his head. The possibilities are endless. That's what I love about pathology."

How could she be so analytical about someone's death? Occupational hazard, obviously. She couldn't do her job if she allowed her emotions to run wild. Plus, I didn't think she'd ever met Tony. "You do make it sound like fun, but I think I'll pass on this one just the same. Too many adventures already in only a couple of days."

She tipped her chin toward mine. "Your face is one of those I presume? I thought about asking, but my mum always tells me I'm too nosy."

"Well, now you can tell her you're the only one who didn't ask or freak out right away."

"She'll be gratified. So, what happened?"

I went over my encounter with the brown pickup and the aftermath one more time. This was becoming almost as much fun as the "When's your book coming out?" question. Although, that one was much less physically painful. However, if I wanted people to stop asking either question, I needed to stay home. I recited a concise version of the story finishing with: "The rescue squad

253

showed up right after I climbed out of the ditch, took me to the hospital, and here I am. Ain't I pretty?"

Ingrid chuckled. "Smashing. Or bootiful as my three-year-old niece likes to say."

Olinski strolled over with an evidence bag containing two cigarette butts. "How's it going, Doc?" He turned to me. "An odd place for a coffee klatch, isn't it?"

"Well, you know me. If there's coffee, I'm in."

He nudged his glasses back up his nose. "I heard there was some in your apartment. Perhaps you should check it out."

I took the hint, waved to Ingrid, and led Savannah out the wrought-iron gate. My mind roiled as we passed the A-frames on Park Street. There had now been two unexplained deaths in less than a week with no apparent motive for either one. Why would somebody kill Tony, the prime suspect in the chief's death? Did this exonerate him, or was it unrelated?

And what about the ink needle in his hand? An interrupted attempt to dispose of evidence, perhaps. But if he would do something like that, why not get rid of the stuff they found in his car? The only logical explanation was a plant by the actual killer, which returned me to the question: who had access to the needle? Only Veronica Winslow, who received the package, Mayor Teresa Benedict, who possessed the key to Veronica's office where the box was stored, and any member of the police force who knew the location of the spare keys to the town hall. That narrowed it down to fifteen or twenty people. Big help.

The only reasonable choice in the group was the mayor. She might've had multiple reasons to kill the chief. He was allegedly her ex-lover who jilted her and then planned to run against her in the next election. He also retained the ability to destroy her marriage by telling her husband about their suspected relationship. Or use the knowledge throughout the campaign to impugn her character, though releasing the information would hurt him, too.

Unless the chief accused her of an affair without naming the other party. Insinuation and innuendo were often more effective than truth. He'd shown a propensity to do anything necessary to achieve his goals in the past. Why wouldn't he do it in this situation? I hadn't found any proof yet they'd actually *had* an affair. Would the chief make one up just to damage the mayor's campaign? If so, how could the mayor prove it never happened?

Still, none of that explained the evidence found in Eric's locker. How would she accomplish that? The cops owned spare keys to the town hall. Did the town hall have a set to the police department as well? Technically, the cops worked for the mayor. Did she bribe someone on the force to shift suspicion to Eric?

Lots and lots of questions, with a side of speculation. Still no answers. As much as I needed to go home and work on my book, that endeavor would be hopeless. The giveaway clue would have to wait a while longer. When we hit Main Street, we turned right toward the diner on the next corner. Angus brewed coffee, too. Perhaps he'd learned something about who ran me off the road.

The Dandy Diner was an empty shell of its lunchtime self. Two couples chatted over their dessert, one couple I didn't know in the back-left corner. Lula Parsons, the secretary at St. Mary's Church, and her husband George occupied the one in the back right. Angus carried coffee for refills and delivered checks for payment on the way out. Two bags sat on the counter next to the register. The grill was clean and unstaffed, and no servers bustled among the tables. In tonight's concert, he was a one-man band.

Savannah and I climbed into an orange booth at the far end of the restaurant, opposite the front door, away from prying eyes and ears. On the wall above my head, the Marlboro Man cantered across the plains into the camera, a lit cigarette clamped between his lips, "Come To Where The Flavor Is" printed below his horse's hooves.

Angus folded into the booth across from me and wiped his forehead with a towel. "I heard what happened. How are you holding up?"

Already? If textile mills were as efficient as his rumor mill, there'd be enough material to clothe the world for free. "I'm all right. I've had an interesting twenty-four hours."

"No kidding. You want something to eat?"

My stomach did a somersault. "No, thanks. I'm still processing everything."

He broke into a broad grin, eyes twinkling. "Might be the perfect occasion for the specialty of the house."

The specialty of the . . . ? Oh! "A grilled-cheese sandwich, and tomato soup, right?"

"That's the one."

I hadn't consumed one of his chase-your-blues-away meals in months. "That does sound delicious, but I don't want you to mess up your grill for me."

He shook his head. "Don't worry, we don't close for another two hours. If you don't dirty it up, somebody else will."

"All right, I'll take it with a Mountain Dew."

Angus scooted off the orange seat. "And I'll bring something special for my favorite girl." He reached over and rubbed Savannah under her chin. "You're such a good girl. How's my sweet baby?"

"Nice to know I'm so easily replaced."

"Not replaced. Enhanced."

Enhanced. Hmmm. Perhaps that explained my emptiness when she stayed at my mother's. She was a part of me now.

Before Angus could start on our dinner, Veronica Winslow came in and stood by the counter. The bags were hers. I'd never asked Veronica about the alleged affair between the chief and the mayor. This seemed like a good time to do that. To perhaps finally put it to rest one way or the other. When she headed for the door, I followed her out, leaving Savannah standing at the door, watching.

"Hi, Veronica."

She turned toward me. "Oh, hey, Jen. I didn't see you. I heard you've had another busy day. How are you?"

"I'm okay, though I suspect it hasn't really hit me yet."

"I'll bet."

I didn't want her dinner to get cold, but I had to ask. "I have a quick question, if you have a minute."

"Sure. Shoot."

"I heard a rumor that Chief Vick and Mayor Benedict were having an affair. Is there any truth to it that you know of?"

Veronica chuckled. "Angus?"

"Of course, but he seemed pretty sure."

"I never witnessed anything directly, but the chief spent a lot of time in her office. Much more than he ever did with the last mayor. Always with the door closed and sometimes after hours. Obviously, I can't say what they talked about or what they were doing after I went home. I was always the last staffer out, though, and they'd still be there. So, if I had to guess, I'd say it's more likely than not. Does that help?"

It wasn't the positive proof I'd hoped for, but if the two public figures were as discreet as they needed to be, it was probably as close I was going to get. "It does, thank you."

She held her bags up. "You're welcome. I'll see you later."

"Definitely. Have a good night."

Savannah's tail swept Angus's floor when I came back in. I slid back into our booth, and she jumped in beside me, sat facing the table, and waited for her snack. The only thing missing was a napkin tucked into her collar. It didn't matter, though. She always cleaned up after herself.

Angus returned with soup and sandwiches for both of us and chicken scraps garnished with crumbled bacon for Savannah. I debated offering her a trade, but she wolfed the treat down before I could speak. I dipped a corner of my sandwich into the soup and lost myself in the swirl of flavors bathing my taste buds instead.

The couple in the left booth rose to leave, and Angus headed for the cash register. While her significant other paid the check, an auburn-haired woman in a pink, tulip-covered frock approached my table. "Hi, Jen. Sorry to bother you, but I wanted to tell you how much I loved your book."

"Thank you," I replied while Savannah stretched her neck to sniff the intruder. She passed the smell test, and Savannah thumped her tail.

"I can't wait until the next one comes out. Any idea when that might be?"

Finally, I had an answer to the dreaded question, like it or not. "Should be out late winter or early spring."

She bounced on her toes and clapped her hands. "Oh, wonderful. I'm so happy!"

Heat crept up my neck into my face.

Angus replaced her at the table. "What was that about?"

I sighed. "The usual. When's the book coming out?"

"Any news on that front yet? I'm excited to see what the twins are up to this time."

Et tu, Brute?

A mouthful of soup took the sting out of my following words. "I received an ultimatum from my publisher, so the novel will be out in a few months if I can meet the deadline."

"Good luck."

"Thanks. Any whispers in the wind about the truck that hit me last night?"

He bit into his sandwich and swallowed quickly. "Actually, someone told me they'd seen an unfamiliar brown pickup in town yesterday. The person thought it looked like Leonard behind the wheel, but he drives a Taurus."

"Perhaps Leonard borrowed the truck. Is he moving or something?"

"Not that I'm aware of. It might not have been him, anyway. The guy I talked to only got a quick peek as the vehicle went by. Besides, Leonard couldn't have run you off the road. He was on duty. On a 911 call at the time, from what I understand. And why would he want to hurt you to begin with?"

I sopped up the last of my soup with the corner of my sandwich. "A 911 call in Riddleton? What happened?"

"Not exactly in town. Somewhere out in the boonies near the line between us and the county jurisdiction. A domestic dispute or something. I don't know who was involved."

"Guess we need to figure out who owns that truck." That sounded like a project for Brittany. Now that she was speaking to me again.

CHAPTER TWENTY-FIVE

Saturday morning dawned with the sun streaming through the bedroom curtains. A spotlight dragging me into the new day against my will. Savannah had wormed her way beneath the covers and squeezed me to the edge, so I had one leg hanging off. Apparently, a queen-sized mattress wasn't big enough for both of us.

The clock on my nightstand flashed 4:45, and I turned off the alarm set for five, which was the only way I could make the runners' new six a.m. start time. Not interested in the song du jour. It would only end up stuck in my head all day. Right now, *coffee, coffee, coffee* occupied my brain space. A craving bordering on addiction. I should start a group: Coffee Addicts Anonymous. We'd have to meet in the football stadium, though.

I crept out from under the bedclothes, hoping my puppy would sleep a while longer. No such luck. The instant my feet hit the carpet, her snout made its first appearance. A flick of the comforter, and the rest of her head followed posthaste.

"Good morning, sleepyhead."

Savannah yawned and stood, blinking at me. Then she leaped to the floor, landed on her chin, and trotted toward the kitchen. I threw on some sweats and trailed her to the food dish. "Nope. Not yet, kid. I'm in no mood to clean up an accident this morning."

I grabbed her leash, made a surprise attack on her collar, and clicked the lead into place without a confrontation. A quick trip around the block solved Savannah's immediate problem, and I took care of mine while she inhaled her breakfast. My face had returned to almost normal with only a hint of residual inflammation, and my blackened eyes had faded to purple. I'd progressed from the walking dead to the walking wounded.

Joining the group for our Saturday morning run remained out of the question, though. My broken beak wouldn't stand for it. A run, slow as I might be, was definitely not in the category of taking it easy. Still, I could drop by for a visit with the gang. Also, since I wouldn't be running, Savannah could come along. We might even walk the path. It wouldn't be the first time Eric and Lacey covered five laps to my one. Even so, we'd likely keep pace with Angus.

I downed my coffee and woke Savannah from her post-breakfast nap. She sniffed her empty food dish, then settled by the door while I collected my keys. The sneak attack system failed this time, but her full-bellied sleepiness kept the skirmish to a minimum.

We strolled down Park Street with the sun rising on my left, and I admired the Independence Day exhibitions, although I hadn't thought about the competition in days. Recent events made it all seem so trivial.

As we approached the park, a sense of dread filled my chest, and the memory of Tony's body entrenched itself in my mind. I stopped. Savannah strained at her leash, excited for a rematch with the squirrel. On the other hand, I would be thrilled to never encounter another rambling rodent again.

Eric and Angus waited at the gate, early as always. Angus sported his running sweats—gray pants with an oversized sweatshirt that rested at mid-thigh. Eric wore his Christmas colors—green shorts and red Riddleton Jackrabbits tank top, white towel draped around his neck.

Their smiles lifted some weight from my chest, but anxiety lingered deep in my psyche. What grisly discovery would we make today? Silly idea. I'd been to the place a hundred times since I'd moved back to town and had only one negative experience. No reason to believe in a repeat. Still, the doubt remained.

Angus reached for Savannah, scratching the base of her ears. "How's my girl this morning? Are you having a good day?"

I pressed my lips together. "I'm fine. Thank you for asking."

Angus ignored me, and Eric said, "I didn't think you'd be here this morning."

"I needed to get out of my own head for a while. I can't run, but I thought a walk would do me some good."

"Well, I'm glad you came. How are you?"

Me too. Butterflies fluttered in my stomach. "Much better, thanks. The ice and ibuprofen are doing the trick."

Angus, reluctantly abandoning the puppy, squeezed my arm. "Happy to hear it. You look a lot healthier than you did yesterday."

Savannah swiped his knee with her paw. I shortened her leash. "That's not saying much. Did you learn anything else about that truck?"

"Not yet."

Eric arched his eyebrows. "What've you heard so far?"

"Somebody thought they saw it in town Thursday, and it looked like Leonard was driving, but I haven't been able to confirm that," Angus replied.

"Leonard?" Eric turned to me. "You think he had something to do with your accident?"

"He couldn't have. He responded to a 911 about the same time I was run off the road. A domestic dispute or something."

He propped his foot on the bench and retied one of his high-class running shoes. "Huh. I know a dispatcher. I'll give her a call later and ask about it."

"Why? Do *you* think Leonard had something to do with my accident?"

He grinned. "No, of course not. I have to practice my detective skills. Leave no stone unturned, and all that. Must check out every alibi, right?"

My heart swelled. The way he smiled made me want to play connect-the-dots with his freckles. "Right. Meanwhile, I wish the Sutton County Sheriff's Department practiced your diligence."

"Still no word?"

"Nope."

Savannah jerked on her leash and pranced behind me. I turned around as Lacey approached the sidewalk. "What're you doing here?"

"Thought I'd walk the track, and help you guys believe you're faster than you really are."

She scratched Savannah behind the ears to calm the furry jack-in-the-box. "Thanks. I need the confidence boost after my lousy performance in the race last week."

"Lousy? You were the first woman to finish."

She poked Eric in the ribs. "Yeah, but I wanted to beat the scarecrow here."

Eric's jaw dropped. "Like that was ever gonna happen."

She shrugged. "There's still next year."

We trooped through the gate, and Savannah and I started off down the track while the others went through their stretching routine. No need to put myself through the torture for a change. My muscles had proved to be as flexible as rebar. Stupendous for skyscrapers, but not so much for runners. Not that anyone would ever legitimately call me one of those.

Eric and Lacey breezed by before I achieved the quarter-mile mark. Of course, I had to deal with stop-and-sniff delays. I glanced behind me as Angus puffed around the bend, sweatshirt drenched with a "V" shape originating at his collar, though the sun was still below the tree line.

When Angus caught up to us, he slowed to match our pace. "Hey, thanks," he said.

"For what?"

"Giving me an excuse to goof off. I'm not feeling it, so I'll just stick with you, instead."

Was he serious? No way. He loved his Saturday morning run. More likely, he didn't want me to feel abandoned. "You don't need to do that. We're used to walking by ourselves."

"I want to. That's what friends are for."

Friends? Yeah, I had those now. I smiled at him. "Thanks. I'd enjoy the company."

While Angus nattered about the dress the mayor had torn yesterday, it occurred to me I'd never said those words before. Less than a year ago, the concept of him sticking with me to provide companionship would've made me cringe and search for excuses to leave. Brittany had always been the only friend I could tolerate or who could tolerate me. My life had changed, and strangely enough, I didn't mind.

And then there was Eric. The concept of a relationship with him didn't seem quite so outlandish anymore. Funny how a frightening experience could affect one's point of view. When I found him waiting for me in my ER cubicle the other night, my mood improved dramatically. Did I care for him more than I'd wanted to admit? Possibly.

Angus continued to blather about torn clothing. Did I care about the mayor's ripped dress? Not at all. But Angus wanted to tell me about it, which was fine with me.

A squirrel dashed across the path, and Savannah nearly ripped my shoulder out of its socket, trying to chase it. It was a good thing she was still a puppy. Her full-grown self would've sent me to the hospital with a dislocation. I'd better add leash etiquette to her training schedule, assuming I ever made one.

Eric and Lacey lapped us again when Savannah gave up on the squirrel and stopped to dig for grubs. Short, fat, squishy beetle larvae. Doggy caviar. Frankly, I didn't understand the fascination with either the bugs or the fish eggs.

When Angus started a play-by-play account of Mrs. Simpson's knee surgery, my mind went on a quick excursion to the Davenport residence. I mulled over how the twins would find the giveaway clue hidden between two books in their father's office library. There needed to be a logical reason for one of them to pull a book off the shelf. A difficult one. Better to let my subconscious work on the problem for a while.

I tuned back in to Angus just in time for the grand finale.

"And now she's taken up running. Isn't that amazing?"

I smiled at him, warmth pushing some unease out of my torso. "Wow! That's crazy. Will you invite her to join the group?"

"She's seventy-five years old."

Oops. Guess I should've listened. "I'll bet she's faster than me."

He chuckled. "And me, for that matter. I'll talk to Eric."

About halfway around the track, we spotted the crime-scene tape, which cordoned off the area where Savannah had found Tony. My heart thudded into my breastbone.

Deep breath in, slow breath out.

Angus laid a hand on my elbow. "Are you all right? You've gone pale all of a sudden."

"I'm fine."

He turned to follow my gaze. "Is that the place?"

I nodded.

"Come on," he said and took several steps toward the barrier. "I want to check it out."

I swallowed hard. "We're not supposed to cross the line."

He halted with his hands on his hips. "Since when has that ever stopped you? Aren't you the one who faced down a killer pointing a gun in your face? Or were all the news reports exaggerated?"

"No, but—"

"Let's go, then. The cops might've missed something."

I reeled Savannah in and eased under the tape. She curled her tail over her back, pressed her nose to the ground, and zigzagged toward the tree where we'd discovered Tony.

Angus knelt on one knee and pointed at a dark patch in the grass. "Blood. Is this where you found him?"

"Yeah. He was stretched out on his side, covered with pine needles, the rock they think killed him behind his back."

He peered at the grass. "There's an indentation about an inch deep in the dirt. Like someone dropped the stone from some height."

I squatted beside him, restraining Savannah with a hand on her chest. "Huh. Tony probably wasn't lying here when he died. Unless the killer hit him, then stood, and let go of the rock. I'd think someone acting in the heat of the moment would drop the murder weapon immediately when the horror of what they'd done sank in."

"Could be, but what makes you think it was spontaneous?"

"People planning a homicide don't bring a rock with them. They carry a gun or a knife or something else deadly. Someone who's angry and upset will grab whatever's handy. Tony's death wasn't premeditated in my opinion."

Angus clambered to his feet. "Okay, let's say you're right, and he got into an argument with somebody who slugged him. Tony was what five-two, five-three maybe?"

"Something like that. He came up to my forehead, and I'm five-six."

"Sounds like any man or tall woman could've hit him with enough force to kill if the angle was right."

I scratched my ear. "True, but he was a stocky guy. Strong. He would've fought back."

"Unless he was struck from behind. What if there was no argument? What if somebody snuck up and took him by surprise?"

"In that case, almost anyone could've done it."

He sighed. "Let's see if we can find something to narrow it down."

"The cops crawled all over the place searching for clues. I doubt they missed anything."

Angus grinned at me. "You got other plans for today?"

"Only a date with my manuscript. I guess I can spare some time to scout around a little. Plus, I've got the bionic nose here to help." I chucked Savannah under the chin. "How about if one of us works from the inside out, and the other from the outside in? That way we'll both cover the whole area."

"Sounds like a plan." He headed toward the yellow tape marking the perimeter.

Savannah and I slogged our way around the pine beside us. She explored the grass, I the bark and lower branches that might not have been a priority for the searchers. We worked our way out in wider circles, examining every inch with no results.

Our third trip around brought us to the next tree in line. We repeated our methodology—Savannah covered the ground, which had already been thoroughly searched, and I examined the tree's surface and branches. I quickly checked everything I could observe while upright and had to bend over to work my way down. My back cramped, and I squatted to relieve the pressure. My knees would object when I rose again, but it was the only way to check out the bottom of the tree. Pain later won out over pain now.

The pine stood directly between the crime scene and

the gate, so it was in the path the killer would've used to escape. I paid particular attention to the nooks and crannies of the bark. Perhaps the murderer brushed against it and left a blood trail. At about the level of my mid-thigh had I been standing, a tiny scrap of dark fabric clung to a sharp outcropping. "Angus, come look at this!"

He hustled over. "What?"

I pointed out the cloth. "What do you think?"

"It's definitely small enough they might've missed it in the search."

"Or someone could've left it twenty minutes before we got here."

"Perhaps, but I'll flag down Eric and see what he thinks."

"Good idea."

He started toward the track.

But then I had a sudden thought. "Hey, Angus!"

He turned back. "What?"

"What color did you say the mayor's dress was? The one she tore?"

"Navy blue."

CHAPTER TWENTY-SIX

Eric and Lacey sprinted across the park with Angus behind by much more than a nose. Eric stopped Lacey at the crime scene border and joined me. "Whatcha got?" he asked, sweat dripping off his forehead.

Savannah bounced, as if on a pogo stick, to attract his attention. I held her back and showed him the scrap of dark fabric clinging to the bark. "This might be a clue to Tony's killer."

He wrinkled his nose. "Conceivably, but who knows how long the thing's been there? Someone could've brushed up against the pine while watching the race Saturday. A lot of people hung out here to cheer us on."

"What about the storm we had last Sunday? Would something so flimsy have survived the wind and rain?"

Eric peered at the cloth, forehead resting on the bark. "The cloth's tucked in rather well, so possibly, but I'll call a team out here to collect it, anyway." He retrieved his phone from the holder strapped to his upper arm and waved me away from the area.

I scowled. "Come on, little girl. We know where we're not wanted."

Eric glared at me and spoke into his cell.

We departed the crime scene. Apparently, no matter how much I contributed to the investigation, he still treated me like an outsider. Then he wanted to know why I hesitated to begin a relationship with him. How could I be with someone who didn't trust me?

On the other hand, I didn't wear a uniform or carry a gun. I had no police training or investigative experience. It's not like I wanted to be in the middle of these things but I somehow managed to find myself there anyway. Why? My mystery writer's curiosity, perhaps. It might also be coincidence, but I didn't believe in coincidences. Especially when murder was involved. Chalk it up to bad luck.

I wandered over to where Angus and Lacey huddled together, whispering. "Hey, guys. So much for a relaxing morning, huh?"

"Doesn't seem to be any such thing when you're around," Lacey said with a smile. "You're always stumbling into something or other."

"Keeps life interesting." More than I wanted, for sure. "What do you think, Angus? Is that the spot where the mayor tore her dress?"

He cupped his chin with his hand, elbow propped on his other forearm. "No idea. Could be. Why would Teresa Benedict kill Tony?"

Excellent question. While she might've had motive to murder the chief, no clear reasons had come to light for her to execute Tony. "He had the needle that had probably been used to inject the cyanide into the wine. Perhaps she attempted to frame him?"

Lacey rested a hand on Angus's shoulder. "Homicide seems a little extreme. She could've planted the syringe somewhere without killing him."

"What if she caught him trying to entrap her, and things got out of hand?" Angus asked.

I massaged the back of my neck. "Okay, but why were they together in the park?"

A heavy silence settled over us until Lacey said, "Perhaps one of them stumbled across the syringe somehow and tried to blackmail the other. This would be a perfect place for a clandestine meeting. Nobody comes here at night. Since Tony ended up dead, I'd have to guess he was the blackmailer."

"That makes sense," I said. "Especially given Teresa was one of the people who had access to the needle."

Angus nodded. "And she had the most to lose."

Savannah snagged her leash in her teeth and yanked. Poor baby was bored, but I wasn't ready to leave yet. I handed the lead to Lacey. "Would you hold her, please? I need to talk to Eric for a minute."

"Sure."

"Thanks." I hurried to where Eric stood, still on his phone.

He held up one finger, and I waited while he ended the conversation. "That was my dispatcher friend. The alleged domestic dispute call came from an address abandoned over twenty years ago. The bottom line is, unless a couple of squatters had a violent argument, and decided the best solution was to get themselves arrested for trespassing, the report was a fake."

"Bet Leonard was pissed when he drove all the way out to the boonies for nothing."

Eric kicked a pine cone at his feet. "Yeah, probably. I'll talk to Olinski about the situation."

"While you're at it, ask him if they found any fingerprints or DNA on the syringe in Tony's hand."

273

He ran a hand over his carrot top. "Why?"

I gestured to Angus and Lacey. "We have a theory, and I want to know if we're on the right track."

"What's your theory?"

"Uh-uh. You'll think it's crazy and won't help us."

He opened his mouth to almost certainly tell me to stay out of it, then closed it again. "Okay, I'll see what I can find out, but he most likely won't tell me anything. I'm still suspended, remember?"

He's learning. There was no way I was going to stay out of it after being run off the road. "I understand, but if we're correct, you might be off the hook."

Two uniformed officers approached with a crime scene kit, and Eric threw me out of the roped-off area again. I collected my dog and headed home, late for my date with the Davenport twins. When I was a teenager, my mother told me I should always keep my dates waiting. Make sure they understood I was in control. This was the first time I'd ever listened, but at least it was for an important reason.

Brittany came out of her apartment as we crested the landing. "What're you doing out so early?"

"We went up to the park."

Her mouth fell open. "The doctor told you to take it easy. Running isn't—"

I held up my hand. "I didn't run. We walked around with Angus, that's all."

"That's all right, I guess. You look a lot better, by the way."

"Thanks. I'll be glad to dispose of the ice pack, though."

She tilted her head and studied my face. "You probably can at this point. You're almost human again. As close as you ever get, that is."

"Very funny. I'm as human as any other crackpot you've ever met."

She smirked. "I haven't met any other crackpots."

"Well, this crackpot has some information you might find interesting."

"Oh?"

I crossed my arms.

She crossed her arms, too. "Come on, give. I have to go to work."

"All right. Angus told me he talked to someone yesterday who saw a brown pickup truck in Riddleton Thursday afternoon. The driver supposedly looked like Leonard, but he was at work at the time of the accident."

Her jaw dropped again. "Whoa! That is interesting. Even if it is third-hand."

"Everything from Angus is third-hand, and he's almost always right. Too bad Eric's suspended. We could ask him to search the DMV database. Although, he knows about it, so maybe he'll tell Havermayer. Any idea who the vehicle might belong to?"

"No, but if I have some time, I'll go through the archives. Perhaps a brown truck will turn up in a picture from one of the town functions. Was there anything unique about it?"

"I don't know. I only caught a glimpse out of the corner of my eye."

"Okay. I'll start with the Founders' Day picnic. They hire a photographer to take lots of pictures of the celebration every year."

"Sounds like a plan. Thank you. Call me if you find anything."

"I will. See you later."

She waved and trotted down the steps.

Once inside, I nuked a mug of coffee while Savannah curled up on the couch to recover from her outing. Poor baby worked so hard and never got a minute's rest. I plopped down beside her and reached for the TV remote, then my laptop caught my eye. Nope. Not today. Too much on the line.

I relocated to my desk and brought up my latest chapter. The twins were in the office attempting to puzzle out who'd kidnapped them and left them tied up in the woods to die. One of them had to find the note hidden between two books on the bookshelf.

Dana occupied her father's chair and sipped from the cup of Earl Grey Mrs. Barlow had carried in. "Daniel, do you remember how Father let us play in here when we were little?"

Daniel sat across from her. "Of course, I do."

"You used to hide under the desk, and pretend you were a secret agent."

He laughed. "And you were the enemy spy searching for me."

"When we became too troublesome, he'd give up trying to work, and read Shakespeare to us. He was a marvelous actor."

"The Taming of the Shrew was always my favorite."

"Father's, too. He loved doing the voices."

Her brother set his cup on the desk and went to the bookshelf. He ran a finger along the spines. "Here it is," he said, pulling the book off the shelf. A folded piece of paper fell to the carpet behind him.

"What's that?" Dana asked and pointed to the floor.

276

Daniel glanced down, collected the note, and unfolded it. "The message is from Jonathan, on the company letterhead."

"Father's partner? What does he say?"

"He demanded Father buy out his share of the business."

Now for the sticky part. I had to lead them to the realization that Jonathan had killed their father. First, they had to make the link between this letter and the "Pay up or else!" note. I stared at the screen and waited for the words to fall into my head. Nothing. Not even random letters.

Perhaps closing my eyes would help. The orange glow inside my eyelids reflected the emptiness of my mind.

C'mon, Jen, you can do this.

I drained the last of my coffee and scrambled to the kitchen for a refill. Caffeine might jump-start my dead battery. Something had to. The first draft would be complete after three more chapters, and it all hinged on this one scene.

The microwave did its job while I paced my apartment track. Oxygen and caffeine. The writer's dynamic duo, though not necessarily in that order. I'd bet I was able to hold my breath longer than I could write without caffeine. Although, the results would probably be the same.

Ideas began to come to me as I fixed my coffee. The rhythmic clink of spoon against mug focused my conscious thoughts and allowed my unconscious free rein. The secret place for my best brainstorms. Eventually, some of them worked their way out of the depths, but never without a fight. I donned my mental boxing gloves.

The most promising solution would be for the twins

to compare the handwriting in this note to that of the other two. Their comparison of the first two notes was inconclusive, just like Eric's signatures. Perhaps this letter could tie all three together. Have similarities to both of the others. That might work. Then once they baited the hook, all they had to do was reel in the fish. Jonathan would be on his way to prison for killing Victor Davenport, the book finished, and I'd be out of danger with my publisher.

I settled back in at my desk and tapped away on my laptop keys. The river flowed freely, the current carrying me through the pages. Until a thump on the door claimed my attention. Brittany breezed in before my legs responded to the trigger. "You'll never guess what I found!"

"A picture of the brown truck?"

She narrowed her eyes and pressed her lips together. "Sometimes, you really irritate me."

"In a good way, though. Right?"

"No such thing." She swiped hair off her forehead and removed a portfolio from her shoulder bag. "This photo was taken Founders' Day a couple of years ago."

I covered the ground to the kitchen table in record time, dodging the leaping puppy every step of the way. She'd produced an eight-by-ten of a young man with unruly brown hair leaning against a light-coffee-colored pickup. "Who is he?"

"Turn it over."

I flipped the picture and read aloud the handwritten note in the upper left corner. "Greg Partridge and his brand-new F-150. Founders' Day." I glanced at a beaming Brittany. "Why would Greg Partridge run me off the road?"

Brittany shrugged. "We can't actually be sure it was Greg. All we know is he bought a brown truck two years ago. Even if it was his pickup, we don't know he was driving."

"Someone said Leonard was behind the wheel earlier in the day."

"Yeah, but didn't you tell me he was at work that night?"

I laid the photo back on the table. "I did, but his whereabouts during the time of the accident are in question."

"Maybe so, but his motives are no clearer than Greg's. Why would either one of them try to hurt you? It doesn't make any sense."

"No, it doesn't."

Brittany nudged the photograph back into the folder. "We need to take this to Detective Havermayer."

"Why? This isn't her case. Besides she wouldn't care, anyway."

"Okay, we'll take it to the sheriff's department. It's definitely their investigation."

I barked a laugh. "Yeah, right. They think I was high on something that didn't show up in the toxicology screen and drove myself into the ditch. I still haven't received a call from a detective. The only way I'm bringing them any evidence is if it's positive proof."

She rested her hands on her hips. "And how do you propose to obtain proof?"

"Simple. I'll examine the truck. Since I found brown paint on my car, there has to be silver paint on his."

"Are you out of your mind? If you're right, and Greg's truck is the vehicle that hit you, what makes you think he won't try again? You told me the area was remote. Nobody else around but Tony, and he's dead. Greg could kill you and throw your body in the lake without anybody ever suspecting a thing. Bring the photo to the sheriff."

"Forget it. I'm going to the lake. Nothing you can say will change my mind."

Brittany sighed. "Fine. Then I'm going with you."

"You just got off work. Aren't you tired?"

"Not that tired. I'm coming with you."

"Now who's crazy? Didn't you just finish lecturing me on how dangerous the idea is? Well, you were right, so why would you want to come along?"

"To save you from yourself. Besides, when we run into trouble, and knowing you we *will* run into trouble, two heads are better than none."

I poked her in the arm. "Hey, don't you mean better than one?"

"Not at the moment." She dug out her phone. "Since we'll be in the area anyway, wanna have dinner with my parents?"

"Sure. Why not?"

A five-minute conversation complete, she tossed her cell phone into her shoulder bag and said, "Let's go to the lake."

CHAPTER TWENTY-SEVEN

Brittany insisted on driving, which suited me just fine. Her Chevy Cruze was roomier and cleaner, not to mention less likely to lose its front bumper the first time we hit a pothole. Heavy traffic slowed us down as shoppers desperate to beat the heat in the air-conditioned malls in Blackburn returned home. Large malls were great places to collect characters, but sensory overload encouraged me to keep my trips to a minimum. Like once a year, if that.

"Do you truly think we'll find silver paint on Greg's truck?" Brittany asked, pumping the brakes for a vehicle turning left in front of her.

"I don't know. I have mixed feelings. Finding proof would be terrific, but that side of Leonard's family is a mystery to me. No idea how Greg'll react when we show up."

"With luck, it'll be parked in the yard, and we can sneak in and out unobserved. Then, deliver whatever we find, if anything, to the sheriff, and his deputies can deal with Greg."

As we traversed the dam, the afternoon sun sprinkled glittering light on the water in the distance. "I almost hope we don't find anything because I have no clue why he would do that to me. I hardly know the guy. I've met him twice since coming back to town. Once at the 10k, then again at the fundraiser and didn't speak to him either time. Delete last Saturday from my memory, and I'd have no idea Greg Partridge even existed. Other than seeing him around town occasionally. That doesn't count." On the other hand, there was also that argument he had with Leonard in front of the police station about the birthday party. That was kind of strange, too.

Brittany chuckled. "Same here. We don't exactly travel in the same circles." She glanced at me. "Are you sure you can't think of anything that would make him mad enough to run you off the road? Even something ridiculous that would never bother a normal person? Remember, he's related to Leonard, so anything's possible."

I sighed. "Nothing I'm aware of. How does he even know what my car looks like? Maybe I stole his parking space one day or something."

"Perhaps we're on the wrong track, then. Greg can't be the only one in the area with a brown pickup truck. He's just the only one I could find."

A muffled version of "Send in the Clowns" emanated from my seat. Charlie's ringtone. I pressed my torso against the seat belt, my still-sore ribs objecting, and fished the phone out of my back pocket. "Hey, what's up?"

"You remember how Leonard told you and Lacey he once tried to be an artist but didn't have any success?"

"Yeah, why?"

"I found an ad from an art gallery in Charleston. They hosted a show a couple of years ago, and guess who the star attraction was."

I sat straight up in my seat. "Leonard? Are you kidding?"

"Nope." He read the advertisement. "November twenty-second, blah, blah, blah, blah, a bunch of people I never heard of, and featuring pen and ink drawings by Leonard Partridge."

I shot a puzzled glance at Brittany, though she had no idea what the conversation was about. "Why would he act like he had no talent? I always pegged him as the type to exaggerate his abilities, not downplay them."

"What if he didn't want anyone to know he was capable of forging Eric's signature?"

"Could be. Thanks, Charlie. I'll phone Eric."

I ended the call and relayed the info to Brittany. "I can only think of two reasons Leonard would set Eric up. Either he killed Chief Vick and needed a patsy, or he hates Eric enough to want to implicate him. Neither option makes a whole lot of sense. What do you think, Britt?"

She checked her mirrors. "The situation is more complicated than we thought, somehow. I can't imagine what would drive a cop to murder the chief of police. Besides why throw suspicion on Eric? Aren't they friends?"

"I thought they were. Let's find out what Eric thinks." I pressed the icon next to his picture.

"Hi, Jen. I don't know anything about the fabric yet."

Now that was a fascinating way to answer the phone. Apparently, he believed I only contacted him when I wanted information. It was the same reaction he had the last time I called. Was it true? Did I only call Eric when I needed something? Brittany had accused me of that, too. Something to think about.

I put the phone on speaker. "Hey, you're on speaker with Brittany. And actually, I have news for you this time. Charlie stumbled on an ad for an art show with Leonard as a featured artist."

"He likes to draw. So what?"

"Well, he told me he wasn't good at it, so he gave up and became a cop. Turns out he was talented enough to be featured in a gallery show, so he could've lied because he's the one who forged your signature on the property room log and planted the stolen evidence in your locker. Can you think of any reason why he might do that?"

Silence.

"Eric?"

"I can't think of anything. We get along all right. I was tough on him when he was still in training, but that was my job. I assumed he understood that. Perhaps he took it more personally than I realized."

"Lacey says he's a grievance collector."

"Even if that's true, I never did anything to him to deserve being falsely implicated in a homicide. There has to be something else. Besides just because he's capable of forging my signature doesn't mean he did."

I yanked the seat belt away from my chest and took a deep breath. "You're right. I'll try to keep an open mind."

Eric laughed. "That's not something you do particularly well."

Pissant. "What did Olinski say about the 911 call?"

"He said he'd talk to Leonard this afternoon to find out why he was out on a visit to an abandoned property for over an hour. But a buddy of mine told me Leonard never showed up for work today."

"Weird. Perhaps he had car trouble."

"Without calling in? Olinski'll love that."

Brittany tapped my thigh and pointed toward the upcoming intersection at SR-32-83.

"Hey, Eric, I gotta go. Call me if you hear anything."

"Will do."

"Turn left at the light," I said. "Partridge Road will be a few miles down on the left."

"Got it."

But, of course, she didn't have it, missing the street on the first try, same as I did. A U-turn and a right put us back on track. As soon as the tires hit the dirt, my stomach tightened, and my heart rate skyrocketed.

Deep breath in, slow breath out.

Brittany glanced at me and halted the car. "Are you okay?"

Nope. "I will be in a minute."

She peered out the window. "Where did it happen?"

I gestured to a place about a hundred feet away. "Over there. Let's take a look."

"Are you sure?"

"Yes. I need to get back on the proverbial horse."

She coasted to the general area, and I jumped out the instant the wheels stopped turning. The spot was easy to find, the shoulder grass flattened by numerous rescue vehicles and the tow truck. My gaze followed the trail of mangled vines and uprooted weeds to the bottom of the ditch some ten feet down.

Brittany came up and draped her arm around my shoulders. "Wow, that's deeper than I thought. Can't believe you escaped with only a broken nose and bruised ribs. You really are a walking miracle." She squeezed me tighter. "You must stop taking all these chances, though. Your luck's gonna run out sooner or later."

"Nah, I'm invincible, remember?"

She shot me a sidelong glance. "Uh-huh."

I backpedaled. "All I did was come out to visit Tony. It's not my fault some lunatic decided the road was too narrow for both of us."

She shook her head. "Of course not. Nothing is ever your fault."

What's that supposed to mean? Not getting into it now, though. "You want to check out Tony's place? He did a lot of work to it."

Brittany glanced at the sky. The sun had fallen below the tree line, and dusk set in. "It's getting kind of late."

I checked my phone. "It's only six thirty, it just seems later because of the trees."

"Still, I want to make it out of here before dark. Your friend might come back."

"Not likely, but we can make it quick. Ingrid suggested the park might not be the primary crime scene. Tony might've died at the cabin, and somebody dumped him by that tree." I wiped my sweaty palms on my jeans. Another horse to climb back up on.

"Fine."

We drove a little way down the road, and I got out to search for the sign. Brittany crawled behind me as I hunted for the telltale stack of pine cones. Not sure I wanted to find it, though. It might be where Tony died. However, I was neck-deep in the situation already. No escape now. In for a penny . . .

The shoulder grass flattened out into the driveway. I raised a hand, Brittany stopped, and I kicked some of the cones away to make sure. Yup—25472. We crept down the long, bumpy path. Who kept covering up that sign, though? And why?

Brittany parked where Tony's SUV had been the last

time. The pristine area showed no signs of disturbance of any kind. Whatever had happened to Tony, he was still conscious when he left the vicinity. Unless somebody carried him out.

I inched up the rickety steps, avoiding a Havermayer-style mishap, and tried the door. Locked. Another promising hint. A killer transporting a dead body probably wouldn't bother to secure the building. Especially out here. The closed window curtains obscured the interior from view. No help.

When I landed on solid ground again, Brittany had the door to the outhouse open.

"What do you think?" I asked.

She turned back to me. "About what?"

"The still, silly."

She raised one eyebrow. "What still?"

I trotted over and peered in. The jugs remained along the walls, box of corks in the corner, but an empty space had replaced the still. "It's gone. The old-timey still was here."

Brittany shrugged. "Not anymore."

"Huh. Let's go check out that truck while we still have enough light."

She gestured toward the car. "After you, milady."

"Oh, no, after you."

"If you insist." She sallied to her Chevy, left hand on her hip, the fingers of her right hand pinched away from her side as if holding her imaginary gown out of the dirt, and slipped into the driver's seat.

I laughed, and warmth welled in my chest. I'd missed my friend.

We overlooked the Partridge place on the first pass and had to turn around in the small clearing at the boat put-in. No surprise, given the diminishing light and dense undergrowth along the road. Perhaps we should've skipped the stops on the way. No reason we couldn't come back tomorrow if necessary, though. Finding the proof was nonnegotiable.

The narrow path appeared on the right as if a wizard had removed an invisibility cloak. Brittany and I shared a glance and a shrug before she turned in. Guess we both needed to schedule eye appointments.

We crawled down the cratered driveway, grateful we'd left my mobile disaster area of a car at home. Dislodged metallic bits would've trailed behind us like breadcrumbs. At the top of a slight rise, a distant clearing popped up. Two ant-sized people crossed from left to right.

Brittany stopped the car. "What do you want to do?"

"Keep going. I'll watch for an opening sizable enough to stash the car out of sight. We can cut through the trees, so nobody sees us."

"Are you crazy?"

Here we go again. "No, I'm not crazy. My mother had me tested."

She chuckled and shook her head at the quote from *The Big Bang Theory*'s Sheldon Cooper. "Well, she should've taken you to that doctor in Houston."

"But she didn't, so drive," I said with a smile.

Not quite twenty feet from the entrance to the open space was a footpath, just roomy enough for Brittany to park. I pointed it out to her. "Back in there."

"Back in? You must be kidding."

"We might need to make a quick getaway."

She glared at me over the tops of her glasses, maneuvered the Chevy into position, and cut the engine. We exited the vehicle, careful not to slam the doors, and made our way to the edge of the thicket. Hidden behind an ancient pine tree, tall and expansive enough to block out the South Trust Tower, I peeked out at the clearing.

No sign of the two figures that'd passed through earlier. On the left was an old, weather-beaten barn complete with peeling red paint, sagging roof, and rooster weathervane. Attached to one side was a flat-topped shelter perfect for protecting a vehicle from the sun.

I poked Brittany and pointed. "Look over there. I'll bet they keep the truck under that lean-to."

We hastened across the driveway into the safety of the trees on the other side. From that perspective, a metal building, more than twice the size of the old barn with a large set of double doors in the center and a smaller door to one side, was visible on the right. No rust anywhere, so it had to be relatively new. South Carolina humidity was hell on metallic structures. Vehicles too. The slightest scratch would corrode in a matter of weeks.

Brittany brushed hair back out of her eyes. "I wonder what they're doing in there."

"No telling, but that's the direction the guys we saw were headed, so we'll go the other way."

"Agreed."

We worked our way through the pines, struggling through the leaves, vines, and pine cones. Fallen branches and fear of snakes slowed our progress even more. The sun descended steadily toward the horizon. At this rate, we might be unable to see the vehicle when we found it.

When I picked up the pace, Brittany tripped and lurched into me. We both went down. Pain flashed through my midsection. She squealed and grabbed her ankle.

I hoisted myself to my feet. "Are you okay?"

She grasped my proffered hand. "Fine. Help me up." Once erect, she tested the injured joint. "The ankle's all right. This is ridiculous. Let's get out of here before anything else goes wrong."

"Uh-uh. I'm not leaving without checking for the truck. You wait here. I'll pick you up on the way back."

"No way! You're not going alone."

My protector to the end. "I can handle it. I'll be right back, promise."

"Forget it. Let's go." She took off for the barn.

We hobbled the remaining forty feet without incident. The back door of the structure hung on one hinge, so I whipped out my phone and activated the flashlight for a quick peek inside.

Brittany grabbed my arm. "Wait. Somebody might see the glow and decide to investigate."

Correct, as always. I turned it off and peered into the gloom. Not much of interest. Stalls for nonexistent horses and a floor littered with hay accounted for the musty mildew stench. On the wall beside the door was a saddle that hadn't accommodated a rider's rear end in half a century.

I sidled to the corner of the building and poked my head out. The truck was exactly where I'd guessed it would be.

There was no view of the clearing or the metal edifice from here, which meant nobody could see me, either. The brown pickup absorbed almost all the available space. Pressed against the side of the barn, I sidestepped toward the front of the vehicle. Brittany followed.

When I cleared the passenger-side door, I spotted the building across the way. I held up my left palm to stop

Brittany from following me any further. No sense in both of us risking exposure. My knees popped as I squatted down. A sideways duck walk propelled me to the bumper, where the crumpled headlight had no glass. Beside it, I found a two-inch smear of silver paint. I snapped a picture. With luck, the damning evidence would be visible.

A throat cleared a few feet away. I looked up.

Leonard smiled at me, his service weapon pointed at my head. He held out the other hand. "I'll take that phone, now."

CHAPTER TWENTY-EIGHT

I rose to my feet, hands up, palms forward, and handed over my cell phone. "What the hell, Leonard?"

He stuffed the phone in the back pocket of his uniform pants. "I just caught me a couple of trespassers."

Perspiration pooled under my arms. "We're only trespassing if we refuse to leave when asked. You should've learned that at the academy, Officer Partridge."

The depth of his scowl sent a shiver down my spine. "You always have to be a smartass, don't you, Jen? I can't imagine what Eric sees in you." His lips twisted into a grin that would give a child night terrors. "Then again, he's an ass, too. Maybe you two deserve each other."

"Look, we don't want any trouble. Give me back my phone, and we'll leave quietly, and never return."

"I don't think so." He peered around me. "You! Get up here, and keep your hands where I can see 'em."

Brittany limped past the truck into the open with her hands at ear level. "All right, I'm here, and unarmed. What are you doing? Don't shoot."

Leonard shifted his weapon to his left hand and wiped the moisture off his face with his shoulder, revealing a jagged tear in his uniform sleeve. "I'm not going to shoot you."

"Then put the gun away," I said, unconvinced. I had to keep him occupied until I figured a way out of this situation. He had a tear in his sleeve. We could talk about that. "What happened to your shirt?"

"I had a run-in with a tree."

"Looks like you lost."

"I never lose." He gestured toward the metal building with his pistol. "Enough chit-chat. Move, and don't try anything stupid. I'll shoot if I have to."

Brittany and I exchanged a glance and started toward him. He circled behind us. My mind raced, desperate for a means of escape. We could make a run for the woods and end up with a bullet in the back as a reward. Would Leonard fire at us? Since I had no idea what was happening here, I couldn't answer that question with any certainty. Everything depended on what, or who, he was protecting. I suspected we were about to find out.

Multiple tire tracks crisscrossed the packed earth beneath our feet as if Greg hosted a daily demolition derby.

Brittany hobbled on her injured leg, and I wrapped my arm around her to offer support. Leonard jabbed me between the shoulder blades with the muzzle of his pistol. Pain radiated down my arms.

"Move away from her."

I whirled and glared. "She twisted her ankle. I'm only trying to help."

He raised his weapon to the level of my eyebrows. "She doesn't need any help. Right, Brittany? Tell her."

She grimaced through another step. "I'm fine, Jen. Thanks."

"What are you going to do with us?" I asked him.

"Haven't decided yet. What're you doing out here?"

Better question: what were *they* doing out here? "I was checking Greg's truck for paint transfer to see if he's the one who ran me off the road the other night. Brittany only came along for the ride. Don't you want to know if your cousin was involved in a hit-and-run?"

He lowered his eyebrows. "You two should've stayed home, and minded your own business."

"Ending up in a ditch in the middle of nowhere *is* my business. I have no idea what else is going on here. Let us go now, and we have no story to tell."

He laughed.

"Seriously, you can all carry on as usual. Harm us in any way, and Olinski'll send the whole sheriff's department to comb every inch of your property. I can't imagine what they'll find, but I bet you can."

He shook his head.

"Tell me something. Why did you kill Tony?"

"Who says I killed Tony?"

"Your shirtsleeve."

"Ha. I didn't kill Tony. Or Chief Vick, either, although I thought hard about it."

I stopped, and Brittany almost hobbled into my back. "Why?"

"He was going to fire me. Said I wasn't cut out for the job. I'd bet anything he wanted to make room for his son, though."

"But you don't know that for sure." Except Zach told me his father said as much without naming names.

Leonard grabbed my arm and pulled me toward the building. As we approached the double doors, a smiling

Greg dressed in stained gray coveralls came out the smaller one. "Welcome, ladies. Nice of you to join us."

Brittany and I looked at each other. The lunatic thought we'd come for a dinner party?

Leonard angled around us to stand next to his cousin. "What do you want to do with them?"

"Just leave 'em with me, Lenny. I'll take it from here."

"You promised not to hurt them."

Greg grabbed Brittany by the arm. "And I won't. Trust me. Now, help me get them inside, and you can go. You're late for work. Don't want the new chief dissing you the way the old one did, right?"

He towed a stumbling Brittany through the doorway.

Leonard took my elbow. "Please don't make any trouble," he whispered. "Don't give him an excuse to harm you."

This wasn't the man who marched us over here at gunpoint. *Why the change?* "What's the deal? Why were you so nasty before?"

"The barn has cameras. He heard everything I said, and he was watching. I had to make it look good."

He shoved me into the building. I closed my eyes against the brilliance emitted from the overhead fluorescents. I turned my head away and opened them again. A dozen or so pony-sized copper kettles lined both sides. The covered pots sprouted tubing connected to a six-inch steel pipe running the length of the structure. At the room's opposite end, two cauldrons steamed, each tended by a guy in coveralls continually stirring the contents with a wooden paddle. I suspected I should be grateful I couldn't smell anything through my sponge-plugged nose.

The Partridge clan was still in the moonshine business, only supersized.

Chief Vick must've figured out what they were doing. Maybe even believed Tony had something to do with it when he stumbled on that antique still in the outhouse. Was bootlegging the reason the chief had to die?

Leonard guided me to the left, behind the row of stills. "Don't touch anything. They'll burn you."

"Got it. So, if you didn't murder Tony who did?"

"I have my suspicions but can't prove anything. I caught my sleeve on the tree trying to retrieve a scrap of paper that might've been evidence. Turned out to be a grocery list. Cost me a perfectly good shirt."

I drifted too close to the pipe, and Leonard grabbed me. "Be careful! If you break that Greg'll kill you for sure."

No doubt he told the truth. "Thanks. How does Tony's death connect to Chief Vick's? Did Greg murder them both?"

"I don't think so, but he's involved somehow. The problem is he's family. Greg and I are friends, but if I look too closely, my uncle would assign someone to take me out without thinking twice. This thing is much bigger than you realize. The Partridges have perfected this operation over the last hundred years."

"But you're a police officer. How can you turn a blind eye to an illegal operation?"

He snorted. "I want to live, that's how. You saw what happened to Chief Vick, right? I think he discovered too much about the operation and they eliminated him. It's one thing for the chief to figure it out on his own. If I help, I'm next."

"I get that, but why did you run me off the road?"

"I didn't. That was Greg."

I shook my head. "You were seen driving his truck that day."

"I borrowed it to move some furniture out of storage. I'd never do anything to hurt you. Why would I?"

"I don't know. You tell me."

We'd almost reached the back wall, and Greg had already taken Brittany into the next room. What was he doing to her? My stomach clenched. Question time was almost up. "Who planted the evidence in Tony's car and Eric's locker?"

"Greg took care of that. It was easy—Tony never locked his car. All Greg needed to do was sneak up there in the middle of the night. He's the one who keeps covering Tony's address with pine cones, too. To keep you away. Didn't work, though. You're worse than a bulldog with a bone."

"Thanks. And Eric? How did Greg gain access to the police station?"

"He didn't." Leonard stopped and turned me toward him. "I did it. I forged Eric's signature and put the evidence in his locker. You have to believe me. I never intended for anyone to accuse him of murder. I only wanted to get back at him for the way he treated me when I was in training. I meant it as a prank."

"Some prank. You almost cost him his job and landed him in jail."

"I heard. I'm sorry."

Greg burst out of the back room. "Hey, Lenny! What's the holdup?"

Leonard shoved me. "She's being a pain in the ass, as usual."

I tripped and tumbled face-first into the wall. Fire seared through my nose, and my ribs flared. I struggled to breathe. If I managed to escape this situation, I owed him a solid punch in the eye. Of course, my luck, I'd break my hand in the process.

He dragged me to my feet, aggravating the ache in my torso, and hauled me over to Greg. "Here. You deal with her."

Greg held my gaze, a grin twitching at the corners of his mouth. "My pleasure."

I suspected I wouldn't share his amusement.

The back-room dimensions occupied a third the size of the front. On each side, the six-inch pipes poking out of the Sheetrock drained into tanks equipped with spigots sized to fill individual bottles, which were then capped and stored in segmented cardboard boxes.

Directly ahead, a white van lined with pegboards loaded with handyman-type implements was parked by opened double doors. Five-gallon buckets of paint sat on the floor beside the vehicle, and a ladder fastened to the driver's side roof stretched from front to back.

Brittany knelt inside the van, her hands tied behind her back and attached to a hook. Duct tape covered her mouth. Fear and anguish poured from her eyes.

A mushroom cloud of anger blossomed through me. I jumped into the van and approached her.

"Hold it right there," Greg said.

I stopped in front of a pegboard adorned with screwdrivers, wrenches, and files and glared at him. "What did you do to her?"

"Same thing I'm about to do to you." He retrieved a length of rope from his pocket and climbed up, reaching for my wrist.

"Hey, Greg! Come see this."

He peered out the door toward the voice.

"These bottles are all broken. What do you want me to do with them?"

Heart pounding, I grabbed a small, short file off the board behind me and stuck it in my back pocket. No idea if I'd be able to reach the tool when I needed to, but just its presence gave me some comfort. It could be our only way out of this mess.

"Leave 'em over there, and I'll deal with it in a minute," Greg replied, then turned back to me. "Turn around with your hands behind your back."

His breath was hot on my neck as he tied my wrists tightly together, the rope rough on my skin. He prodded me forward and ordered me down on my knees opposite Brittany. Her eyes closed, her chest rose and fell rapidly. She was alive. I intended to ensure she stayed that way.

Hang in there, Britt. I'll get us out of this.

When Greg jerked my hands up to tie them to the hook on my side, my shoulders and ribs screamed. I sealed my lips. Damned if I'd let him know he hurt me.

"Where are you taking us?"

He picked up a roll of duct tape, tore off a four-inch section, and attempted to slap it over my mouth. "Don't worry, you'll find out soon enough."

I turned my head and leaned as far away from him as possible. "Wait!"

"What?"

"My nose is plugged with sponges. If you cover my mouth, I'll suffocate. You promised Leonard you wouldn't hurt us."

"No problem." He removed a pair of pointy pliers from the board.

"What are you going to do with those?"

"I'm gonna help you breathe. Now hold still or I'll poke your eye out."

I froze and held my breath.

Greg tipped my head back, peered up my nostril, grabbed the end of the sponge, and yanked. Pain seared through my face, then settled into a dull throb. For the first time in days, I could inhale through one side of my nose. I felt almost normal again.

He covered my mouth with a strip of duct tape.

One of his men loaded cartons on the floor of the van. Greg arranged them in the middle of Brittany and me. Two stacks of three blocked the space, creating a cardboard wall. We couldn't work together to break free.

Greg clipped a board into place, sealing us in and fashioning a false back for the compartment. Darkness enveloped us. I had two feet side to side to maneuver in, give or take. When I lifted my head, barely a quarter inch of room remained between me and the boxes. Not a lot to work with, but it had to be enough. Our lives depended on it.

Thuds indicated they'd reloaded the paint buckets. Preparing for departure to who knew where to deliver six cases of moonshine. Who would need bulk bottled moonshine? Restaurants and bars came to mind. I couldn't imagine a stupendous demand for the product, however. Unless the patrons didn't know what they were getting.

Sweat beaded on my forehead. The air grew thick, difficult to pull into my lungs. I twisted my wrists to gauge the rope's flexibility. Not much. Could I reach the file in my pocket? Almost, but not quite. My only hope was to free myself from the hook.

Deep breath in, slow breath out.

The driver's side door opened, and someone climbed in, rocking the van. I waited for a matching shift from the passenger side. Nothing. I exhaled. At least we only had one captor to deal with. Two against one, except I still couldn't reach Brittany on the other side of the barricade if I *did* manage to break loose. Still, the file was a bit of hope for me to hang my hat on. If only I had a hat.

The engine fired up, and the back doors slammed. I swung on the hook as the vehicle lurched forward. My shoulders and wrists squealed, but the movement inspired a surge of possibility. If the ropes glided freely around the hook, I might be able to slide them off. However, since I wasn't privy to our destination, I might not have much time to work. I needed to move fast.

My head bounced like a bobblehead doll as we jolted down the driveway, increasing my neck and shoulder stress. I tried to follow the twists and turns of our route while waiting for the brainstorm gods to present me with a way to escape my bonds. No success on either front. Lack of familiarity with the area quickly led to abject confusion. After a while, though, the smooth pavement and steady hum of the tires made it clear we traveled on the highway. The radio blared some country song I didn't recognize.

I rocked back and forth on my knees, the rope sliding on the hook, which built momentum, and steadied my nerves. As calm as possible under the circumstances, I trapped a deep breath, yanked my arms up and forward, and smashed nose first into the stack of cartons. The duct tape stifled my shriek. I panted puffs of air through my nose until the agony subsided.

What was plan B? I had no clue, but protecting my face no matter what would definitely be included. The only way to do that was to prop my forehead on the box, then try again. I braced my head and gritted my teeth against the discomfort. A three-count later, I leaned forward and bent my elbows to slip the rope off the hook. It rose, but not far enough. Too much tension on the cord.

Plan C. Repeat steps one and two, then lean toward the wall to release the pressure for the final pull.

Okay, prop head, three-count, lean forward, bend elbows, lean back, pull up, hands free!

Halfway there, but cutting through the rope would be a long, slow process. Did I have enough time?

I inserted two fingers into my back pocket and fished for the file. I blinked away the perspiration that dripped into my eyes. Pinching the implement in my fingers, I drew the tool out of its hiding place until the top of the handle hit my palm. A quick shift and the file was wedged between my thumb and forefinger, upside down. All that remained was to slide it under the rope and saw like my life depended on it.

CHAPTER TWENTY-NINE

Every stroke of file against rope resulted in a millimeter of progress, and another layer of skin scraped off my forearm. Adrenaline masked the burn for the time being. The van might stop to unload the cargo at any time, leaving us at the mercy of the guy in the front seat. I intended to be ready for him.

There'd been no sound of movement from Brittany since we left. I implored her to be okay. To believe otherwise would throw me into a panic. Anything that happened to her tonight would be my fault. I'd never be able to live with that. What would I tell her parents? Or Olinski?

I sawed steadily until the van stopped, then started moving again. We'd exited the highway. I'd run out of time. I forced the metal strip back and forth, ignoring the jabs into my flesh. Were they drawing blood? That would be the least of my problems if I wasn't free by the time the man opened the panel.

The blade broke through the last strand as we chugged to a standstill, and the engine stopped. Low voices wafted through the compartment when someone unlatched the back doors, but I couldn't make out the words. The vehicle rocked as the paint buckets skidded over the floor and out. Not long now.

I couldn't risk him noticing I'd freed myself until I cut Brittany loose. I put my hands behind my back and grasped the hook with a forefinger, approximating the position I'd been in when he last saw me, and waited.

The board that separated us from the rear section disappeared, and a heavy-set man in jeans and a dirty white T-shirt looked from me to Brittany and back again. He set his finger against his lips. "Not a sound out of either one of you. Get it?"

I nodded and assumed she did the same. No dome light illuminated the compartment, and we remained shrouded in darkness. He handed off a case of moonshine to someone I couldn't see. Five repetitions completed the delivery.

The man replaced the divider, slid the paint buckets back into position, and closed the back doors. After he climbed back into the cab and started the engine, I released my hold on the hook and ripped off the duct tape. The sting reinforced my decision to never have a mustache wax.

When the van rolled into the street, and the radio came on again, I risked a whisper. "Britt, are you okay?"

"Mmmmm."

I crawled to her side. "I'm going to pull the tape off. Keep your voice down."

She nodded.

As gently as possible, I peeled the adhesive away from her lips. "Better?"

She sucked in a deep breath. "Yes, thank you. How did you free your hands?"

"I stole a file. Lean back so I can lift you off the hook."

304

She complied. I lifted her hands free, then said, "Turn around so I can untie you."

Brittany shuffled around on her knees, lost her balance, and bumped into the wall separating our compartment from the cabin. We stiffened, staring wide-eyed at each other. I held my breath until certain there'd be no response, then let it out in a rush.

"Sorry," she whispered.

I patted her shoulder. "No harm done. Let's release you in case he's looking for a safe place to pull over. We'll have to get through him to escape."

After she completed her rotation, I went to work on the bindings. The file remained in my pocket, but using it would take longer and cause more skin damage. The knots were tight but not impossible. Clearly, Greg hadn't anticipated our ability to reach them. It took me a few minutes, but eventually, Brittany massaged her wrists and stretched her legs out. I sat opposite her and alternated my legs with hers. Now we had to make a game plan.

"Here's what I'm thinking," I murmured. "Safe to say he's not just taking us on a sightseeing trip. We'll overpower him when he comes to let us out of the van and run."

"Are you sure we can take him? He's kind of big."

"He's expecting us to be incapacitated. If we rush him as he removes the board, he'll be off-balance, and have his hands full. We come at him with maximum force, scream to freak him out, then knock him down, and take off. What do you think?"

Brittany chuckled low in her throat. "You make it sound so easy. I'm a reader not a runner. Also don't forget, I have a bad ankle."

Running my hands down her lower legs, I compared them to each other. "It's a little swollen, but I don't think anything's broken. Can you grin and bear it?"

"I may bear it, but I refuse to grin."

"Fair enough. Let's try to get a little rest while we can."

I closed my eyes and focused on the highway hum to keep my mind from wandering into the oh-my-God-he's-gonna-kill-us zone. No way I would let that happen. It was one thing to put myself in danger, but I'd dragged Brittany along this time. She trusted me, and I'd let her down. I had to make things right.

If I had my cell phone, I'd call for help. But what would I say? I had no idea where we were. But they could triangulate our location if I could stay on the phone long enough this time.

"Britt, do you have your phone with you?"

"No, I left it in the car. Didn't think I'd need it."

So much for that. "Yeah, I don't have mine either."

The drone diminished, and the van stopped, then turned. Had we reached our destination? Best to be ready, just in case. We might only have one chance to overpower the driver and break out. We had to make the most of it.

I patted Brittany's good leg. "Looks like we're almost there."

"I wouldn't mind knowing where 'there' is."

"Someplace out in the woods where our bodies will never be found, I'd imagine."

Brittany chuckled. "Gee thanks. That makes me feel better."

"Well, if we time this right, his intentions won't matter."

We rearranged ourselves onto our haunches, one on each side of the van. As soon as the board separating us from the back moved, we'd spring, knock the man down, and clear the way to freedom. That was the plan, anyway. My plans had an annoying habit of going awry, however. We'd better be luckier this time.

We decelerated again and bounced over a rough road. I leaned against the wall and put a hand up to steady myself. "Yup. We're definitely out in the middle of nowhere. Did you bring your compass?"

"Nope. Left it with my phone. Didn't think I'd need that, either."

"Well, you were clearly never a scout."

"Right back atcha." She squeezed my hand.

The tires stopped bouncing. We braced ourselves against an almost-circular turn, and the van backed up to a halt. Locking eyes with Brittany, I stood, hunched over at the waist.

Go time.

The back doors creaked open. My heart threatened to burst out of my chest. We rocked as he climbed in. The scratch of paint buckets against the floor marked his progress. Within a minute, he panted outside the panel. I focused on the edge.

When the first hint of light appeared, we sprang into the board, yelling as loudly as we could. My ribs screamed as all the air rushed out of my lungs. Our combined weight toppled him. He grunted and went down. We scrambled on all fours, the wood biting into my knees.

He clutched my pant leg. My jeans weighed down my hips as I struggled to jerk free. "Britt, he's got me!"

Brittany turned and slammed her hand down on his wrist. His grip loosened. I jerked free and leaped out the back, Brittany right behind me. I landed on my feet, arms rotating for balance. She went down and grabbed her ankle. Behind us, the driver clambered up, hand on the back of his head.

I hoisted Brittany up by her shoulders, wrapped my arm around her waist, and half-carried her forward. "C'mon, Britt, hang with me. We gotta put some distance between us and him." My knees buckled under the weight. I struggled on. A peek to get my bearings brought a ramshackle barn into view.

A whistle sounded behind me. I jerked my head up and turned around. Greg Partridge stood next to the van, gun in hand. I tore my vision away from the pistol long enough to establish we'd ended up right back where we started. Greg had sent us on a joyride with no joy, for what purpose I couldn't fathom. Only to keep us out of the way? Nothing else made sense.

Teresa Benedict came out of the bottling room and lingered beside him, arms folded across her chest.

Why was the mayor here?

The icy glitter in her eyes raised the hair on my neck and instilled more fear in me than the loaded weapon trained in my direction.

Brittany balanced on one foot, her injured ankle now double its normal size, and draped an arm across my shoulders. I gave her a quick squeeze.

I jutted my chin and focused my gaze on Greg. "What do you want with us?"

He brandished the gun. "Want with you? Hell, I wish I'd never met you. Now I have to kill you, and you only have yourself to blame."

My face flushed with anger. "We didn't know anything until you sent Leonard out to capture us. If you'd left us alone, we could've taken our picture, and skedaddled.

The worst that would've happened was a ticket for reckless driving. This is *your* fault."

Greg took a step toward me. The mayor held him back. "Everybody calm down," she said in her soothing politician voice. "There has to be an answer that works for everyone."

"There's only one solution to this problem," he said, pulling his arm out of her grasp. "They have to be eliminated."

Teresa turned her frigid glare on him. "We can't keep killing people."

He returned her hostility. "What do you mean 'we'? The first two are on you. You started all this. Now I'm stuck cleaning up *your* mess."

Brittany's eyebrows shot up. "Is that true? Did you kill Chief Vick and Tony, Teresa?"

Blood rushed into the mayor's face. "Of course not! I'm not a monster."

I changed the subject. If I could keep her off-balance, she might slip up. "What's your interest in the Partridges' bootlegging operation, Mayor?"

"Don't be silly. I have nothing to do with it."

"Then, why are you here?"

Her voice rose half an octave. "Why am I here? To look for you. I heard you were missing. I wanted to help."

"Who told you we were missing?"

She took a step back. "I don't remember. Angus, maybe."

Except Angus didn't know where we were. "What made you think to look here?"

Her eyes fired icicles at me.

Greg stepped between us and pointed to Teresa. "Enough of this nonsense. Go home, and check the balance in your campaign fund or something. I'll take care of these two."

Campaign fund?

The connection between the mayor and the moonshiner became clear. The mysterious contributions everyone wondered about came from Greg Partridge. A payoff for Teresa keeping the police from looking too closely at his operation. Chief Vick wouldn't back down, so she killed him to protect her cash cow. But how to prove my theory?

Teresa took two steps toward the Expedition parked on the side of the building where the bottles were packaged, then turned back. Her mouth was set in a straight line across her face. "I didn't kill Tobias Vick."

I stared her down as the pieces tumbled into place. "No, you made Tony eliminate the chief, then you murdered Tony to keep him quiet."

Her shoulders drooped. "Tony's death was an accident. I don't expect you to believe me, but he fell on that rock. Yes, I shoved him, but he hit his head when he went down. He wasn't supposed to die." A single tear rolled down her cheek. "I never meant for him to die."

"Okay, but how did you get him to kill the chief for you?"

"He had no choice, really. He was laundering money for Greg, the same as I was. If the chief figured it all out, Tony would go down too. It was the only solution, and he knew it."

She trundled, head down, toward her car.

I stopped her. "Teresa!"

She turned.

"Who threatened my dog?"

310

"I did, but I never would've hurt her. I just wanted you to leave us alone. I knew how stubborn you could be."

"It backfired on you."

"Yes, it did."

Greg waved his gun in the direction of the bottling room. I had to think fast. The man was desperate enough to follow through and crafty enough to bury us somewhere we'd never be found. Or dump our well-weighted bodies into Lake Dester. Either way, we'd die, and he'd get away with murder.

I had to stall. "Hey, Greg! What did you do with the still that used to be in Tony's outhouse? I kinda liked that thing."

"Me too, but I couldn't risk the new chief picking up where the old one left off. It was that still that got Vick started in the first place." He grabbed my arm. "Now get moving!"

I crossed my feet in mid-stride and feigned a stumble. Brittany, who I still supported with my shoulder, went down with me.

Greg guffawed.

As I helped her up, I whispered, "Follow my lead. When I tell you to, run as fast as you can to the nearest exit. Try to get back to the car."

She nodded.

Now I only had to figure out what to do next. I searched my memory for the layout of the other room. Stills lined the walls, six-inch pipes alongside. No help there unless I could detach one of the conduits leading from the still to the tube running from one room to the other. The middle of the room was empty. At the front, the two kettles filled with whatever the men were stirring with the oar-sized wooden paddles. Would anyone still be there?

311

We slogged through the bottling room. Greg poked me in the back once or twice to speed us along, but Brittany's ankle bulged like it'd swallowed a softball. Our only hope for escape was if Brittany was exaggerating the extent of her injury. If this really was the fastest she could move, my plan had no chance.

As we approached the door between the rooms, I incorporated my favorite writer's trick: distraction. "Just out of curiosity, Greg, why did you leave the bottle and glass in Tony's car? You had to know he could make a deal and tell the police about your operation."

Brittany and I stumbled through the doorway. My gaze flew immediately to the kettles. They appeared empty, the oars resting across the tops, the men tending them gone.

Greg scoffed at my question. "I had nothing to worry about. Tony laundered money for us. Besides, he knew if the state didn't kill him for murdering the chief, my father would for cutting a deal."

He strode across the threshold right behind us. I grabbed a paddle and yelled, "Run!"

Brittany took off toward the exit.

Greg raised his arm to fire at her.

I slammed the oar down on the gun.

His pistol fired into the floor, fell, and skittered away. He shoved me against the cauldron and dove for it.

My makeshift weapon bounced away as the air whooshed out of my lungs. No time to rest, though. I jumped on his back, impeding, but not halting, his forward progress.

He grunted and bucked. I held on like a three-year-old playing horsy.

I scrabbled over his head and lunged for the pistol,

stretching as far as I could. My ribs and face throbbed, but I had to keep going. I pushed forward.

Greg seized my leg and yanked me back.

My sliding left hand nudged the paddle. I rolled on my side, grabbed it with my right and swung, palms stinging as I connected with the side of his head.

He screamed and clutched his ear. Blood poured through his fingers.

I leaped to my feet and ran, snatching up the gun on the way. A glance back revealed Greg on hands and knees, struggling to stand. I jerked the door open, slamming it against the wall.

Brittany had progressed about two-thirds of the way across the clearing. I sprinted to her side, and she threw an arm over my shoulder. After a quick check for Greg's whereabouts, I half-carried her to where we'd parked her Chevy.

I loaded her into the passenger seat with her swollen foot propped on the dashboard. As I made my way to the driver's side, Olinski and a once again uniformed Eric pulled up in a black SUV, light bar flashing blue into the night.

He had a knack for showing up when I needed him most. I might have to keep him around after all. "What are you guys doing here?"

Eric jumped out of the Suburban. "Brittany's parents called when you two didn't show up for dinner or answer their calls. Are you okay?"

"Yes, but how did you find us?"

"We tracked your phones."

"Thank you." I handed him Greg's gun and waved him away. "Go find Greg and Teresa! I'll take Brittany to the hospital."

Olinski hit the gas before Eric was entirely in, spraying dirt on me, which blended nicely with all the grime I already wore. My latest fashion trend.

When I settled in the car, the seat hugged me like an old friend. Brittany rested with her eyes closed, finally safe again. After all the times she'd taken care of me, it was my turn. I cranked up the engine and bumped down the road.

CHAPTER THIRTY

A cloudless, sunny sky presided over the Riddleton Fourth of July parade. Once again, I found myself surrounded by densely packed humanity on the sidewalk in front of the town hall. But this time, it felt like home.

I stood beside Brittany, who sat in a wheelchair Olinski had rustled up for her, so she didn't have to use her crutches. I swallowed back my guilt. If I hadn't encouraged her to run on her injured ankle, she might not have needed surgery for torn ligaments. Of course, she also might be dead.

"Fantastic parade," I said. "Everyone went all out this year."

She smiled and tilted her head back. "The town needed it. Especially the ovation Anne-Marie received all the way down the route. A true demonstration of solidarity."

"I don't know. They might've been applauding that '65 Mustang she was riding on. It's really nice of Principal Goldfarb to let the grand marshal use it every year. I'm not sure I'd let anyone else look at it, let alone sit on the back of it."

She poked me in the leg. "That doesn't surprise me."

"Ha ha. I haven't seen Olinski. Is he here?"

"He had some paperwork to finish up. Should be done any minute."

"I can't believe how attentive he's been since you got hurt. I hardly recognize the guy I dated anymore. When do the wedding bells start ringing?"

She lifted her eyebrows and stared at me over the top of her glasses. "No time soon, for sure. He *has* been sweet, though."

"To you perhaps. He's mad at me for putting you in danger."

"He'll get over it. Eventually. Besides, it was my idea to go with you."

"Tell *him* that."

"I did." She touched my arm. "I'm almost finished with those chapters you sent me. They look pretty good for a first draft. I'll send them back, with comments, when I'm done. Are you going to make the deadline?"

I smiled. "I am. I have two more chapters to go, and I should be done with those by the end of this week. That gives me a month for the rewrites before I submit. My editor is going to have a lot of work to do, but at least it'll be finished."

Brittany shot me a sidelong glance. "It's good for her. She needs to earn her keep, anyway."

"Don't tell *her* that!"

Newly appointed acting mayor Veronica Winslow and Eric slid in beside us.

My shoulder brushed Eric's. "Good morning, Madam Mayor."

Veronica rolled her eyes. "Knock it off. I was only

316

selected because the council couldn't agree on anyone else."

"They agreed on you rather quickly from what I understand. Have you considered running in the election?"

"What? No way. I'm no politician."

Eric crossed his arms. "You wouldn't be laundering money through your campaign, either. Definitely a plus. I'd vote for you."

She shook her head. "I didn't realize that was the only qualification."

I shot her a grin. "Well, you also haven't killed anyone."

They both groaned.

"Too soon?"

"Yes!" they chorused.

"Sorry. Too much excitement, I guess."

"Where's Savannah?" Eric asked.

"I had to leave her home. It's too hot for her to be out here for any period of time. Even this early in the morning."

"Makes sense."

"You know, I never did ask you what Leonard was doing on that 911 call."

Puzzled, he dropped his eyebrows and tilted his head.

"The one he had the night I was run off the road? At the abandoned property?"

"Oh yeah, I forgot about that. Apparently, the woman's grandfather died, and left the house to her. She and her fiancé fixed it up, and decided to move in after the wedding. They had a huge fight over where his recliner fit into her decorating scheme. He wanted the chair in the living room. She opted for out on the curb for pickup. Leonard did a terrific piece of work talking them down."

"Sounds like he was getting better at his job."

"He wasn't my favorite person, but I'm a little sorry he forgot the oath he took as a police officer."

Veronica laid a hand on my arm. "Didn't he pull a gun on you, Jen?"

"Yes, but since he was also under threat from his family and never actually used it, I refused to press charges. I guess Olinski fired him, instead."

"He had no choice, really. Leonard knew what his family was doing and who was behind the murders, and didn't say anything to anyone. That's an ethics violation," Eric said.

"And he planted the cyanide in your locker."

"Yeah, that too."

Olinski squeezed in on the other side of Brittany as the Ravenous Readers float went by. Lacey had decorated her husband's pickup truck, and Charlie stood in the back dressed as Thomas Jefferson waving a copy of the Declaration of Independence. My heart grew as I took in the smiling faces around me. I was part of a group for the first time in my life. I had people to support and protect me, and I'd gladly do the same for each of them.

Veronica nudged me. "Shouldn't you be up there, too?"

"I'm hanging with Brittany in case she needs anything. Besides, the float was all Lacey and Charlie's idea, so I wanted them to have the spotlight."

Eric enfolded my hand. I not only didn't mind but even entwined my fingers with his and waited. No panic. No overwhelming urge to run away.

What's happening to me?
He looked at me and smiled.
For the second time in less than a week, I kissed Eric.
Only, this time, I meant it.

ACKNOWLEDGEMENTS

A special thank you to my agent, Dawn Dowdle, and my editor, Cara Chimirri, along with the rest of the Avon team. None of this would've been possible without them.

Also, Misty Adams, Ann Dudzinski, Julie Golden, Dawn Miller, Suzanne Oldham, and D.L. Willette, all of whom suffered through the first draft and contributed greatly to the finished product.

And, of course, my furry best friend, Sadie, who lay by my side through every word.

**She can write the perfect murder mystery . . .
But can she solve one in real life?**

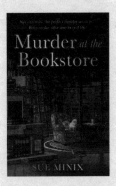

Crime writer Jen returns to her small hometown
with a bestselling book behind her and a bad case
of writer's block. Finding sanctuary in the local
bookstore, with an endless supply of coffee,
Jen waits impatiently for inspiration to strike.

But when the owner of the bookstore dies
suddenly in mysterious circumstances, Jen has
a real-life murder to solve.

The stakes are suddenly higher when evidence places
Jen at the scene of the crime and the reading of the
will names her as the new owner of the bookstore . . .

Can she crack the case and clear her name,
before the killer strikes again?

**Don't miss Sue Minix's debut cosy mystery
– available now!**